Praise for
A Conversation in Blood

"If you enjoy storytelling with the content sensibilities of *Game of Thrones,* then imagine George R. R. Martin forced to write while strapped to the front of a War Boys' car going 100 mph, pumped full of Jolt Cola and Pixy Sticks with Metallica blaring from the speakers and you approximate the full Egil & Nix experience that [Paul S.] Kemp delivers."
—*Rebels Report*

"Paul S. Kemp's no-nonsense writing style, the quick/action-packed pacing, and the strength of the characters makes for an engaging read that will keep you turning the pages."
—*Cinelinx*

"Fast-paced and entertaining, *A Conversation in Blood* masterfully blends magic with sword and sorcery in a way that is accessible to readers."
—*Nerdophiles*

"This is an adventure perfect for fantasy fans and action-movie lovers. It will take readers on a wild ride with heart-pounding fights, harebrained schemes, and several laugh-out-loud moments."
—*Booklist*

BY PAUL S. KEMP

The Tales of Egil and Nix

The Hammer and the Blade
A Discourse in Steel
A Conversation in Blood

Star Wars

Star Wars: Crosscurrent
Star Wars: Riptide
Star Wars: The Old Republic:
Deceived
Star Wars: Lords of the Sith

The Sembia Series

The Halls of Stormweather
Shadow's Witness

The Erevis Cale Trilogy

Twilight Falling
Dawn of Night
Midnight's Mask

The Twilight War

Shadowbred
Shadowstorm
Shadowrealm

The Sundering

The Godborn

Anthologies and Collections

Ephemera
Realms of Shadow
Realms of Dragons
Realms of War
Sails and Sorcery
Horrors Beyond II
Worlds of Their Own
Eldritch Horrors: Dark Tales

A CONVERSATION IN
BLOOD

AN EGIL & NIX NOVEL

PAUL S. KEMP

DEL REY • NEW YORK

2017 Del Rey Mass Market Edition

Copyright © 2016 by Paul S. Kemp

Published in the United States by Del Rey, an imprint of Random House, a division of Penguin Random House LLC, New York.

DEL REY and the HOUSE colophon are registered trademarks of Penguin Random House LLC.

Originally published in hardcover in the United States by Del Rey, an imprint of Random House, a division of Penguin Random House LLC, in 2017.

ISBN 978-0-425-28549-7
Ebook ISBN 978-0-553-39201-2

Cover design: Beverly Leung

Cover illustration: © John Picacio

Printed in the United States of America

randomhousebooks.com

2 4 6 8 9 7 5 3 1

Del Rey mass market edition: August 2017

For Jen, the Knights R&R, and the Ladies D and S

ACKNOWLEDGMENTS

Foremost to my readers. Thank you so much. And a hat tip and my most sincere gratitude to Ms. Brackett, and Mssrs. Leiber, Howard, Burroughs, and Moorcock.

A CONVERSATION IN BLOOD

PROLOGUE

BEFORE

Nix bounded backward but the creature's thick arm and fist caught him squarely in the torso and audibly cracked his ribs. The force of the blow drove the breath out of him in a pained gasp and knocked him back into the hard metal of the wall. The moment he hit the wall the edges of his broken ribs ground coarsely against one another. He tried to seal off a shriek behind clenched teeth, but it slipped the reins of his control and the force of the scream misted the air before him in spit and blood. His legs would not hold him up and he slid down the wall to the floor, gasping but trying not to, each new inhalation a knife stab of pain in his chest.

"Nix!" Egil shouted.

Nix couldn't see his friend; the huge, misshapen bulk of the creature, the leftover of the Great Spell, blocked Egil's body from view.

The creature roiled toward him, one lumbering step, another, the movement of its form under its filthy, bloody cloak more like a landslide than ambulation. Nix knew he was going to die. Pain and blood loss blurred his vision, shrank his field of view down to a tunnel in which he saw only the creature, the otherworldly creature, as it advanced on him.

Its movement allowed Nix to see Egil behind it. His friend was down on all fours, but favoring an arm, bleeding, beaten, his forehead wrinkled by pain. The eye of Ebenor, tattooed on his pate, the symbol of his faith in the Momentary God, a farce of a deity that Egil somehow ennobled, was smeared with blood.

"Over here, creature!" Egil said, visibly working up to an attempt at standing. "Over here, you fakking thing!"

The creature stopped, its bulk rippling under the filthy cloak it wore. It turned to face Egil with whatever passed for its head.

"Get up," Nix said to Egil, the words barely a whisper. "Get up, Egil."

And Egil did. His huge muscles bunched as he lifted the mountain of his frame, put a leg under him, and used his remaining hammer as a crutch to get himself upright. He inhaled, gripping the hammer in his right hand, the veins in his arm standing out like cordage. His left arm hung limp at his side, broken or dislocated at the shoulder. The look in his hooded eyes promised an answer in violence, and so did his tone.

"That's right," the priest said softly, staring at the thing. "Over here."

The creature tensed and roared, the sound coming from a dozen mouths, a cacophony of rage and frustration that somehow reminded Nix of crashing surf, an elemental sound, the sound of something inexorable, unstoppable. Egil did not blanch in the face of its anger.

"Likely we'll do this again sometime, creature," Egil said, raising his hammer and spitting in the creature's direction. "Or maybe we won't. Either way, you don't clear today without first answering to me."

The creature took a halting step toward Egil, the singular

priest of Ebenor facing the singular horror of worlds gone by. Nix used his hands to shift his weight but even that slight movement caused bone to grind against bone. He hissed with pain but fought through it, tried to maneuver himself so that he could get his feet under him, to rise and stand with Egil, but the prolonged agony nearly caused him to pass out. He could barely breathe. He felt as though a boulder were on his chest, and he knew what it meant: Blood was filling his lungs. The sound he'd heard that reminded him of surf wasn't the creature; it was his respiration, his impending death.

Again? he wondered.

Maybe.

Probably.

Nix saw Egil's tracheal lump work as the priest swallowed some hard truth. Egil glanced first at Nix, then off to his right, and said, "Do it if you can, Jyme. Do it now."

The words and what they implied opened a path through Nix's pain and brought him a moment of clarity.

Jyme's voice carried from outside Nix's field of view, though Nix knew that Jyme stood at the place that was no place, that was every place, that was the *only* place, the Fulcrum.

"I don't— How?" Jyme asked.

Once again Nix pressed his hands on the cold floor, tried to move his body so that he could see Jyme, but the pain brought another scream. He faded, unconsciousness beckoned, but he held on, *forced* himself to hang on. He blinked hard, shook his head, and raised a hand feebly in Jyme's direction.

"Small changes," he said, but his broken chest could make the command little more than a strangled whisper that ended in a bloody, painful froth. "Only small changes, Jyme."

The creature roared, took another step toward Egil.

Jyme spoke again, his voice wearing a hint of panic. "I don't know the fakkin' words, Egil! This is Nix's play, not mine. Nix, what are the words? Can you hear me?"

"Just look at them," Nix whispered. The words would almost read themselves. Jyme just needed to look at them.

"You don't need to know them," Egil said, his tone strangely calm. The priest eased himself to his right, filling the space between Jyme and the creature. "Nix already activated them. Just read the stanzas like Nix said. You can fakking read, Jyme. Be the damned hero, now. That's what you wanted."

"Small changes," Nix murmured, though he was drifting and the words came out a half moan. He cursed himself for not having told them enough. "Anything more and we don't know what will happen. Everything could be lost. Small changes, Jyme. Small."

Maybe Egil heard him mumbling, for the priest glanced at him and they shared a look that spanned years, maybe worlds. Egil gave him a single nod, a gesture that said everything between them, and turned his heavy-browed gaze away. His nostrils flared and he squared up to the creature, the same way he'd squared up to everything they'd ever faced.

Nix's eyes were heavy, closing. The pain subsided, a bad sign. He heard Jyme speak but the words blended together, a rising surf again. Or maybe that was his failing lungs.

Nix heard Egil shout and the sound pulled him back from the edge for a moment. Bleary-eyed, he watched the priest charge the monstrous creature, lone hammer held high.

The sight made him smile softly.

Whatever happened, he hoped he and Egil would meet again forever.

Jyme stood inside the socket in the floor, and the shimmering, translucent column of light that descended from the ceiling illuminated him, exposed him, separated the world he knew from the world he didn't. At moments the light seemed present, at others, gone. At moments he felt present, and then gone himself. The whipsaw made him dizzy, made his footing questionable, his stomach queasy. There were writings on the smooth walls, etched or scratched into the metal by many different hands. There were images, too, alphabets he didn't know, things he could not make sense of, that were not to be made sense of, that he feared looking at too long.

Worlds gone by, he thought, recalling Nix's phrase.

How many times? How many?

He stood on the spot, what could only be the spot, a hole in the world, a socket in time. It made him feel strange to stand there. He felt looked at, no, looked on, no, *looked through*, like he was barely there, like something he couldn't begin to comprehend—some potential—filled the space all around him. The clock was some kind of spyglass or foci that had led them to the place that was no place, to the Fulcrum, where the universe looked down on men and laughed. For some reason he thought of the tattoo on Egil's head, the sign of Egil's faith, the eye of Ebenor, who was god for a moment and only a moment. A ridiculous, futile moment, no doubt.

The creature's roar brought him back to the present. His mind had been drifting, as if infected by the place, its potential.

Be the hero.

His own thinking, haunting him, mocking him.

He might have already failed a hundred times. He couldn't know.

Small changes. Small.

A temptation burrowed its way to the forefront of his brain. Make a big change. Be a lord or king or a god. Destroy the creature, the afterbirth, the palimpsest, whatever Nix had called it. It would all work out.

Nix's admonition warred with that thinking. Little changes or everything is at risk. Minimize unforeseen consequences. Just put in a contingency, Nix had said, a dependency woven into the fabric of the world. A small thing to help us along.

Jyme watched as the irate creature flung Egil's corpse against the wall of the room with no more effort than if the priest had been a child. Egil's body hit the stone with a dull thud, left a smear of blood on the wall, and flopped grotesquely to the floor by Nix. The priest's hammer rang as the head struck the stone. They were dead, and in death the same as in life: side by side. Jyme was alone.

Be the hero.

Those were his words, or at least his thinking. And he meant them. And they teamed with Nix's admonition and won the war against temptation.

He licked his dry lips and had to work to slow his breathing. Sweat soaked his jerkin and tunic. His legs felt as though they'd give out at any moment, as though he'd slip off the spot, lose his footing somehow, and fall forever. He was still exhausted from the climb. And he was frozen by the weight of what he needed to do. He was paralyzed by the uncertainty of whether he should do it at all.

No, he knew he should do it. He may have already done it. Or maybe Nix had already done it. But the Jyme of right now didn't know what would happen, and the not-knowing terrified him.

The magic of the place-that-was-no-place stood the hairs on his neck on end, caused his skin to tingle. Fear magnified the sensation. He held the plates in his hands, their metal warm and vibrating, slippery, their potential already awakened by Nix.

They felt alive in his hands.

The world, *this* world, awaited his decision.

They'd fakked it up, the three of them. Fakked it up good. Everything they'd done had been for nothing, at least this time.

How many times? How many times? He felt like he was missing something, something important.

"Shite, shite, shite."

The hulking creature—Jyme still didn't know what to call it, not really—turned on the barrel-thick trunks of its legs and faced him. Its hood had fallen away, revealing the misshapen horror of its head, the congealed mien of four or five human faces. Slobber dripped from one of the mouths; blood dripped from another; rotten teeth poked out of all of them, the angles wrong, grotesque. The many mouths inhaled and exhaled in rhythm, causing the creature's form to heave and roll. Jyme winced at the sight of it. It was as otherworldly and impossible as this place.

Most of the bloodshot eyes in the lumpy egg of the creature's head moved about seemingly at random, though one pair managed to stay focused on Jyme. The mouths opened, strings of spit and blood stretched between the ruined lips, and they spoke together, but not quite in unison.

"Give us what I want I will we will do it you don't know how to do it I must we must do it!"

Hearing its voice steeled Jyme to his task. He inhaled, lowered his chin, rummaged deep into his being to find the courage, and eyed the horror.

"Fak you, thing. We go again."

All the eyes widened and looked at him, focused on him, and it lumbered toward him.

Jyme looked down at the plates, the writing—the script had changed to the common alphabet—and recited the stanzas as the creature began to scream. The words poured from him, easy, simple words, nothing like he would have expected, and he felt the power gathering. He tried to picture in his mind what he needed to picture, tried to imagine what he wanted, only small changes, a little help for them next time through. The huge creature closed on him, the clubs of its fists raised to strike.

Be the hero.

"No!" the creature said. "It must not no we I must no stop stop stop!"

As the remaking neared completion, Jyme realized his mistake, *their* mistake, the mistake they'd been making each time.

He made the change.

Be the hero.

CHAPTER ONE

NOW

Rain soaked him and grunts leaked from between the rotted, misshapen teeth of his mouths and all he could do was smell the world and blink in the downpour and the night and all he could do was walk and seek and try to keep the grunts from becoming moans and the moans from becoming screams, and there was no release reprieve rest but only the monotony of fear and constant pain and solitude and despair.

One clubfoot after another sank deep into the mud of the road he should not travel the road but he had lost his way in the rain and found himself on the road and now he did not want to get off the road because it must lead somewhere and somewhere drew him because he otherwise had nowhere to go forever. He'd had a name once, or names. He'd known them long ago but he could no longer remember them. They were buried under the chaotic heap of his thoughts and memories some his own some others he was a vestige a leftover an afterbirth the price.

Afterbirth afterbirth he was the Afterbirth, a necessary by-product to the process but irrelevant after. Afterbirth, that was his name now.

He murmured the words maybe or just thought them or moaned them it didn't matter because he was the afterbirth the leftover. Strange worlds lived in his memory but he could not know if they were his memories because he recalled only vignettes and they all melded and made no sense and so he moaned at the building pressure of the past and so he was the Afterbirth. He didn't know why he existed but knew only that the world he walked was not his world and it never could be his world.

He could smell himself the odor of his flesh and robes and realized he could smell others too others not far off. He had missed them in the rain and now he was too close to their sweat their shit their menstrual blood the road dust the wretched debris of the world in which he was the most wretched of all and the world was not his world for his world was gone in the casting of the Great Spell.

He should get off the road and remain unseen on the edges in the shadows where he always hid, where he stayed out of sight because he feared life in a cage and because he knew the words of the Great Spell were lost and so the remaking could not be cast again. He diverted toward the side of the road, thinking to shelter in a copse of trees—

"You a'right there?"

The voice shocked him stopped him in his steps and the mud gripped his sodden boots and his sodden thoughts drifted for a moment out of the mire of their despair to focus on the crispness of the moment. He blinked and blinked under the depths of his hood and cloak, his body heaving, his mouths open and pulling in wet breaths.

"I was askin' if you were all right," the voice said again, as a short, stout man stepped out from the deeper darkness under the copse of trees to one side of the road. The man was looking down as he stepped out, adjusting his breeches as if he had just relieved himself. His body was a normal body not an afterbirth not an unmade. A dagger and a short, wide-bladed sword hung from scabbards on his belt and a wide-brimmed floppy hat and trail cloak shielded him from the rain. He was a man of this world and the man looked up and was talking to him, to him, the man talked, spoke to him, perhaps because it was too far for the man to see him very well in the dark. The man had disease in him, eating at him from the inside, the Afterbirth could smell it. He would die soon, probably in great pain. The Afterbirth envied him and hated him for his mortality and weakness and normalcy.

"Sky's taking a piss, yeah? I like a little privacy when I do the same. Can take me a while, if you take my meaning. We probably shoulda just stayed nearer the caravan."

The man rummaged in his pocket for something as he approached, and the Afterbirth was rooted to the earth and when the man was close enough to see the Afterbirth, to take in his size and form, he stopped in his steps and the stink of fear rose on him.

"Uh . . ."

Even in the dark and the rain the Afterbirth could read the horror as it took root and grew on the man's bearded face and his eyes widened into shadowed, startled holes. The man took his hand from his pocket, took a tentative step back, and swallowed. The smell of fear-summoned sweat surrounded him like a fog now.

"What in the Gods are . . . ?"

The Afterbirth started to answer, for a moment forgetting himself and thinking he could converse with this frail man. A dozen mouths opened at once, emitting a rain of words in languages the Afterbirth alone spoke and the man lurched back as if the words had struck him a physical blow. He stumbled, mouth open, eyes wide, his face a mask of raw fear, and still the Afterbirth gargled and babbled and growled at him.

The man whirled and ran, babbling and garbling himself, syllables in the inarticulate language of terror. He slipped in the mud and wet as he went, and the wind tore his hat from his head, and it blew to the Afterbirth's blocky feet, stuck against his boots as if the gust were presenting him with a gift. He bent and picked it up in his twisted fingers and placed it on his head but it was too small of course and the fact enraged him for no reason that he could say except that rage and loneliness and despair were the only things he ever felt with clarity and he hated the world and those who lived in it and those who could feel and those who could die.

The man he'd frightened was shouting as he ran up a rise and out of sight off the road. "Up and armed! There's something out here! A creature! Up and armed!"

Shouts answered the man, the barking of dogs, the sounds of alarm building.

The man had spoken true, for the Afterbirth *was* a creature, but hearing the dying man say it of him put a flame to the kindling of his ever-present anger and he vented it in a growl, a wet, guttural sound issuing from his mouths and promising blood. He snarled and moved after the man, toward the shouting, toward the stink of them all, the trunks of his feet sticking in the mud as though the world itself—not his world but *theirs*—was trying to slow his pursuit and let time diminish his rage. But nothing could diminish it, nothing except that he somehow be unmade and thus made free.

More cries and shouting carried from beyond the road, and the Afterbirth heard the ring of metal, smelled the rush of adrenaline, the acridity of controlled fear.

He lumbered up the rise, hand over foot, slipping in the wet, his heavy tread putting dents in the soil. He could see well in the dark, and as he crested the rise he saw the caravan's camp before him, a dozen wagons on the grass of the plains, the circle of them ringing two large campfires, the milling silhouettes of two score people framed against the light of the flames. They darted about in alarm, several of them gathered around the man who'd fled from the Afterbirth. A few were shouting, pointing back toward the road, and the whole camp had the frenetic feel of a disturbed hive. They couldn't yet see him through the night and rain but the dogs that caught his scent barked and growled from within the ring of wagons. The horses, too, must have smelled him, for he heard their frightened whinnies and saw two of them rear up, pulling against their traces.

He moved in his ungainly fashion toward the camp, growling, and the sound of his voices was the inarticulate roar of worlds long gone. The animals in the camp went mad at the approach of him. The two horses that had reared now screamed, snapped their traces, and galloped off into the night. More shouts from the men and women. Dogs crouched and barked and growled to hoarseness but kept their distance. He got close enough that the glow of the firelight showed him to them.

"There! Over there!" shouted a man from within the gathered crowd, pointing at the Afterbirth.

"Kill it!" yelled another.

A dozen men holding sharp steel broke away from the rest and rushed out toward him. He picked up his pace, mumbling, and rushed headlong at them. They slowed some when they saw his size, and he smelled the fear on them. He ran into the crowd of them and hit them like a tide, trampling one, smashing another's skull with a blow from his fist. He didn't bother to defend himself as the rest of the men shouted and slashed and stabbed. Blades sank deeply into his flesh, the angry rhythm of violence, but he only heard it. He felt none of it, could feel none of it. The world could mark him, scar him, but could not hurt him. He was in the world but not of it. He could feel only the pain of his unending existence, the isolation of being entirely, utterly, forever solitary.

And anger. He could feel the anger.

Dogs rushed out, hackles high. They snarled at him from the edge of the melee, foaming at the mouth, but kept their distance. Women screamed, gathered children to them. Another horse broke free of its tie and bolted off into the night. The camp was in chaos. Men not yet in the fray shouted and sprinted toward him. Something disturbed one of the bonfires and a shower of sparks went up into the night, temporarily casting the whole of the area in an unearthly orange glow.

He lashed out with a thick arm and struck a man on the head, sending him careening backward and down. He bowled another man over as the man drove a thick-bladed sword through his abdomen, the blade scraping the teeth of one of his mouths. He roared and stomped on the downed man, crushing him underfoot.

"It should be dead!" another man shouted, slashing at the Afterbirth's neck.

He grabbed the speaker by the throat, lifted him kicking and gasping from the ground, and squeezed until he felt something give way. The man went still and the Afterbirth threw the corpse into another man, knocking him down, then stomped that one to death. Throughout he moved inexorably toward the circle of wagons, leaving broken bodies in his wake, the pressure in him creating the need to do violence.

"It can't be killed!" someone screamed. "Run! Run!"

The barking of the dogs grew crazed, terrified, the screams of the women and the wails of the young likewise. The acidic stink of pure terror filled the air and yet more men ran toward him, another six, shouting, blades in hand. They chopped and stabbed but he took the blows and killed them each in turn, one after another, breaking bones with his fists, crushing bodies under his boots. Their blows put gory ravines in his flesh, but only for a moment before his otherworldly nature sealed the gashes to scars.

Crossbow bolts thudded into his flesh from somewhere

within the ring of wagons. He felt the vibration of their impact, but no pain. He tore the bolts from his flesh, stabbed a young man through the face with one of them, drawing ever closer to the wagons. He could smell a few people hiding within them, terrified.

"Burn it!" shouted a woman, and another echoed her shout. "It's the only way!"

Another took up the call to burn him, another.

He trampled another man and ground the corpse into the rain-soaked earth. He broke the skull of another with a blow from his fist and lurched into the bright firelight within the ring of wagons, roaring.

His cloak was torn, the hood that normally shrouded his visage knocked back from the combat, and in the light of the bonfire the remaining caravanners saw him clearly. They froze for a moment, their faces sculpted into looks of horror and disgust. He murdered the quiet with a growl from his ruined lips and malformed mouths.

At that, most of the survivors turned and fled, some screaming, some in silent terror. Those who remained wavered, holding blades or clubs in drooping grips. Two men, however, found their nerve and hurriedly lit torches from the fire. Their bravery spread to some others and postures straightened. The men advanced, the flames dancing wildly in the rain as the torches shook in their hands.

The Afterbirth charged at the nearest of the men, the clubs of his fists held high. The man lurched backward, stabbing defensively with his blade and torch. The sword went into the Afterbirth's stomach and out his back; the torch put flames to his cloak, and the frayed material, though wet, caught fire. The Afterbirth ignored the blade and the flame and drove a fist into the man's face. Bones crunched. Blood sprayed and the man fell in a heap.

The other man, who'd circled behind the Afterbirth, cursed

and jabbed him with his torch. The cloak burned in another place, the fabric curling and smoking.

"Die, demon!" the man said.

The Afterbirth spun on the man, who tried to retreat but slipped in the wet grass. He backed off crabwise, his expression a mask of terror, but was too slow. The Afterbirth grabbed him up by his jerkin, lifted him overhead, and cast him several strides away into the bonfire. Another cloud of sparks exploded into the night, carrying with them the screams of the man, the smell of burning flesh. The man writhed for a moment, dislodging some of the logs, then went still.

The Afterbirth's cloak smoked and burned but fire could harm him no more than could steel. He let his clothing burn, framing him in flames, and roared.

Those who had found their bravery behind the torch-armed men turned and fled into the night.

The Afterbirth didn't pursue. Instead he rampaged among the wagons. Fire blistered his flesh only to reheal as he overturned crates and shattered urns, tore off doors and smashed in walls. He found a few elderly hiding in the wagons and beat them lifeless, letting their pain serve as a proxy expression of his own. His burning cloak had spread flames from him to the wagons and soon he stood naked and solitary amid a growing inferno. The flames sputtered and danced and raged against the rain. The smell of blood and death and smoke filled the air.

His chest heaved with exertion. He looked around upon the fire-lit slaughter, his anger slowly draining away, the pressure of his hateful existence eased, at least for a time.

He'd murdered more than two dozen, murdered them because . . . because . . .

Because the world shouldn't exist, because he shouldn't exist, because he didn't know why he walked the world, didn't know why he was forced to live with no respite and no hope of escape and he should not be in the world that was not his world and the pain should not be his pain and he needed it to stop stop stop.

He shouted his frustration into the sky for several minutes, his mouths wailing, doing battle with the rolls of thunder as the rain increased.

And when he was done and his rage had reduced down to mere despair, he found a new cloak among the wagons that could cover his malformed body and resumed his walk.

His body carried more scars but his hope was unincreased.

"Afterbirth," he muttered again and again.

He was the Afterbirth.

And he did know why he existed. He had no purpose, no reason for being. He walked the earth that was not his, aimless and alone.

He existed only because of the Great Spell and he was its afterbirth.

Raised voices and a man's drink-sloppy laugh carried from the hall through the closed door, startling Nix awake. He jerked in the cushioned chair, instinctively putting a hand on the hilt of one of his daggers. The voices receded, the laughter died, and he blinked dumbly in the dim green moonlight that filtered through the shutters and stained the room in viridian.

For a moment the remnants of a dream clung to his consciousness—he recalled a steaming swamp, a throng of reptile men in outlandish robes speaking a language he could not understand, a great spell of some kind or other, screams, but whether of exultation or terror he could not be sure. He tried to hold the images in mind because in his sleep-addled haze they seemed important somehow, but wakefulness gradually pushed them away, turned them to ghosts that leaked through the seams of his memory. He sat up as the real world exorcised the dream. He wiped drool from his cheek and oriented himself.

He'd fallen asleep in the worn, overstuffed chair beside Kiir's bed. She'd been febrile, bothered by bad dreams, and unable to sleep. Tesha had given her the night off to get well and Nix had offered to sit by her bedside until she fell asleep. He had little else to do, with Egil off on one of his drinking binges.

Kiir lay there now, her slim form wrapped in blankets, her breathing regular, her long red hair a cloud on the pillow.

Nix still felt discomfited from the dream, and the unhelpful green light of Minnear gave the room a surreal, unnatural feel. He ran a hand through his thick hair.

"Fakking moon," he whispered. He hated sleeping in the light of a full Minnear. It had given him nightmares ever since the events with Blackalley. He pushed those memories from his mind on the double quick.

He yawned and the yawn turned to a burp and he winced at the fishy aftertaste of Gadd's eel stew, which he'd forced down as supper hours earlier. Likely the squirming fruit of the Meander had done his dreams few favors, too. No doubt, he'd be resurrecting the stew by way of fish-flavored belches for the next several hours.

He solemnly swore then and there to keep future suppers restricted to meat that walked rather than swam, ideally accompanied by liquid composed of hops and fermented wheat. He put a hand to his chest: So oathed.

He glanced at Kiir, her body a shapely rise under the thin blankets, and it hit him that he was sitting watch in a chair beside a beautiful woman's bed instead of trying to charm his way into it.

"Huh," he said, vaguely surprised at himself.

Had he gotten respectable somehow? Honorable? If so, when the fak had *that* happened?

Somewhat disgusted with himself, he looked about the floor for a bottle of spirits, anything to kill the taste of eel stew. Seeing nothing, he could only endure the taste while he coexisted with his own nobility of character.

He was turning into Egil, was what was happening. And that was because Egil was turning into something else, and one of them had to carry the weight of respectability in their partnership. The priest, the sole worshipper of the dead god Ebenor, who'd been a god for only a moment, hadn't been himself since the events with Rose and Mere and that fakking serpentman mindmage in the Deadmire. Rose had been inadvertently caught up in an assassination plot by the Thieves' Guild, and had been afflicted with a condition that only a powerful mindmage could relieve. So Egil, Nix, and Mere had journeyed to the Deadmire, seeking the legendary mindmage Odrhaal, all the while pursued by agents of the Thieves' Guild, intent on killing Rose as the sole surviving witness to the assassination attempt. The three had eventually found Odrhaal deep in the Deadmire and he'd fixed Rose, but at a price. The sisters had opted to stay as apprentices to the serpentman mindmage, and Odrhaal had placed false memories in the surviving guild men. Egil still regarded the events as a failure, and felt as though they should've killed Odrhaal rather than let Rose and Mere go. Nix, however, knew that they'd had no choice. They were no match for Odrhaal.

Still, Nix had no way to know if the choices they'd made in the swamp had been of their own free will or if they'd been manipulated by Odrhaal's mind magic. It ate at him sometimes. It ate at Egil worse, no doubt because it reminded the priest of his failure years earlier to keep his wife and daughter safe. Egil had grown increasingly taciturn recently, and drank even more than usual. Nix had been of little use in helping his friend navigate through his despair.

His train of thought caused something from his dream to try to bubble its way back up to consciousness, but it slipped away before breaking the surface. He shifted in his chair to get more comfortable, failed in the effort, mentally cursed the chair for being terrible as a chair, and watched Kiir sleep, as he'd promised.

The chair attempted to cramp him into standing but he refused out of spite and soon drifted off despite his discomfort; his last thoughts before sleep took him hovering in a half dream state in which he imagined a great war between armies of wizards and serpentmen, all of them wielding the green magic of the moon, the power of it beyond anything Nix had ever seen, and in the process destroying the world.

He awoke sometime later to hear Kiir mumbling and making small, alarmed noises. He opened an eye to make sure she was all right. Nix could not tell how long he'd dozed, but Minnear still polluted the room in a miasmic glow.

She was still sleeping, waving a hand in front of her face as if to shoo an insect. Lines furrowed her brow, and her lips turned down in a frown. She moaned and mumbled. Her gestures sharpened, her tone grew louder, and her body spasmed as if she were pushing something away.

"No!" she said. "Stop!"

Nix roused himself fully, wincing at the cramp in his back. He leaned forward and placed a hand on her forearm. His touch stilled her, but her brow furrowed more deeply and she shook her head.

"No. No."

"Kiir," he said, and gently shook her. "Kiir, wake up."

She opened her eyes and for an instant they looked filled with terror, but when she registered Nix's face, her location, she relaxed. She covered his hand with hers.

"You're all right," he said. "Fever dream?"

She nodded. Her touch was warm, still somewhat feverish. "I'm so thirsty."

"I can go get you some water."

"No, don't leave. What's the hour?"

"Dunno for sure. Late, though. Nightmare, was it? You were shouting. Small wonder you've slept so poorly of late."

She looked past him at the wall, her eyes distant. "Not a nightmare so much . . . just a dream. I've had it often lately."

"Well, not a nightmare is good, yeah?"

She brushed a few wisps of sweat-dampened hair from her face and gave him an absent half smile that highlighted her freckled beauty. Were he a lesser man, then and there he'd have been tempted to ask her if he could share her bed.

"I wouldn't say 'good,'" she said softly. She focused on him and smiled more broadly. "Thank you for staying, Nix."

He felt his cheeks warm and pulled back his hand to give her space. "Of course. I said I would."

"You did."

The moonlight colored her skin but did not damage her beauty.

He cleared his throat. "So, are you . . . going back to sleep, then?"

He winced at himself for asking, but he couldn't help himself. She was beautiful and he wasn't *that* good a man. He just wanted to give her an opening.

She sighed and pulled the sheets tightly about her, closing her eyes. "Mmmhmm."

"But you still want me to stay?" he said, then hurriedly added, "In the chair, I mean. Which is an awful chair."

"No, you can go if you want, Nix. I know that chair isn't comfortable. I'll be fine now."

He sighed, adjusted his expectations, and eased back into the chair, determined to once more do battle with its cushions. "I think I'll stay until you fall back asleep at least. Then maybe go have an ale and see if Egil returns. What was the dream about? I've been having a few of my own lately."

She didn't open her eyes, just nested more deeply into the bed. "That we were the dream," she said quietly. "That nothing was real and everything was a dream."

Nix blew out a soft whistle. "Well, that's fakkin' disquieting." He thought it somehow echoed his own dream. "It's this moonlight, yeah? Some are more sensitive to it than others. No one should sleep bathed in this green."

She opened one eye and smiled. "Not alone anyway." She lifted the covers slightly. "Join me?"

The sudden turn took Nix by surprise. He'd been hoping for the invitation but hearing it made him flush and he stuttered with the effort of forming an answer.

"But . . . I . . . you said . . ."

Kiir laughed. "I was teasing you, Nix Fall. You should see your face when you think about sex." She slackened her expression and looked at him sidelong, a bit oafish.

"I look like that? Really? Hells. Given how often I think about sex, people must think I look a lout more often than not."

"Well," she said. "Maybe not quite that bad. Anyway, I'm not asking for marriage here. Just sex. I know what this is."

"I . . . you do? Because I'll own I'm not sure I do. I feel a bit like a nervous first-time hob right now. That explains my expression maybe."

She chortled. "You're so silly about some things."

He frowned. "Seems I'm not having my best night. Silly, now?"

She propped herself up on her elbow. "Yes. Especially about women. I know you like me. I know you think I'm pretty. But I also know why you're hesitating."

"You do?"

"Yes! I see the way you look at her. Everyone sees it! Including her."

By "her," Nix knew that Kiir meant Tesha, who managed the Slick Tunnel for Egil and Nix and allowed the two of them to get away with precisely nothing.

"What exactly do you think you see?" Nix asked. "Because I don't even know what I feel about her."

"Ha!" she said, and collapsed back into the covers. "Yes, you do."

"No," Nix insisted and meant it. "I like her, true. And respect her. And I think she's beautiful and . . ."

Kiir stared at him, her delicate, plucked eyebrows raised knowingly.

"Shite," Nix said. "I guess I do know a bit of what I feel, don't I?" He sighed. "Well, I didn't realize I was so obvious. I guess this means I won't be joining you, alas. But not because I'm not tempted," he quickly added.

She laughed. "Maybe you're not as inconstant as she thinks."

Nix's mood took an instant turn. He leaned forward in the chair, elbows on his knees. "First, where in the Pits did you learn that word? Second, inconstant? Me? She thinks that? I'm as loyal a man as there is. Save Egil maybe."

Her expression told him her mood had turned, too. She stared at him hard, her mouth pressed into a tight line. "To answer your first question: I know the word because I'm a prostitute, not an idiot. And to answer your second: Neither she nor anyone questions your loyalty generally. She questions it when it comes to women. Because your eye wanders, yeah? Because you are tempted, yeah?"

"I . . ." He trailed off, unable to gainsay her words. He sank back in the chair and crossed his arms over his chest. "Actually that's fair. But it's only because you're all so lovely! How's my eye supposed to stay in one place? And why does everyone know everything about me except me?"

"Ha! You're not hard to read, Nix."

Nix went on as if she hadn't spoken. "And the word galls, like something Egil would say. Inconstant. Did she use that word specifically?"

Kiir rolled her eyes. "Gods."

Nix leaned forward. "Did she?"

"Being honest," she said, and blew out a sigh, "I don't remember if she used that word specifically. But that was the sense of her meaning. Let's be done now, all right? I'm tired. We can talk tomorrow."

"Hrm. All right, fine," he said, and stewed in silence as she settled into the blankets, turned her back to him, and eventually fell back asleep.

When he was sure she was in a deep sleep and not revisiting her dream, he rose, made an obscene gesture at the chair for being so damned uncomfortable, stretched, and walked out of the room into the dark hall. He gently closed the door behind him, turned, and almost walked into Vella as she led a glassy-eyed middle-aged hob toward her room. The woman moved as quietly as a thief. She was taller than Nix, with raven hair that reached her waist, and colorful floral tattoos that covered both her arms from shoulder to wrist.

"Nix," she said in her husky voice, by way of greeting.

"Do I look inconstant to you?" he said to them. He stood back and held out his arms so they could regard him more easily.

"Huh?" the hob said, squinting, his voice slurred from Gadd's ale and the late hour.

Vella stared hard at Nix while she put a protective arm around the hob. "Ignore him. He babbles. Come on, my lovely. Vella has lessons to teach you."

She challenged Nix with her eyes to say anything more and he didn't take the dare. He watched her walk away, the dark dress she wore hugging the pronounced curve of her hips, and wondered what it would be like to bed a woman with legs so long.

And then immediately cursed himself for being fakking inconstant and constantly tempted. Wandering eye, indeed.

From down the hall he heard the hob say to Vella, "What does *inconstant* mean?"

"Shh," she said, and took him into her room.

Muttering to himself, Nix descended the large central staircase that led down to the soft glow of the lantern-lit common room. The smell of stale tobacco and eel stew hung thick in the air, the atmosphere spiced with an undercurrent of sweat and the pungency of the pisspots, which given the hour were probably filled to capacity.

"Inconstant," he said to himself.

The clay lamps on the tables and the glow of flames in the large hearth overwhelmed the green glow of Minnear coming in through the leaded glass windows—the ornate glass of the windows a reminder that the building the Tunnel occupied had once been a nobleman's manse. Judging from the mere handful of patrons still at the tables, Nix figured it had to be near the third hour past midnight. Almost closing time.

One serving girl worked the few occupied tables, and two working girls, Lis and Arris, lingered by Gadd's bar, looking lovely but tired, wrapped too tightly in their figure-hugging dresses, and obviously ready for the night to end. Gadd tended his cups and bottles with his usual diligence and Nix wondered if the towering, dark-skinned Easterner ever slept. Nix didn't see Tesha on the floor and that was probably just as well. As irritated as he was, he might have started a fight with her over her word choice.

Three hard-looking drunks sat at the corner table near the Tunnel's double doors and talked and laughed loud enough to irk Nix, but he fought down his impulse to confront them and instead went to the bar. The girls smiled at him and he smiled in return.

"Doing all right?" he asked.

"Tired is all," Lis said, and Arris nodded agreement.

Nix made homage to the fading, stained portrait of pig-faced Hyrum Mung, the lord mayor of Dur Follin, which hung on the wall behind the bar. They should've taken it down—Mung was a contemptible figure when he wasn't comical—but the painting had become something akin to the Tunnel's mascot.

Gadd, in a sleeveless tunic and stained apron, put a tankard of ale in front of Nix and smiled his mouthful of filed teeth.

"Obliged," Nix said. He raised the tankard to the painting.

"To the ugliest man in the room," he said. He took a draught and immediately felt better. Nothing topped Gadd's bitter ales.

"Is that anise in there?" he asked Gadd.

Gadd grinned and nodded. "Like it?"

Nix nodded in return. "I believe I do."

"You look bothered," Lis said to him. She took the seat beside him and blew a wisp of her long dark hair from her face. She took his tankard in hand and took a sip, nodding approvingly at Gadd.

"You do indeed look bothered," Gadd said.

Gadd usually played as though he couldn't speak Common, mostly to further his mystique among the patrons as a savage foreign beer alchemist, but Nix knew the man to be articulate. He knew little else of Gadd, though, only that his history was somehow tied up with Tesha and the distant realm of Jafari, and that he could handle a tulwar when necessary.

Nix started to answer, but instead belched up another fishy cloud.

Lis winced at the smell and waved a ringed hand before her face. "Gods, Nix."

"Blame Gadd," Nix said. "It's his stew I'm raising from the dead." He took another gulp of ale to chase the taste of the burp, then said to Gadd, "It's well that you make such excellent ale, my friend, because your stew is most, most wanting."

"Excel in one thing and be content," Gadd said in his thickly accented Common.

"Something from your homeland?" Lis asked him.

Nix pointed at him with the tankard. "And where is that homeland again? And how the fak did you get all the way here? And what's your history with Tesha? And what *in the name of the Gods* did you do to so curse that eel stew?"

Lis and Arris giggled.

The men on the other side of the room laughed louder, one of them hitting the table for emphasis. Once again, Nix resisted the urge to tell them to quiet down.

"That story's for another time, Nix Fall and Lady Lis," said Gadd. "As for the stew, I take no responsibility. The eels that come out of the Meander are bottom feeders. They eat shite and taste similarly. But they're cheap in the fish market and that's why the stew is on the house."

Nix said, "And that's also why, despite being free, a full pot sits even at this moment over the fire, stinking up the room." He burped again, eliciting moans from the girls. "The drunks are smarter than me when it comes to culinary choices, it seems."

"I stick to bacon and eggs," Lis said, fidgeting with the charm of Lyyra, the goddess of sensuality, which she wore on a chain that hung from her neck.

"Wise," Nix said somberly. "Where's Tesha?"

"Retired for the night," Lis said.

"Wasn't feeling well," Gadd said, then quickly added, "But not because of the stew."

Nix grinned and shook his head. "Look at that. Even Gadd jests now. The world's gone upside down." He turned serious. "She doesn't have Kiir's fever, does she?"

"No," Gadd said. "Female matter."

"Ah," Nix said.

"Speaking of fever," Arris said. "Is Kiir all right?"

Nix nodded. "Fever broke. She'll be fine. Sleeping now."

Lis eyed him sidelong. "It was kind of you to watch over her. You'd be welcome to watch over me sometime, too, fever or no."

Nix dropped a fist lightly on the bar in mock anger. "You see? You're lovely and you're flirting. I know it's only half-sincere, but even so. This is why it's so hard."

"Already?" Lis asked coyly, eyeing his groin.

Nix smiled and shook his head. "Everyone with the jests, now. Must be the hour." To Gadd: "What about Egil, then? Seen him?"

Gadd's expression fell and he shook his head and Nix knew what that meant. Likely the priest would stumble drunk into the Tunnel around daybreak, if he got back at all. Or he'd pass out in the street. Or who knew what else? Nix knew he ought to go find the priest and he would. But before he did he took another swallow of ale and turned in his seat to face Lis and Arris. "Tell me something, do I seem inconstant to you? Because—"

"Yes," said Lis.

"Very much so," Arris added.

"Damn it," Nix said, and Gadd chuckled, the sound a deep rumble.

"But we still love you," Lis said.

"And I, you," Nix said with a harrumph.

The men in the corner table again laughed loud and long, and the sound was as irritating to Nix as a pebble in his shoe. He'd had enough.

"Isn't it closing time?" he said to Lis.

"Nearly," she said and yawned as though to make the point. "Those ones have been here going on three hours. Loud, they are. Rude, too."

One of the men at the table suddenly pushed back his chair, turned his head, and puked all over the floor. Lis and Arris exclaimed a collective, "Eww," and looked away. The other two laughed at their nauseous friend. Gadd cursed in his native tongue. The serving girl—Nix had forgotten her name—looked at the bar for guidance.

"Can't handle his drink is what!" said one of the three, and the other guffawed. Even the puker laughed.

"Well, clean that up, girl," one of the others said to the serving girl.

"No doubt they drank your stew," Nix said to Gadd, by way of a final shot as he bounded from his chair and strode across the room. He put a hand on the arm of the serving girl and said softly, "Go on over to the bar, now."

The puker didn't see him coming, but the other two did.

"She gonna clean this up?" one of them asked. His eyes were too close together over a protuberant nose, and he had a long, narrow, pox-scarred face that reminded Nix of a crescent moon.

Nix ignored him and stepped beside the puker, taking care not to soil his boots in the vomit.

"Stand," Nix said to the man.

"Who in the Hells are you?" said the third man.

Nix hadn't walked across the floor intending a heated confrontation necessarily, but with one seeming imminent, he found he welcomed it.

"I'm the owner," Nix said, then to the puker, "One of them, anyway. Stand the fak up, I said."

Balding and grizzled, the man wiped his mouth with his sleeve, turned around in his chair, and looked up at Nix through bleary eyes. "What's this bother now?"

"He didn't mean nothing by the puke," said moon-face.

"I guess I mean nothing by this, then," Nix said, and kicked the puker's chair leg, spilling the chair and the man. When the man hit the floor, he put a hand in his puddle of puke.

"Aw, fak! Look at this now! That's disgusting."

"Hey!" the other two said to Nix, and started to stand.

"Stay in your fakkin' seats," Nix ordered them, pointing a finger.

The puker was trying to rise, but before he could Nix grabbed him by his vest and pulled him to his feet.

The man visibly winced in the face of Nix's fish breath.

"Fak, man," the puker said, turning his face to the side. "Your breath."

"Yours isn't flowers, either, friend," Nix said. "Smelling, as it does, of puke. Now . . ."

Nix forcibly turned the man around, grabbed a handful of trousers, and hoisted him high enough to elicit a high-pitched yelp.

"As I said, I'm the owner and that's my floor you puked on. I frown on that generally. I frown on it particularly when the puker behaves like a bunghole slubber. Now, you outstayed your welcome a while back and the puke just mortars tight the point."

"I didn't puke on purpose!" the man protested, his voice an octave higher than it had been a moment before.

"It just came on all of a sudden like," said the third man, and pointed with his thick, hairy arms at the hearth. "Probably that eel stew."

Nix sympathized with that, but he was in a mood, so he hitched the trousers up higher.

"My balls, man!" wailed the puker.

"Your balls are leaving," Nix said, leading the man toward the Tunnel's double doors. "Along with the rest of you. And if you puke on my floor on the way out you'll not only clean it up yourself but you'll empty the pisspots as added penance."

"Come now!" the man said. "What'd I do to you?"

Halfway to the door, Nix looked over his shoulder back at the table. "You didn't hear me? You two slubbers, too. Out. We're closed. Gadd, close up."

"There's still patrons here," the moon-faced one said, and he pointed with his chin at the other table across the common room, where a couple of drunks slouched in their chairs, snoring. Not even the tumult had awakened them.

"And we still have our ales," said the other, holding up his tankard. "We paid."

"Too bad," Nix said. "We're closed and you're leaving."

He watched as Lis hitched up her dress and hurried up the stairs, taking them two at a time, probably to inform Tesha what was happening. Gadd stood with his hands on the bar, glaring at the men, pointed teeth bared in a grimace.

"Bunghole," the larger one said to Nix, but both of them rose, muttering at each other. Nix noted the blades on their belts, their scowls. Both were bigger than Nix and neither was as drunk as the puker.

"He just puked, is all he did," said moon-face. "Not the first to do so in here, I'd wager."

Nix propelled the puker the last few steps to the doors, stepped out onto the porch, and shoved him into the street. The man stumbled, tried to catch himself, failed, and fell face-first in the road. He was spitting mud as he whirled and stood on wobbly legs. He glared at Nix through drunken eyes and drew his blade. It stuck for a moment in the scabbard before he got it clear. Minnear still rode the sky and cast the world in green, irritating Nix still more.

"Come on, you fakker," puker said, holding his blade inexpertly.

Nix burped, cursed the stew anew, and bounded down the stairs and into the road, in no mood to take lip from some drunk slubber. He drew his own blade and the man visibly quailed.

Nix had no intention of killing the man, of course, but thought maybe the man could afford to be taught a small lesson.

"We see how it is, now, don't we?" said a voice from behind him, the voice of the big, moon-faced one. "That's the way you want this to go, then. Taking a run at a drunk man, are you?"

The puker firmed up to hear his friends backing his play, and a dumb smile split his muddy face. Nix turned to see the puker's two companions standing on the porch, a promise of violence in their scowls, blades already in their fists.

"Things took a turn, yeah?" said the puker, grinning.

Nix nonchalantly drew a dagger to pair with his sword. "Things do often take a turn, I've found. Seems to be my luck of late. But listen, I can't just teach lessons to all three of you. This goes the way it looks and I'll probably need to kill two of you. You clear on that? You want to talk among yourselves a moment and decide who'll die?"

"Listen to this one," said the big, hairy one to moon-face.

"He's got big balls, I'll give him that," said moon-face.

"Bigger than your pukey friend, to that I can attest. First-hand, as it were." Nix shrugged. "I guess I need to start working on my explanation to the Guard for the two or three bodies they'll soon find. I'll start with something like: They were bunghole slubbers, Goodsir, and no one will miss them, and they got what was coming after a fair warning."

The big one smirked and the two started down the two steps of the porch, spacing themselves to come at Nix from different angles, while the puker eased forward from behind.

Nix spun and flung his dagger. It speared the puker's thigh and he went down screaming.

Nix drew a second dagger to replace the first and smiled at the other two. Their confidence and their advance both faltered.

"You need to move faster," Nix said. "Because things always seem to take a turn back, yeah? That seems to be my luck, too. You boys maybe rethinking things? It's not too late. You can get out of here with bruised pride, a stuck leg, and nothing else."

"Fakker stabbed my leg!" said the puker.

"That's obvious to all of us," Nix said to him. "Gods, man."

"Get him!" said the puker, but still the two hesitated.

Just then a sound came from within the Slick Tunnel, a prolonged howl tinged with madness. The two men tensed, went wide-eyed, and backed quickly away from the doors, but still staying well away from Nix.

"I may have to take back that bit about it not being too late," Nix said, and Gadd burst through the double doorway, his pointed teeth bared in a grimace. The tulwar he gripped in his hands was nearly as long as Nix was tall. He raised the sword high and lunged first at one, then at the other of the two men, both of whom immediately turned and bolted in opposite directions. Gadd pursued the big one for a few strides, howling wildly.

"Don't leave me, you fakkers!" said the puker, but they didn't so much as slow and the darkness soon swallowed them.

Nix looked back on the puker, his face pale from pain and fear and blood loss. "Looks like you need better friends."

The man clambered to his feet, favoring his bad leg, Nix's

dagger still half-buried in his thigh. He looked at Gadd as the big man came back, then at Nix, fear in his eyes.

"Don't let that savage kill me!" the puker said.

"I'm not sure I could stop him if he had a mind," Nix said. "But I think you'll live to see the sun, at least if you get that leg stanched. Just tie it off above the wound." Nix reached into a belt pouch, withdrew a silver tern, and tossed it to the man, who caught it despite being drunk and wounded. "Go see one of Orella's saints. They'll take care of you, even at this hour. Go on. Limp along out of here and don't come back. Not ever."

The man backed off slowly, favoring his wounded leg. He took a bite of the crown, his eyes registering surprise when the give showed it genuine.

"And probably you should make some new friends who won't run off on you," Nix said, as the man continued his retreat. "And also maybe drink less and in general be less of an arse. No one likes an arse. Oh, and don't puke on people's floors. No one likes that, either, least of all me."

"It was the fakkin' eel stew," the man shot back, backing away now as fast as his wounded leg would allow.

Gadd growled and the man turned and scrambled away.

"Keep the dagger," Nix called. "You pull that out now and you'll die in the street." Nix turned to face Gadd, whose pointed teeth glowed white in the dark oval of his face. "You heard him, yeah? It was the eel stew. That makes this whole thing your fault."

"Gofti!" Gadd said, still grinning. "No one made you pick a fight. But did you see the look in their eyes when I came through the doors? Like children, they looked."

Nix grinned. "I saw it. In fairness to them, being charged by a tall dark-skinned man with sharpened teeth and an absurdly large blade would cause any sensible person to move in the other direction."

"Hmm. I suppose this is true."

"Do you need someone to decapitate to calm yourself down

or . . . ? I'm sure we could catch up with that limping puker if need be."

Gadd laughed aloud.

"Anyway," Nix said as he scabbarded his blades, "obliged for the aid. And *gofti*? What is that?"

Gadd's broad face twisted up with thinking and he said, "It is like when Egil says *bah*."

"Ah. That I know well. 'Gofti' it is, then. More from your homeland, yeah?"

"Yes."

"Which is where again?"

Gadd crossed his arms across his chest and shook his head in the negative.

Before Nix could say anything more, Tesha bustled out of the Tunnel's doors in a loose nightdress, her long dark hair hanging wildly to her shoulders, questions and anger brewing in her dark eyes. Lis hovered in the doorway behind her. Tesha took in Nix, Gadd, and the tulwar and asked, "Is anyone dead?"

"No," Nix said. "And have I told you you look lovely?"

"Too often. It's starting to lose its meaning. Have you undermined business with . . . whatever happened here?"

Nix looked down the road, back at Tesha. "Maybe with three slubbers, but otherwise, no. I doubt those few drunks inside even woke up. And Gadd and I are unharmed, thank you for asking."

Tesha ignored him and said to Gadd, "I've told you to keep your distance from them, haven't I? It's bad enough I've got the two of them intimidating patrons. I don't need you doing the same or getting caught up in their schemes."

"I don't intimidate anyone," Nix said. "I'm fakking charming is what. And schemes? Really?"

Gadd stood up straight and looked at Tesha down the length of his wide nose, a small act of defiance. "He needed aid and I gave it. He's a friend."

Tesha's mouth tightened.

"I didn't need it," Nix said. "But appreciate the gesture nevertheless."

Tesha exhaled loudly. "Is the Watch coming or can I go back to bed?"

"Watch isn't coming," Nix said. "Uh, at least I don't think."

"Fine." She brushed some stray hairs out of her face. "Good night, then."

She started to turn away, but halted when Nix asked, "Are you feeling any better?"

"What?"

"I heard you weren't feeling well," he said. "Are you all right?"

She turned and looked unsure of what to say. "I'm . . . fine. Yes. Thank you. Where's Egil?"

"I don't know," Nix said. "Drinking somewhere."

"Well, maybe you should go find out where?" she said, eyebrows raised. "Being his friend, and all."

"Maybe I should," Nix said.

She stomped a foot and pursed her lips. "Good."

"Good. And I'm not inconstant."

That last took her by surprise, to judge from her expression.

The two drunks who had been sleeping at tables staggered past her, muttering apologies. Once they were past she said to Nix, "No, you're not. And I'm glad you're all right. Both of you. Now I'm going back to bed." To Gadd, she said, "Close up. Clear the house, give any hobs upstairs notice that we're closing, and let's get everyone some rest. Everyone sleeps in an extra hour tomorrow. I'll make my bread come breakfast." She looked skyward. "This fakking moon."

"That's what I said!" Nix echoed. "And I'm glad you're feeling better, if I didn't say it already."

She turned and went back into the Tunnel, leaving Gadd and Nix standing outside.

"I like her," Nix said.

"I know," Gadd said. "I'll leave back doors open for you and Egil."

"Well enough," Nix said. "Listen, I feel obliged to say that you're *not* lovely when you're angry. You know that, yeah?"

Gadd laughed aloud once more.

Nix headed out. He smiled as he went, pleased that Tesha had acknowledged that he wasn't inconstant.

His night had taken another turn for the better. Now he just needed to find Egil and drag him home. Hopefully his luck would hold.

CHAPTER TWO

Ool's clock chimed the third hour past midnight, the sound deep and resonant in the quiet darkness of streets long ago abandoned to night's small hours. The towering stone spire of the clock rose high above the city's skyline, an ancient finger pointed at the stars. Minnear had nearly set, surrendering the sky to its sister moon, Kulven, and its soft silver glow. Likewise, the linkboys had surrendered their charges and the charcoal in the torch cages atop the streetlamps had burned down to glowing nubs as Nix made his way along Dur Follin's shadowed streets.

The faint, slow beat of drums carried from somewhere to the south, probably from the Low Bazaar, which never slept. The sound reminded Nix of a heartbeat, like the city's pulse. Most of Dur Follin was either abed or drunkenly ensconced at their taproom of choice, though the occasional pedestrian or carriage moved slowly through the cobblestone streets.

Nix spotted furtive, cloaked figures on business he assumed to be illicit, passed two smiling but fatigued parties of wealthy scions slumming until dawn on this side of the Meander. Nix kept his distance from the hard-eyed, suspicious bodyguards orbiting the entourage. From time to time he saw a teamster moving goods across town to the river markets, taking advantage of streets unclogged with traffic, and Nix twice spotted members of the Watch in their orange tabards.

As ever, drunks and the poor lay here and there at the mouths of alleys or in darkened doorways, little more than human jetsam trying to catch some rest before the poke of a watchman's truncheon awakened them and ordered them along. Dogs barked in the distance; rats skulked in alleyways.

Nix hit several of the taverns and inns along the Dock Ward in which Egil sometimes drank or picked a fight, but the priest wasn't at any of them. They all smelled of fish and seaweed and sweat and Nix cursed Egil for making him abide the stink. The one-eyed tapkeep at the Rotted Onion said Egil had been there until about midnight.

"Drunk?" Nix asked, wincing as he burped up Gadd's stew yet again.

"More sad'n drunk, I'd say."

Nix laid a couple of commons on the scarred wood of the bar before leaving, then worked his way east through a few more establishments. Each one took him farther from the river and the Archbridge, farther from the wealthier west side of Dur Follin and closer to the Poor Wall and the Warrens. It was as though he were tracking the movement of poverty. As he moved east, each establishment was a bit more run-down than the last.

Egil was in none of them. As Nix exited Tevin's Taphouse, a breeze from the south bore the faint, charnel reek of the distant Deadmire, recalling to Nix's memory Rose and Mere and Odrhaal.

Once more his dream tried to surface and once more it failed.

He was soon sweaty and tired and irritable, and by the time

the more immediate stink of the Heap did battle with and de-feated the fainter, rotting smell of the Deadmire, he'd about had enough. He resolved to check a couple more places and leave off for the night. Egil knew how to take care of himself, and Nix was not his keeper.

He was close to the Poor Wall by then, the high, crumbling stone line that separated the desperate poverty of the Warrens from the rest of the city. Through a break in the buildings ahead he saw the rise of the Heap framed against the moonlit sky—a huge mound of rubbish that looked and smelled like a giant had shat on the city.

Nix stopped in the middle of the street, put his hands on his hips, and stared at it. He had spent his youth living hand to mouth in the Warrens, picking through the refuse of the Heap, wallowing in its stink. The mound seemed to him to have shrunk over the years, but that couldn't be right. It had to be just that he'd grown. Either way, seeing it put him in mind of his childhood, which put him in mind of Mamabird. She'd been ill of late. He'd been meaning to check on her. Might do Egil good to see her, too, if Nix could find him.

Nix turned a corner down a narrow, dimly lit street that ran parallel to the Poor Wall. Two-story buildings lined it, all of them built so close together they might as well have been joined. Nix smelled chimney smoke, a skunk's spray, and spotted a cat as it darted out from under the skeleton of a dying tree and crossed the street ahead. Farther down the block he caught sight of a lone man walking down the opposite side of the thorough-fare. The man, too small and not stumbling enough to be Egil, seemed to register Nix at about the same time.

Nix thought nothing of it until the man hooked his left thumb on his belt while putting his right hand in his trouser pocket, one of the signals guild thieves used to identify them-selves to one another. Nix always made it a point to know the identifying gestures, which changed from month to month.

Nix didn't answer the identifier in kind but picked up his

pace and cut across the street to intercept the man. The man slowed at Nix's approach. He put a hand to a hilt on his weapon belt and looked past Nix, head cocked, sniffing for an ambush. Nix did the same and saw no sign of anyone else. He kept his hands at his sides and free of steel for the moment.

"No danger here, friend," Nix called, his voice carrying in the quiet. He stopped five paces from the man, who stood a head taller than Nix and looked almost as wide as Egil under his hooded cloak.

The man stopped, too, keeping the distance between them.

"Nix?" the man asked, and Nix recognized the sloppy, wet tone.

"Trelgin?"

Trelgin was Seventh Blade on the Guild's Committee, answering directly to the Upright Man, Rusk. Egil and Nix had played a role in Rusk's ascension to head the guild—though Rusk wouldn't remember it that way—but they'd also killed a good number of guild men in the process, so feelings remained raw.

"You're a long way from home, Trelgin," Nix said, staying coiled. "Guild house is back in the Dock Ward. Aster whispering mysteries in your ear and telling you to come across town? Or did Rusk just run you off, finally?"

Trelgin took his hand from the hilt of his sword and lowered his hood. A palsy had afflicted Trelgin at some point in his life and caused the left half of his face to droop like melted wax. His speech was halting and every fourth or fifth word came out wet and loose.

"I'd say the same about you being far from home but then I can smell the Heap in the air plain, so I guess a little Warrens rat like you ain't quite so far from your den after all, huh?"

Nix smiled. "I'd reckon what you smell is the drool leaking out of the corner of your mouth, or maybe it's your upper lip, smelling, as it does, of shite, which is what comes of having your nose up Rusk's arsehole more hours of the day than not.

Isn't that about the state of things? Seventh Blade's a shite job, isn't that what you guild boys say? I just didn't know you meant it literally."

Trelgin's droopy face spasmed, as if trying and failing to look angry. "Fak off, Nix Fall. I'll be on my way, if you don't mind."

"No need to run off, Trelgin," Nix said, sidestepping to put himself in Trelgin's path. "I'm just in a mood, is all. Listen, you or any of your boys see Egil tonight?"

Trelgin tried to look sly behind his droopy features. "I saw him, sure."

Nix waited a beat before saying, "You going to tell me where, or do I need to knock out your teeth and inquire of them individually?"

Trelgin's face managed to twist itself into a scowl. "You try that sometime, Nix. Things might not end as you think. And I'll tell you, certain. Your boy's at the Masquerade last I saw. Drunk. Got some difficulties, too."

Nix understood his point. "How many difficulties?"

"Five when I left. Neighborhood toughs. Just slubbers. Been building up in there awhile. He should have just walked on, though maybe walking's not something he can manage at the moment. Or maybe a scrum is what he's looking for. Why don't you go there and get in the mix? Maybe you and Egil both get clicked, save me some trouble. I'll throw a pray to Aster that things end just so. Anyway . . ."

Trelgin started to walk forward, as though he'd push through Nix, but Nix gave no ground. He put a palm on Trelgin's chest, halting him, and stared into his face.

"You could have lent a hand, Trelgin. Sent a guild man to come get me. Even walked him out of there. Either would've gone a long way with me."

Trelgin's lips curled into something Nix figured was a sneer, though it was hard to tell. "I'm not some second-story man you can intimidate or a two-common fen you can sweet-talk. You and him are nothing to me until you're not. And right now, you're still not. So fak you and your way, and take your hand off me."

Nix pointedly did not remove his hand. "No, fak you, you droop-faced bunghole. I could slit you open right now, unzip your stomach before your hand ever went to blade. Maybe you ought to throw a pray I don't?"

Trelgin held Nix's eyes but swallowed hard. "Try and we'll see."

A long moment passed before Nix said, "You owe him and me for not leaving you dead that last time on the street."

"Seemed more the opposite to me," Trelgin said, leaning into Nix's hand. His breath smelled of onions and beer. "I had twenty boys with crossbows aimed at that carriage you were guarding. And anyways, I just paid on that debt by spilling where he was."

Nix couldn't argue that. He removed his hand but did not step aside.

Trelgin sniffed, made a show of straightening his cloak. "And since when did that priest need looking to by me or anybody else? Ain't you the two who stormed the guild house over a match job gone wrong? What in the Pits happened to you?"

Nix let the question go unanswered. It wasn't so much what had happened to *them,* but what had happened to Rose and Mere. Egil felt like he'd failed them, the same way he'd failed his wife and daughter years before, and he was the same way now as he'd been when he and Nix had first met in that lockup long ago. The priest was over his head in self-pity, with his nose in a tankard and his head in the past more often than not.

As for Nix, he was . . . restless, unfocused without Egil. He didn't do well standing still, especially when he disliked the ground he stood on.

"Any guild men in the Masquerade still?" Nix said. "Wouldn't want to cut one on accident."

"Nope. We don't do business inside. Just collect on the protection there."

"All right, then," Nix said, and slid slightly to the side to allow Trelgin passage, a small gesture to show respect. "Be seeing you, Trelgin. And . . . thanks."

Trelgin's eyebrows rose in surprise. "'Thanks' is what he said. Huh. Well, all right, then."

With that, Trelgin brushed by him—close, to make a final point—and they parted. Nix made for the Masquerade.

The Masquerade was a ramshackle hole of a tavern that leaned against the Poor Wall like a drunk, the kind of place that stayed full until the sun rose and scattered the patrons like insects afraid of the light. A crooked sign hung from rusted chains above a moisture-swollen wooden door that strained against the jambs as if trying to escape the place. Filth covered the writing on the sign, but the faded image of a mask was visible. Shutters hung askew from their hinges, somehow reminding Nix of crooked teeth. Lamplight, smoke, and the murmur of alehouse conversation carried through the windows in the front. Birds roosted on the roof near the single chimney, fluttering at the noises below, and some slubber was pissing against the wall, humming loudly to himself as he went.

Nix stepped across the street, around a few piles of horse dung that awaited the morning's dungsweepers, hopped over a prone body—who might also be awaiting the dungsweepers, depending upon whether he was drunk or dead—and pulled open the door of the alehouse.

The place stank of some acrid incense intended to hide the reek of urine and sweat. Large, exotic masks of demonic faces hung from the walls, with candles mounted behind them to make the eyes glow. No doubt the proprietor purported them to be from some land abroad, though all of them were likely bought in the Low Bazaar from some second-rate peddler. Smoke fogged the air. Games of cards and dice went on at a few tables, but most faces were turned toward the rickety wooden bar, where

Nix spotted Egil, and heard the rising, anticipatory volume of a brewing confrontation.

The priest sat at the bar in a light cloak, his broad back to Nix, his eyes staring at the wall behind the bar, fixed on nothing, his hand around a tankard, his huge form testing the rickety stool upon which he sat. Nix didn't see the priest's hammers near to hand.

The barkeep was not in evidence, but a group of five men stood around Egil, their body language and eager nudges announcing an expectation of violence. The largest of them, a towering man with long black hair and a thick beard, stood beside Egil, glaring into his ear. The man wore a leather vest over his tunic, and a low-quality dagger hung from his belt. A neighborhood tough, as Trelgin had said, probably looking to make a rep with his crew.

Nix took stock of the seated patrons—saw none that looked tested, and thus none that concerned him—and started forward. Disbelief stopped him in his boots when the large tough said something sharp to Egil, slapped the priest on the back of his head, and yet remained upright. Egil barely moved and the group around him laughed. The tough hit him again, again, and Egil did nothing.

The priest was further gone than Nix had realized.

"This one's dumb, yeah?" the tough said, and his fellows guffawed.

"Dumb, right," said one of the others. "Haw!"

"Nothing!" Nix shouted, to get the attention of the onlookers and the toughs. "And I mean nothing . . ."

Faces turned toward him, all but Egil's, and a quiet descended on the room. He spoke more softly, staring straight at the big fakker who'd struck Egil.

"Nothing irritates me more than a pissdrip would-be slatboard king making noise in some shithole like it matters. Like *he* matters, when, in point of fact, he does not."

For a moment no one spoke. The toughs looked at one another in puzzlement.

"You're too dumb to understand that, I'm guessing," Nix said.

"He call this place a shithole?" one of the men said to another.

"He called us pissdrips, I think," said the big one.

"Let me clarify for the slow-witted among you, which I'd wager is each and every one," Nix said. He never took his eyes from the big one. "I called *you* a pissdrip. You, the tall one with the dumb look and the pig nose. The rest of you girls aren't worth my calling anything at all."

"He called us girls now?" said one to the other.

Some of the seated patrons chuckled. Egil didn't move.

The big one's face wrinkled in anger and he took a step toward Nix. "That's a big mouth on such a little man."

"And that's a little brain on such a big man," Nix returned. "Maybe you should come quiet me down?"

"I think you don't know who you're sassing, little man."

Nix took a few steps forward, picking his way through the tables. He put a hand on his sword hilt. "Oh, about that you're wrong. I know precisely what you are. You're a type, boy. And you'd do well to stand down lest you get hurt. Priest, you about ready?"

Egil didn't even turn around. "I don't need any help here, Nix."

"You sure?" Nix snapped. "Because it looked like maybe you did, in that you allowed this pig-snouted, poorly dressed, dull-witted fakker to slap you in the head not once but thrice and still remain on his feet. How drunk are you, man?"

The big one looked from Nix to Egil, then nodded knowingly. "I see how it is, then. You two a couple?"

Laughter from the rest. Even a chuckle from the tables.

"Fak's sake," the priest said. He slammed the rest of his ale and stood, his stature dwarfing that of the five toughs, even the big one. "Fine, then."

The big tough turned on Egil, putting a pointed finger in the priest's face. "You ain't goin' nowhere, slubber. Sit down or I'll—"

Egil loosed a punch into the man's gut so hard that the wind audibly went out of him as he doubled over. The priest grabbed him by his long hair, pulled his head upright, and head-butted him squarely in the face. Blood sprayed, bone crunched, the man went limp, and Egil let him fall to the floor.

The other four hesitated a moment before going for blades. Nix bounded forward and slammed the pommel of his dagger into the back of the nearest one's head, felling the man like a brained pig, then drove his heel into the knee of another, tearing gristle and buckling him.

"My knee! My knee!"

"I've been hard on legs tonight," Nix said, by way of apology.

Egil turned and squared off against the other two and they backed off a step, blades only half-drawn. No one at any of the tables stood. Most looked away.

"That's wise, boys," Nix said to the two remaining toughs, as he stepped on the unconscious man he'd downed. "You skin that steel and you'll have to be carried from here, same as them."

They let their blades fall back into their scabbards and showed their hands.

"My knee is ruined!" cried the wounded one. "Kill those fakkers!"

Nix stared down at the man. "Another word and I'll quiet you for good. That's the mood I'm in. You hear?"

The man opened his mouth, thought better, and slammed it shut, glaring at Nix.

To Egil, Nix said, "Can we go?"

Egil looked at the three downed men, at the bar, at Nix, and shrugged his mountainous shoulders. They exited the alehouse while the toughs collected their fallen and their dignity.

"Two unconscious, one groaning on the ground, and two to tell the tale," Nix said. "Seems a decent night's work. Unless you killed that big one?"

Egil ignored the question. "I know what you did there, Nix."

"I had to wake you up somehow. What the fak are you doing? Sitting there like that?"

"I didn't ask for help or for waking up. This is my own business."

"No, it's not," Nix said. "You let that little slubber hit you on the head three times and did nothing. That looks bad for you, but also for me. People think of you, they think of me. Wake the fak up, Egil. To preserve my reputation, if nothing else. Pits, I ran into Trelgin coming in here and that droop-eyed arse called your nerve into question. Him."

Egil looked up at Kulven. "Trelgin. Fak him. I don't care what he thinks."

Nix nodded knowingly. "And that right there is the problem."

"So you say," Egil said.

"Damned right, so I say."

They walked together in silence for a time before Nix said thoughtfully, "You know, we're spending too much time in alehouses. For it we get nothing but hangovers and fights. Two for me tonight alone. I say we get out and do something."

Egil said nothing, so Nix pressed.

"You open to that or not? No shrug. No grunt. A word or words by way of answer."

Egil looked at his knuckles and Nix wondered what he was thinking.

"You can't keep blaming yourself," Nix said. "You open to something, is what I'm asking."

Egil gave a slow nod. "I suppose I am. Getting away from . . . this." He made a gesture with the shovels of his hands that took in the whole of the city. "Would be welcome."

"Good," Nix said. "Otherwise I'd have to recruit Gadd.

He's solid, but an unnerving fakker, what with those teeth and tattoos and all. You're just the sole priest of a dead god. I'm used to that. Anyway, good, this is good." He nodded, relieved. "I'll find something for us. We'll do it and it'll be like . . . before."

"It'll never be like before," Egil said.

Nix didn't fight the sentiment, though it pained him to hear Egil give it voice. "Fair enough. But maybe it'll be better than now, yeah?"

"Can't be worse."

"You've some blood on your head there," Nix said.

Egil wiped his brow, looked at the red smear on his fingers. "Not mine."

"I didn't figure so," Nix said. "Listen, I have an idea."

"That I did figure," Egil said. "You've been building up to that 'I have an idea' tone of voice. Last time I heard it we ended up sideways of a demon in the tomb of an Afirion wizard-king."

Nix grinned. "You say that as though it wasn't fun. Wasn't it?"

"It was. Seems a long way back now, though."

"Aye. And as it happens, you have the same tone of voice at times," Nix said. "Last time was . . ."

He caught himself before he said it, but Egil said it for him. "Blackalley."

"Right," Nix said, thinking of Rose and Mere and Odrhaal and his dreams. "But anyway I do, in fact, have an idea."

"And the tone proves a prophet."

"Right," Nix said.

During their travels through the Deadmire, they'd found an intriguing set of enspelled metal plates, inscribed in a language Nix had never before seen. When they'd returned to Dur Follin, he'd stowed them away, and in the haze of grief and drink he and Egil had lived in after losing Rose and Mere, he'd mostly forgotten them. But he figured there had to be something to them. Even if it just led to them chasing the wind for a time, it would at least give them something to do. An adventure was what they needed to recover themselves. Like old times.

"Say it," Egil said.

"I will," Nix said, nodding. "But I want to let it simmer for a bit. There's a thing or two I need to do first."

Ool's clock started sounding the fifth hour and that gave Nix another idea. "What do you say we go see Mamabird?"

"You heard Ool's contraption calling the hour, Nix. Wholesome people aren't awake now."

"In your case that's true, but not in mine, nor in Mama's. She wakes ahead of the fifth hour every day to get breakfast ready for the flock."

Egil grunted. "That woman's better than we deserve. You know that, yeah?"

"No argument."

Mamabird had saved Nix when he was young, plucked him from scavenging the Heap, given him a home, and helped instill a moral code. The man he was today he owed to her. She provided both Egil and Nix something akin to a home, or at least a home base, someplace they could return to that stayed the same even when the world changed. They saw her only rarely, but still . . . she was home.

Nix said, "Under the present circumstances maybe seeing someone better than we deserve will do us both some good. Besides, Tesha was irritated when I left the Tunnel. I'd just as soon not return there yet."

Egil nodded. "She'll be sleeping, though, yeah?"

Nix shrugged. "Who can say? Anger might keep her awake. It's possible I ejected someone from the Tunnel and shed his blood in the street."

"Hmm," Egil said. "That sells it. Mamabird's it is."

Nix smiled. They'd faced demons and devils both, but neither of them cared to stand before a wrathful Tesha if they didn't have to.

"She said I'm inconstant," Nix said.

"Tesha?" Egil said, his tone serious. "About women, she meant, or more than that?"

"Just women, I think."

"Well, I guess she's right about that, yeah?"

"No," Nix objected, "she's not right about that. Well, possibly she's somewhat right. But you're of little help. And she took it back anyway."

"Did she?" Egil sounded skeptical.

"She did. You know what? Remind me not to drag you out of bars anymore. Henceforth I'll just leave you there to wallow in a tankard and get slapped around by slubbers."

Egil sighed. "Point taken. I'd have beaten those five eventually. Even drunks have limits. I was just . . ."

"Punishing yourself," Nix said. "Guilt's as much your companion as me these days, Egil."

Egil cleared his throat. "So are we going to see Mama or not?"

"We are," Nix said. "Inconstant. Bah. That's nonsense."

"As between the two of us," Egil said, "I'm the only one permitted to say 'bah.'"

"Gofti," said Nix.

The half-asleep guards at the Slum Gate yawned as Nix and Egil approached. Nix knew the Slum Gate was a punishment post for the Guards. The shift ended at dawn and from the bored look of them, the guards were counting down the moments.

"Business in there?" the graying, bearded sergeant asked. He looked them over, his mouth tightening as he took in Nix's blades.

"I grew up in there," said Nix.

"Why in the Hells would you want to go back, then?" the sergeant asked, then shrugged. "You know what? Your business and none of mine." He stepped aside, signaled for the gate to be opened. "Good eve. Or morn. Whatever the fak it is."

As they walked through the gate, Nix heard another one of the guards say, "That's Egil and Nix, ain't it?"

A short, potbellied guard poked his head out of the shack, nodded, and said, "I heard they ain't as tough as once supposed."

The gate closed behind them and they stood in the Warrens, the arsehole of the city.

"You hear that slubber?" Nix said to Egil.

Egil grunted.

"I blame you," Nix said, and tried to leave it at that but couldn't. "It reflects on us both, see? Because we're a team, man. A pair. No one thinks of Nix alone. Or Egil alone. Only Egil and Nix. Or, if they're smart, Nix and Egil."

"You already said as much earlier," Egil answered.

"It bears repeating."

"We aren't married, Nix."

"No," Nix said. "We're more than married. We're brothers. Aren't we?" Egil's pause irritated him, so he grabbed the priest by the shoulder and turned him so they were looking each other in the face. "Aren't we?"

The priest nodded. "We are. I'm just . . ."

Nix softened his tone. "I know what you are, and I sympathize, but fakkin' get it together, man. We lost the girls. I don't like it, either. And we didn't even lose them, really. They were never ours to lose, and they made the choice to stay with that . . . thing. What can we do?"

"Nothing," Egil said, wincing at the memory. "But it still feels wrong. The stink of the Deadmire is in the air here and all I can think is . . . we were wrong."

"Wrong things happen all the time. We adapt and move on."

Egil inhaled deeply, blew it out. "Some things are more wrong than others."

Nix could tell from the furrows in Egil's brow and the pain in his eyes that he was thinking not of Rose and Mere, but of his wife and daughter.

"Aye to that," Nix said and thumped his friend on the shoulder. "Some things are more wrong and then some. Let's get to

Mama's and get a reminder that there are bright spots in the world yet."

"Aye," Egil said, and Nix thought he sounded half-convinced. "We could go back to the swamp. Retrieve them."

Nix had entertained that idea often enough over the previous months. "No, we can't. You know what that mindmage can do. We were lucky to get clear the first time. We go back there, we don't come back. Worse, us going back might put Rose and Mere at risk, too. It was their choice, Egil. Theirs."

"Bah."

"Bah, indeed." They continued on, Nix burping the while. "Maybe they'll come back to us sometime."

"Maybe," Egil said.

Walking the trash-strewn, packed-earth streets of the Warrens always turned Nix vaguely morose, and discussing Rose and Mere had only amplified the feeling. The maze of tightly packed shacks and huts were the undrained dregs of Dur Follin. They just remained there within the Poor Wall, festering, multiplying, bugs in stagnant water. Poverty begat itself, and was multiplied by debtors and criminals fleeing into the Warrens from creditors and the Watch, by immigrants to Dur Follin being shunted there from the docks and gates unless they were able to pay the required head tax. The Warrens seemed never to change. They were as perpetual as human misery, and seemed to Nix to have existed longer than Dur Follin itself.

He'd grown up amid the filth, the abandoned child of a prostitute, and he still hated it. But it spoke to him somehow, too, and he refused to move too far away from it out of fear he might not hear its reminders. The core of him would always be the scrawny, perpetually hungry orphan who scoured the Heap, scavenging the trash of his betters for anything he could eat or sell or use. He supposed he'd never leave that behind, no matter where he went, and he was glad for it. He'd killed a man in the Warrens once over bread, an act that could have hardened him or softened him.

If not for Mamabird, it would certainly have been the former.

With Mamabird's help he'd managed to get out of the filth and become who he was, but he knew that he was unusual. Most of the Warren's denizens would never leave, would never know anything but hunger and violence and deprivation. They'd live in squalor and die the same way, rarely venturing outside the Poor Wall. Their world was small and dirty, and it could have been his, would have been his, if not for Mamabird.

"I've gone from scavenging the Heap to scavenging tombs," Nix said thoughtfully. "Not much changes, I guess."

"Bah," Egil said, his voice loud in the quiet. "We don't scavenge tombs. We explore them and liberate their treasures."

Nix guffawed. "By scavenging them, though, yeah?"

"Bah," Egil said again, but with less conviction. "You twist words to fit your mood. Besides, we do other things, too."

"Example, if you please."

"Bodyguard work," Egil said after a moment.

"And how has that gone for us?" Nix asked, recalling the events with the Night Blade.

Egil grunted. "Not well, I'll own. But we're also property owners."

"And I'll ask again, how is that working out? Without Tesha, we'd have no patrons and would already have lost everything."

Egil said, "The point remains, though. We've done and do other things. Maybe not as well as tomb robbing—"

"Scavenging."

"*Liberating*. But we do them. And hiring Tesha shows our skill at spotting talent."

"To recap, then," Nix said, adopting the tone of one of his instructors from his days at the Conclave. "We are excellent tomb robbers, mediocre bodyguards, and property owners who run their property poorly, and at least one of us is a terrible priest. Sound right?"

"Fak you and your terrible priest," Egil said, mirth in his

tone. "And while you freely utter blasphemous words against my faith, you neglect to mention that at least one of us dropped out of the Conclave and is thus a failed student of wizardry."

"I didn't drop out, but was expelled, which you well know."

"So you say."

"I do," Nix said. "I'll add as a final point in our favor that we at least curse quite well."

"No fakking disagreement there," Egil said, nodding. "We make fair drinkers, too. Points for that."

"Points for that," Nix agreed. "Let's hang our cloaks on those pegs and consider ourselves once more worthy of the world."

He held out a fist and Egil tapped it with his own.

Thin-walled shacks and decrepit buildings, many just skeletons of old lumber, formed a maze of narrow, crooked streets. Piles of smelly, unrecognizable debris dotted the way. The hour left the unlit streets haunted by poverty but otherwise mostly deserted. Fire pits glowed in the occasional alley, with dark forms huddled on the ground around them. Rats and cats and feral dogs prowled the ruins, fighting the perpetual war among their kinds.

Nix kept his wits about him as they walked. The denizens of the Warrens were desperate but generally not stupid, as someone would have to be to take a run at him and Egil. Still, he saw no need to take chances.

A shout sounded from somewhere off in the night, followed by a woman's scream.

"Odd to see you with no hammers," he said to Egil, lowering his tone instinctively.

"I own it feels odd to be unarmed."

"If we get sideways of someone, maybe just clench your fists and shake them in earnest."

"Aye," Egil said.

As was his habit, Nix did his part to ease the life of some lucky few by dropping silver terns now and again as he walked.

He thought of the coins as seeds, and hoped they sprouted something in whoever found them, even if it was only a moment of relief.

"Terns or royals?" Egil asked.

"Terns," Nix said. "People would kill each other over gold. Nowhere to spend it here, anyway. Guards at the gate caught them with it, they'd never be able to explain it. Silver's hard enough. I'd do more but . . . you know."

He made a gesture that took in the whole of the Warrens.

Egil nodded somberly. "Things are what they are, Nix. We can't change the world."

"No," Nix said. "We just live in it and make our way. But being the charming fakker I am, it seems to me I ought to be able to change it."

"Well, that 'fakker' part has the right of it, anyway," Egil said.

"You're saying I'm not charming, priest? As though you could judge?"

"I am so saying and so judging."

"Fak you," Nix said.

"So much for charming, eh? And thus my point is made."

"Hardly," Nix said, "seeing as how I offered that well-deserved curse with a rakish, nay *charming,* raise of my eyebrow."

"So you say."

"I am so saying," Nix said with a nod, imitating Egil's tone. Nix thumped the priest on the shoulder. "See? Things getting well back into square with you already. I like it. You get those hammers back on your waist and I'll vow all's well in the world."

"'All's well' goes too far, but I take the point. You know, every time we enter the Warrens you talk incessantly."

"I do," Nix acknowledged. Talking kept him from thinking too much, remembering too much.

"Though I guess that's little different from just about anywhere we are," Egil said.

"And here we are," Nix said, gesturing ahead.

Mamabird's neatly kept, if slightly decrepit home stood like an island of order in the chaotic desolation of the Warrens. An ancient wooden fence delineated her small plot and garden, and even thugs treated it as sacred ground. Nix worried often that someone would break the unwritten rule of the Warrens— that Mama was untouchable—but his concerns so far had proven unfounded. Perhaps no one wanted to get on the wrong side of him and Egil, or perhaps Mama commanded that much love and respect. Nix figured it was probably the latter. He and Egil had long ago stopped encouraging her to move out of the Warrens; she would not even consider it.

A lantern burned on the wooden porch of her home, casting its light out into the darkness, a beacon for the lost children of the Warrens. Mamabird lit it every night. A gray cat sat in the glow, cleaning its paws. Another two lounged on the roof eaves. No doubt another dozen that Nix couldn't see lurked about the house. Mama loved her cats second only to her chicks.

Lamplight leaked through the slats of the home's closed shutters.

"See?" Nix said, nodding at the light inside the house. "Didn't I say?"

"You did."

By unspoken rule, before approaching the house they stopped in the street and faced each other.

"So?" Egil asked, squaring up to Nix so that Nix could see him clearly in the moonlight.

Nix looked him over. The priest looked disheveled, tired, and unshaven. "You look not quite yourself but not so far from it that she'll worry overmuch. There's nothing for the stubble, but tuck in your shirt, maybe button your vest, and straighten the cloak. You stink only a bit, so that's something. You have smudges on your head that look vaguely like an eye."

"Fak off."

Nix smiled. "Me?"

Egil looked down on Nix. "Close up the top button on your shirt. Run a hand through your hair. That's better, though you still look vaguely rodentish."

"And fak off to you, too."

With that, they walked to Mamabird's house and took the three steps up to the porch, where Nix rapped lightly on the door. The cat on the porch looked upon them with indifference.

Inside, the floorboards creaked and Mamabird's voice carried through the wooden door. "Who's out there now? You need help, little one?"

Nix smiled, as that was the same question she'd asked years ago when he'd first knocked on her door.

"It's Nix and Egil, Mama," Nix said. "Sorry for the hour—"

The door opened immediately—as ever, she did not lock it—and there Mamabird stood, covered in a faded smock and stained apron, her girth filling the doorway, her thick gray hair pulled up in a bun. A wide smile deepened the wrinkles around her mouth and eyes, and her chin pulled back into its folds. Nix could not help but smile in return.

Like the Warrens, Mamabird seemed never to change. Nix liked to think the light in her spirit froze her age in place. She held out her arms, stepped forward, and embraced them both at once. She smelled of garlic and sweat and home.

"My boys! Now what brings you here this early?" She released her embrace but kept a protective hand on each of them. "Some trouble?"

"No trouble, Mama," Nix said.

"Well, ain't that a first?" she said.

"Everybody's funny tonight," Nix said, and Egil chuckled. "Something in the wind maybe. Anyway, we just wanted to see you is all."

A cat darted out as they stood there. Another darted in, an orange tabby.

"And maybe have some soup," Egil added, breathing in the aroma of Mama's soup, the smell drifting through the doorway.

"Well, you get on in here and see me then," she said, pulling them by their hands into the house and closing the door behind them. "I'll serve some soup directly. My chicks are still asleep upstairs so we'll keep our voices low."

CHAPTER THREE

Aragged oval carpet covered the stained, age-worn wooden floor of Mamabird's front room, and a hodgepodge of chairs sat about the room or faced the small hearth. Mama went to the large soup kettle hanging from a hook over the fire. "I was just reheating the soup from last night. I'll make a new pot later this morning. Onions are thriving this year. Potatoes, too. Sit, boys. Or we can eat in the kitchen?"

"Here's fine, Mama," Nix said.

They sat in the chairs before the hearth while Mama ladled soup into two wooden bowls, then handed one to each of them. Nix's chair had uneven legs and Egil's creaked ominously upon taking his weight, but neither of them cared. They were as much at home here as they were anywhere, and the soup—tepid potato and onion—sent Nix back into his past.

"Delicious," Egil said, and Nix agreed.

For a long time they simply sat together in the glow of the firelight, talking of the Warrens, Nix's childhood, Mama's herd of cats, the garden . . . and nothing else mattered. Nix felt a twinge of sadness when the light of the rising sun started to creep through the shutters.

He summoned his courage and finally asked, "How are you feeling, Mama?"

"Me? You always ask that, Nixxie, and I'm as healthy as ever. How're you two?" She reached over and took Egil's hand in her own. "Especially you, young man? You always seem weighed down by something. More so than usual this visit. You could tell me, you know, let me share the burden. That's why Mama's here."

Egil smiled and placed his huge hand over hers. "Just being here lightens the burden, Mama. It's enough."

"You should've seen him hours ago," Nix said. "The priest wears his melancholy like armor."

She never took her rheumy eyes from Egil. "You weren't one of my chicks when you were a boy, Egil. Not like Nixxie. But you are now. And you know my door is always open."

Egil nodded and smiled, a genuine smile that Nix was pleased to see.

"A crack in the armor, mayhap," Nix said, and drained the last of his third bowl of soup.

Before Egil could answer, a thin waif of a girl descended the narrow, creaky stairs into the room, yawning as she came. She stopped cold when she saw Egil and Nix and Mama.

"It's all right, Kinnen," Mamabird said. "These are friends of Mama's."

"Hello," Egil said, turning in his seat, testing the wood's resolve.

"Why are you up so early?" Mama asked her.

"Bav is snoring," she said, but kept her eyes on Egil. "Is he a giant, Mama?"

Mamabird laughed, and it turned into a raspy cough. "Well, I guess he is, but he's a nice one. That I know for certain. You go straighten your pallet now, and try not to wake the other chicks. Breakfast soon."

"Yes, Mama," Kinnen said, and turned to go, eyeballing Egil over her shoulder as she went up the stairs as though he were some creature of myth. Egil stared after her a long moment, thoughts churning behind his eyes. When he turned back, his face was thoughtful.

"You do so much here," the priest said to Mamabird.

"As much as I can," she said cheerfully. "That girl, Kinnen, she had a rough go but she'll be fine now. You all right, Egil?"

"I am," Egil said with a nod. "I think I am."

After finishing another half bowl of soup and a bit more conversation, Egil and Nix stood. Nix would have sworn Egil's chair sighed with relief.

"You don't want to stay and see the rest of the chicks when they rise? They grumble about their chores more'n even you did, Nixxie."

"I doubt that," Nix said. He knew well that the boys and girls Mama fed and housed worked for their keep, sweeping, patching, tidying, and otherwise keeping the flotsam of the Warrens away from the island of Mamabird's home. He'd hated it in his youth, but it had taught him valuable lessons. "But we do need to head out. Deeds to be done, adventures to be had; you know how we are."

"You are the same silly boy as ever," she said. She stood and hugged him hard. "I miss you."

"And I, you," Nix said. "Which is why I return here when I need to set my world right."

She hugged Egil in turn, and Egil held on to her longer than Nix had ever before seen.

"You remember what I said now," she said to him. "And remember that the world needs its giants, too. Don't you let it beat you down to size."

"All right," the priest answered. "Thank you, Mama."

Before leaving, they each emptied their pockets of terns and commons and handed them to Mamabird. She would not take them, so they placed them on the hearth, as was their habit.

"Hear now, you can't keep giving me all your earnings," she protested. "How will you eat, yourselves?"

Nix smiled. "Does Egil look like he's missed meals, Mama? We're fine. And it pleases us both to help you some so you can help them some."

"Aye," Egil said. "Very much so. Maybe Kinnen can have a dress?"

"Maybe she can," Mama said with a smile. "I love you both."

They answered in kind and after leaving, they walked in silence for several blocks. A few denizens of the Warrens, up with the dawn, watched them pass. Dogs skulked out of their path. The Heap rose to their right, gulls wheeling around it like a snowstorm in the morning air. The dungsweepers would be coming through the Slum Gate in their wagons within an hour, bringing the night's refuse. The Warrens would be waiting to receive it, as ever.

Nix shook his head. "Odd that that run-down home and an old woman in the Warrens feels like the center of the world."

"We all need a place," Egil said. "This is yours."

"Yours, too, I'd say."

"Maybe," Egil said. "Anyway, I needed that. Should've come sooner. Better than another tankard. Thanks, Nix."

Unused to the priest's sincere thanks, Nix managed only, "Yeah. Of course. Uh, anyway, always good to see Mama."

Egil nodded. "It is. That woman never sets foot outside the Slum Gate, lives in a hovel, will barely take our money, and yet does more good than us."

Nix pursed his lips. "We back to this again? I won't dispute she does more good than us or anyone I've ever known. But we do some good."

"Example, rogue."

"Shite, man, I don't know. We treat the working women and men in the Tunnel fairer than they used to get. We've beat a few arseholes who'd earned it. We saved Rose and Mere from their brother and . . ."

The moment Nix said it, he wished he hadn't. He trailed off, cursing himself in silence, wary of Egil slipping back into despondence.

"It's all right," Egil said, reading Nix's silence. "We did save them. And then we didn't, and maybe they saved us. Either way . . ."

"Either way," Nix agreed, nodding. "You know, our lives revolve around a handful of women. That seem right to you? Odd at all?"

Egil shrugged. "Seems mostly right to me."

"Seems right to me, too," Nix said. "Just struck me of a sudden, is all. And speaking of, let's go see one of them. I'm sure she has some anger to vent on us. Maybe the sun will have dissipated it some. I'm going to blame you for everything. Fair enough?"

Egil chuckled and they moved through their waking city toward Tesha and the Slick Tunnel.

The same group of guards remained at the Slum Gate, dark circles under their eyes, faces slack. The potbellied one elbowed his fellow as Egil and Nix approached. The sergeant was not in view. Nix figured he was probably sleeping in the small guardhouse, one of the benefits of rank.

"Concluded your business, have you?" the potbellied one asked.

"Mostly," Egil said. He walked up to the guard and added, "I have need of your truncheon."

The man looked baffled. "What's that now?"

Egil did not wait for permission and snatched the surprised guard's wooden truncheon from its loop.

"Hey now!" the guard said, and one of his fellows looking on advanced a step. Nix was not sure of Egil's play, but positioned himself in the path of the other guard. He held up a finger, leaving unspoken the "Be smart, now."

Egil took the short, thick club in his hands and snapped it in half while staring into the potbellied guard's face.

"Oaken truncheons ain't as tough as once supposed," Egil said, loud enough for all of them to hear. "Nor are mouthy Orangies at the Slum Gate supposed tough at any time. You in agreement?"

He dropped the pieces at the wide-eyed guard's feet and took a step forward. The guard, of course, faced with the bulwark of Egil's form, took a step back. His fellow behind him stood frozen. Before matters could progress further, the sergeant's voice carried from the shack.

"All right. You made your point. Move on, now, before this goes another way and I have to arrest you."

"*Try* to arrest us," Egil said.

"My try is awful persuasive," the sergeant said, stepping out into the street. The sergeant was taller than Nix, short gray hair and beard trimmed neatly, hands scarred. He scratched his beard indifferently.

"He really dislikes truncheons," Nix said of Egil.

The sergeant smiled. He was missing an eyetooth. "And mouthy watchmen, it would seem."

"So it would," Nix said, and nodded at the gate. "We'd like to walk through that gate now. Done?"

The sergeant walked past the potbellied guard and up to Egil, into Egil's space. Nix prepared for the worst. The other Orangies took heart and closed around, put hands on blades, wolves circling.

"I guess that depends," the sergeant said. "We done?"

"I guess that depends," Egil said, his voice tight, his body coiled.

"That one there," the sergeant said, and jerked a thumb over his shoulder to indicate the potbellied guard. "He didn't mean no insult before. At least not one that needed answer."

"Disagree," Egil said. "I think he did. And I think it did."

"Well," the sergeant said, "maybe you've given answer enough already?"

"Maybe," Egil said.

"See, boys," the sergeant said to the rest of the watchmen, "this is Egil and Nix, and by all accounts they've seen some scrums. And men that have seen some scrums, they don't like to be called slubbers, even by implication. And when they are so named, that needs answering more often than not. Make sense?"

Assent around, even from the potbellied one, who made eye contact with no one.

"Maybe you've seen your share of scrums, too?" Egil said.

"Maybe I have."

Egil took a step back, his body visibly uncoiling. "Then to answer your question, I'd say that we're done. And my apologies for the ruckus."

"And my apologies for the thoughtless words of my man." He turned and walked back toward the gatehouse. "Open the gates, boys, and wish these citizens a good day."

The guards did as instructed, even insofar as offering grudging "Good days."

With that, Egil and Nix left the Warrens behind.

After they got out of earshot of the guards, Nix said, "No doubt after that demonstration truncheons all over the city will now speak our name in fearful whispers. Well done, priest."

Egil laughed. "Sergeant showed some steel, though, didn't he?"

"Aye," Nix said, and tapped his temple. "Noted for future use. That one's not the usual type of slubber banished to duty on the Slum Gate. He's got balls. Probably got sideways of someone with rank."

"Sounds like our kind," Egil said.

"Aye, that."

They reached Shoddy Way just as Ool's clock rang the seventh hour. Up the street they could see Gadd sweeping the porch of the Tunnel. A few donkey-pulled wagons made their way along the road. A pair of heavyset laborers in smocks and tool belts walked along, chatting, one of them smoking a pipe.

Nix caught a whiff of something exotic cooking in the Low Bazaar, which was not far from the brothel.

Gadd saw them coming, raised a hand in greeting, and watched them approach.

"Gadd holds his broom the same way he does his tulwar," Egil said.

Nix chuckled. "I'd be unsurprised to learn he's killed a man or two with that broom, too."

When they drew near, Gadd studied their faces, nodded, said, "Good to see you're both well."

"'Well' is maybe a bit much," Nix said, suddenly feeling very tired. "But better."

"Aye, that," Egil said, running a hand over his head. "Better, indeed."

"And walking, at least," Gadd said.

"Walking," Egil agreed, and thumped Gadd on the shoulder.

"Our priest has had a vision," Nix said to Gadd, by way of explanation as they walked inside.

The Tunnel had not yet opened for business because Tesha had given everyone an extra hour of sleep, but inside the working men and women sat at the tables eating a breakfast of eggs and sausage. There'd be a line for the washbasins out back.

Everyone at the tables nodded or smiled or greeted Egil and Nix and they returned the gestures. Nix saw Kiir seated with Lis and they went to her.

"You're feeling better, I see?" Nix said.

She smiled, still looking a little pale, and brushed her hair from her face. "Much. You should get some breakfast. Tesha's bread is so good. The Watch never came. Last night, I mean."

"That's good," Nix said.

"Good until we actually need them to come," Egil said.

"When would we ever need them to come?" Nix asked.

Egil shrugged. "Eh, fair point."

The smell of cooking eggs, sausage, and Tesha's beloved warm flatbread carried through the open door behind Gadd's bar. Tesha hawked over the workers' food intake, always making sure everyone ate well. She'd be out in the fenced area behind the brothel cooking over the fires.

"I need sleep more than food," Nix said.

"Likewise," Egil said. He cleared his throat. "And maybe it's best she not see us just yet."

"Maybe it is," Lis said with a laugh.

"Too late," Kiir said, nodding at the door behind Gadd's bar.

"Shite," Nix said.

Tesha walked through, holding a board piled high with flatbread. Her dark hair was pulled up and she wore no makeup. One of Gadd's aprons, much too big on her, covered her day dress. She set the bread down and caught sight of Egil and Nix.

Nix gave her a crooked smile and half wave. Her expression was unreadable.

"She doesn't look angry," Egil said out of the corner of his mouth.

Nix nodded. "That's worrisome."

Tesha crossed the common room to stand before them. "No more bodies, I trust? Nothing I need to worry about that will come back here?"

"No, nothing," Nix said.

She waited. "That's it?"

"For now," Nix said. "I'm honestly too tired for conversation. Egil can give details."

Tesha turned to the priest. "Well?"

"Ask Nix," Egil said, and yawned. "I need to sleep."

"You also need to reconsider the recent course of your life," Nix added.

Egil nodded. "And that, too."

"Though maybe that happened already," Nix said, and winked at Tesha. "That's what happened to us. Our priest found religion at last."

"And now I'll find a bed," Egil said.

Tesha did not budge from before them, halting Egil's attempt to head to his room. An angry line formed between her dark eyes.

"To be clear: I'm not a fakkin' prop in your banter. I asked a question. Kindly answer it."

They looked at each other, eyebrows raised, then back at her.

"What's the question again?" Nix ventured.

"What is going on with you two? I don't mean last night. I mean generally."

Egil sighed. "Ah. Well enough. I'm drinking too much and fighting too little. Been going on awhile now, as you suggested. Nix tried to shake me up by picking a fight, knowing I wouldn't stand by and watch someone else I care about get hurt."

"Someone else?" Tesha interrupted. "You mean Rose and Mere?"

Egil nodded. "That's who I mean."

Tesha's expression softened. "I see. So, is it fixed? Or is Nix going to keep moping around here bothering customers while you spend every night drinking or stumbling or both?"

"Fixed, I think," Egil said.

"Moping?" Nix asked. "Me?"

"Listen," Tesha said to Egil, her voice still soft. "I don't know what happened with Rose and Mere after the four of you left here and I don't need to, but I doubt either of you stood by and let them get hurt. You want some advice?"

"Not especially," Egil said.

"Give it to him," Nix said. "I want to hear it."

She glared at Nix. "It's not just for him. So drop the smug tone. It's for you, too."

Nix frowned. "I don't want to hear it as much now."

Her face darkened. "You are difficult to talk to, Nix. Anyway, here it is. Find something to do, somewhere to go, something worth fighting over, or for. Sitting in brothels or taverns or whatever, that's not the two of you. And you know that. That's why you hired me to run this place. But lately the two of you spend more time here than ever. You bother the patrons, distract the workers, and do yourselves no good. Go do whatever it is you do, yeah?"

"That's what I was just saying earlier," Nix said.

"Then you were right," she said. "And that's a first."

Nix made as though she'd stabbed him through the chest.

Egil put his hands on her shoulders and looked her in the eyes. "I hear your words and I agree with them. But I'd like to go sleep now, yeah? I think I may actually sleep well for once."

She almost smiled. "Yes. Go. And I'm glad you're all right."

"Both of us, you mean," Nix added.

"Maybe," she said.

Gillem, one of Tesha's working men, who was sitting at a nearby table and who'd overheard the conversation, said, "I'm thinking maybe you two boys belong in a bed together, what with all the caring and understanding and watching over each other and whatnot. I could even join you. We'd make a party of it."

"You'd like that," Nix said.

Some of the girls tittered. Even Tesha smiled.

"I would," Gillem said with a grin. "You game?"

Egil harrumphed and Nix shook his head. "I credit you're a handsome man, Gillem, but as a rule the only depths I care to plumb are found on women."

"Likewise," Egil said.

"Well, that's a shame," Gillem said, and gave an exaggerated sigh. "Maybe another time."

"Maybe you should just have some sausage and say no more," Lis called to Gillem.

He took a forkful and said, "I was trying to do just that."

Nix faced Egil. "You see?"

Egil's face twisted into a question.

"This is a nice place now," Nix explained. "A home for them. And that's good we've done. Remember that. Go get some sleep and then shave and clean yourself up. I'll have something for us when you awaken."

Nix went to his quarters but did not bother sleeping. He was tired but too fidgety. He felt like he'd gotten things sorted with Egil, with Tesha somewhat, with the world even. Things were back as they should be. He hadn't realized how much he'd needed to move, to act, to do anything, really. Recognizing that fact was freeing. He and Egil had thought they could retire to a quiet life as property owners. They'd tried it, but neither of them was meant for a life of leisure and contemplation, nor one of sitting about. The stillness would ruin both of them. Egil would die of drink and Nix would die of boredom. They needed adventure, challenge, action.

Of course, that meant they would both probably die in a tomb somewhere, unremarked by anyone.

Nix shrugged. He supposed there were worse ways to die.

His room in the Tunnel was away from the working rooms, in what had once probably been the servants' quarters in the basement. Long ago the Tunnel had been a noble family's manse, before the wealthy had built new homes across the Meander and sold their old ones off to guilds and well-to-do merchants, who then sold them to less savory sorts. The building had changed hands many times before Egil and Nix, who were, perhaps, the least savory of all the building's owners.

His small room held his bed, a night table, and a curio cabinet that had taken his fancy a few months earlier. In it he kept trinkets from his and Egil's adventures. It held a few ancient coins, frayed books written in languages long forgotten, rolled scrolls, small serpent statuettes from Afirion, a knife crafted of an unidentifiable metal but which seemed to never lose its edge, a handful of ivory chessmen from Jafari, a necklace of pointed teeth he'd taken from a brutish half giant in the hills north of Dur Follin, the talking, ever-hungry key he hadn't fed in so long that it had gone quiescent. Properly fed, the key could open almost any lock, though negotiating with the thing over what it wanted to eat often proved tedious. In some ways the cabinet was not unlike his satchel of needful things, the bag he always carried and in which he secreted essential gear and his magical gewgaws. Both cabinet and bag held the mementos that defined his journey through life, those in the cabinet a link to his past, those in the satchel a connection to the present.

What was not in the cabinet or the satchel were the golden plates he'd taken out of the sunken ruins in the Deadmire. Those he'd placed in a locked, lead-lined chest he kept at the foot of his bed. In hindsight, he didn't know why he hadn't put them in the cabinet. Maybe he'd always known they were too valuable for mere display. Maybe he'd always assumed, at least before today, that they were connected to his future, not to his past or present. Maybe he'd wanted them out of sight because they reminded him too much of Rose and Mere.

"Gods," he swore, shaking his head. He was becoming Egil, sitting alone in his room, turning maudlin and waxing philosophical. All he needed was a bald head and a dead god to worship. If he didn't take care, soon he'd be melancholy all the time and grunt replies to questions.

He scooted to the end of the bed, found the chest's key on the ring he kept in his satchel, and opened it. To the eye it appeared empty, but he knew better. He reached in, felt for the enchanted wrap, almost as large as a blanket, that blocked enchantments and could be seen only with peripheral vision, and lifted it out. As an extra precaution he'd placed the plates in the wrap. He unpeeled it to reveal them.

The thin metal plates shimmered like liquid in a shaft of morning light that stabbed through a slit in a window. The plates were golden in color, though Nix knew the metal wasn't actually gold. It was too hard, impossible to mar, unbendable despite being as thin as parchment. He had no idea how someone had carved the tiny characters on them, each delicately engraved, written in a spiral pattern from the inside out, the alphabet one that Nix didn't know, the script covering the entirety of the plates.

He avoided staring at the characters for more than a few moments because when he did they lost their separation and bled into one dizzying, blurry spiral that made him feel like he was falling, slipping into some maelstrom.

He had only the two plates. He'd left several behind in the ruins and wished now that he hadn't. Of course, at the time he and Egil had been pursued by a bizarre monstrosity, so he considered the urgency justified.

He ran his fingertips over the characters, feeling the grooves and whorls. His fingers tingled; the hairs on his arms stood on end. For a brief, rash moment he was tempted to speak a word in the Language of Creation to activate the plates but he resisted the impulse. He should get some idea of what they did first. And for that, he needed to engage the services of Kerfallen the Grey Mage.

He bound the plates back in the enchanted wrap and it was as though they'd disappeared from the world. He placed them inside his satchel and just like that, they moved from his future to his present.

As he stood to go, he considered grabbing the talking key out of his cabinet, but he decided to leave it, at least for the moment. It was part of an old adventure, and he was interested in a new one.

He headed out for the Low Bazaar.

The Afterbirth leaned against the earthen wall of a damp cave in the bank of a river, rocking, muttering from his mouths. He'd sheltered in a cave, as he often did, to avoid being seen. He could not be harmed but he could be held and the fear of an unending life living alone in a cage sometimes paralyzed him, tempted him to live his perpetual existence alone underground, but something in him still longed to walk the world and so he did.

He could smell the dankness of the cave, the pungency of the fungi sprouting from the walls, but mostly he could smell himself, the blood of others still on him, the filth of years and leagues and unending existence.

Dawn lit the cave mouth in dull gray, coating the forest outside in morning light. He smelled the promise of rain in the air. Perhaps he would remain in the cave another day or perhaps he would walk the world or perhaps he would dig into the world and dig and dig until he revealed the treasure of another world, lost worlds, his world, anything but this one. He groaned and moaned and rocked and was alone and the morning gave way to the brighter light of afternoon and still he sat.

He smelled the bear long before he saw it, but eventually the huge shadow of its form lumbered into view and darkened the cave entrance. The Afterbirth ceased muttering and looked up and the bear stopped, not entering the cave, nose raised, chuffing. The Afterbirth stared at it, waiting, knowing it could not see him but that it could smell him, sense the danger of him.

The bear's hackles rose and a rumble from deep in its chest announced its fear or aggression or both and the Afterbirth shifted his weight and answered with a low growl of his own and started to rise and the bear froze for a moment before it whined, turned, and bolted.

The Afterbirth stared after the bear a long while, then, alone again, alone forever, he returned to sitting, to rocking, to moaning and pain and despair.

Hours or days or weeks later something jolted him from his torpor a smell a hint a memory of something he never imagined smelling again. At first he did not believe it and yet it pulled him to his feet and he breathed deeply, greedily, mouths drooling, gibbering, gasping at the faint promise carried in the air. He rushed outside the cave, nearly tripping as he went, babbling, startling birds out of trees, breathing deep, sniffing frantically, trying to isolate the smell and hold it in his nose in his mind to follow it and find it. He noted its direction west and south and despite the bright light of day he ran pell-mell through the forest after it, heedless of whether he was seen, pulled along by the smell like a fish hooked on a line. He tore through underbrush, snapped tree limbs, and at his approach the alarmed animals of the forest retreated to their dens and holes and lairs.

He muttered as he went, his mouths grinning and slobbering and a strange new feeling blossoming in him, a feeling that had a name he'd once known but had not experienced—hope.

For the smell on the wind was a scent not of this world but of the Great Spell, carrying with it the hint of his world maybe or something close to it. And if there was an end for him or a new beginning for him then it would begin there, with the Great Spell. He raced after it, laughing and . . .

And then it was gone, cut off, vanished as if it had never been.

He slowed then finally stopped running and stood there, slouched, alone in the forest, panting, disbelieving. Had he tricked himself into hope, had the smell never been there at all?

"No no no no," he said, his mouths turning the word into a chorus. He had smelled it, the taste had been too acute, too certain, not a phantasm but real.

And now it was gone.

He fell to his knees with a moan and almost started rocking almost surrendered once more to despair and nihilism but the flash of hope he had felt kept him from surrender.

He stood, breathing heavily, growling, the sound quieting the forest around him, even the insects.

He started walking again, hypersensitive to smells. The direction from which he had caught the scent of the spell was fixed in his memory. He would walk that way until the end of time if necessary and hope—hope!—to once again catch the scent.

Nix heard and smelled the Low Bazaar blocks before he saw the colorful tents and stalls that dotted the huge, open-air fair and market. The late autumn breeze bore the smell of sizzling meat, tobacco, bonfires, spices, and incense. Drums, flutes, stringed instruments, and the low, steady buzz of the crowd lent the bazaar a distinct voice. A wooden fence surrounded the grassy, treed plaza between Endel's Ride and Shoddy Way, but the inexorable growth of the bazaar was gradually overwhelming the fence. Dozens of tents and wagons stood outside the wooden perimeter, offering goods, hawking nuts. A few entertainers worked outside the fence, too, including a fire eater in motley who expelled a mouthful of flame to the delight of the children watching nearby. Within the fence, of course, stood the city within a city of tents, lean-tos, huts, and semipermanent shacks.

In any given day, at one point or another, most of Dur Follin's population passed through either or both the Low Bazaar and the fish market in the Dock. Nix fell in behind a donkey-pulled wagon filled with fresh-picked wildflowers, paid the copper entry fee to an Orangie to get through one of the gates, and dove into the crowd.

Clouds blocked the morning sun, but the atmosphere in the bazaar was festive. Pennons and flags snapped in the breeze. Acrobats and jugglers stood here and there amid the tents, entertaining the passersby, busking for coin. Streamers and ribbons hung from trees under which musicians played in groups of two or three, and storytellers stood on barrels, busking for donations by spinning tales. Goods of all sorts filled the tables and stalls, from pots, to tobacco, to knives, to bundles of fabric, to baskets of vegetables and fruits. Everywhere vendors hawked wares, services, and entertainment, and laborers and farmers and merchants moved wheelbarrows of goods to their stalls.

Nix remembered the first time he'd seen the bazaar. He'd

climbed the Poor Wall and snuck into the city proper and stared agawp at the sheer scale. The amount of food and goods crammed into one area had seemed to him surreal. He stole six apples that day and ate them in an alley that smelled of urine. They were the best apples he'd ever had. He'd returned to the Warrens later that night, his eyes opened to new possibilities. Mamabird had taken him in soon afterward, putting his life on a new path.

As he moved through the throng, Nix noted the pickpockets who worked here and there—guild men, he figured. He warned them away from him with a knowing look and firm shake of his head. He stood on his tiptoes and on barrels and crates every once in a while, scanning the crowd for one of the agents of Kerfallen the Grey Mage. The towering agents had no stall or tent, and instead just wandered the bazaar awaiting a hail from someone in the know.

Nix bounded off a crate and tossed a copper common to an old man selling apples and gourds.

"I just want the two," Nix said, taking an apple in each hand. "You keep the difference."

"Generous, goodsir!" the old man said.

"Eh, could be I owe you from a while back."

Nix ate the apples while he walked the crowds and searched. He soon found what he sought. Ahead, a tall, hooded figure moved methodically through the crowd. It acknowledged no one and eyed no wares. Nix cut through the vegetable stalls to his right so that he could intercept the agent. When he stepped in front of it, it stopped and regarded him with a tilted head.

The agent, an automaton of Kerfallen's creation, stood a hand taller than even Egil and Nix felt as small as a boy standing before it. Presumably Kerfallen had made the agent tall so as to stand out in the crowd and be easily spotted in the bazaar, but Nix figured there was at least some overcompensation to their stature—Kerfallen himself stood no taller than a dwarf, though he had pride enough for a giant.

The slack, androgynous, otherwise expressionless face of the agent looked out from its hood at some point above and behind Nix. Nix found the wizard's agent unnerving. It was like talking to a corpse.

"Do I actually have to say it?" Nix said, knowing that what he said was somehow communicated through the automaton's ears to Kerfallen. "Doesn't our long-standing relationship move us past these silly rituals, wizard?"

The automaton looked down so that its unblinking eyes, brown and as empty as those of a fish, met Nix's. It said nothing, just stared and waited. After a few moments, it lifted up its head and started to turn away.

"Fine," Nix said irritably. "The magery of Kerfallen is without peer in the Seven Cities of the Meander. I offer coin for his boon and counsel."

The automaton turned back and extended its right hand, palm up. The flesh looked as dull and old as wax. Nix pulled a small bag of royals and terns from his belt pouch and laid it on the automaton's palm.

"Terns and royals in equal measure," Nix said.

The creature secreted the bag within the folds of its cloak and looked at Nix, waiting.

"I don't want an item," Nix explained. "I have some objects and I need to know what they are or where they come from originally or anything at all that you can tell me about them. If you don't know anything, you indicate as much, yeah? I don't want a bunch of cryptic riddles and talking in circles. If I wanted that, I'd spend a copper common on a Narascene seer. Done?"

The automaton stared down at him a long moment, then slowly nodded.

"Good," Nix said. "Let's move out of the thoroughfare, though."

Trailed by the automaton—Nix did not like having the thing at his back—Nix picked his way through the crowd and tents and moved off to the side, to stand near the wooden fence that bordered the bazaar. As ever, there were passersby around, but far fewer, and none paid them heed that Nix could see. It was as private as they were going to get outside. Nix put a copper common in the palms of three boys idling near the fence and told them to be off. They thanked him, asked no questions, and sped off instantly to spend their windfall.

After they'd gone, Nix reached into his satchel, found by touch the cloth-wrapped plates, took them out, and unwrapped them. He used his body and the wrap to shield them from any onlookers, but that meant getting close to the automaton, which he disliked. The construct smelled of leather and metal and didn't breathe that Nix could tell, and the lack discomfited him.

The sun glinted on the plates as he showed them to the automaton. The construct stared at them for a long moment, entirely focused.

"The script on them is unknown to me," Nix said. "But I was hoping—"

With a suddenness that startled Nix, the creature lurched forward a half step and bent low to study the plates more closely. Nix's innate caution caused him to back up a step, but the automaton just leaned farther forward, its gaze never leaving the plates.

"You can stop right there," Nix said, and the creature did. "I like my space, is what."

Nix held the plates forth and let the creature study them for a long while. Passersby looked at him queerly and he felt ridiculous standing near the fence making inquiry of a magical construct that looked about ready to fall over onto its own face while the activity of the Low Bazaar went on around him.

"I think that's enough," he said finally. He took another step back and shoved the plates back into his satchel without wrapping them in the enchanted cloth.

The automaton watched them disappear into the satchel, then stood upright and looked him in the face.

"Well?" Nix asked, not knowing entirely what to expect. After all, he'd never heard the automaton speak, though he knew Kerfallen heard everything said to the construct and that the wizard was capable of responding through its mouth. The automaton looked at Nix, at the satchel, back at Nix.

"Can you help or not, wizard?" Nix asked, impatient.

The automaton's eyes went from dead to entirely vacant. Whatever force had enlivened the construct left its glassy eye. Its posture slackened, like a pavilion tent that had lost a pole.

"What the—?" Nix said, leaning toward it, but he might as well have been looking upon a statue. He eased a bit closer. "Hello? You there? I paid in good coin, wizard, and if you don't have an answer, just say as much, but don't—"

The automaton's head snapped up and its eyes fixed on Nix. Its mouth opened and Kerfallen's deep voice emerged from it, the sound hollow, as if he were speaking in a vast, empty room.

"You must give me the plates, Nix," the automaton said, holding out a hand and taking a step toward Nix.

Nix instinctively stepped back, a hand on the hilt of his blade. "No, I don't think I'll be doing that. You stand there or I'll take the head off your agent, wizard."

The automaton stopped, slack face fixed on Nix.

"What are they?" Nix asked. "Tell me that. Then we can talk about their disposition."

A long pause before, "They're beyond you. For your own good, give them to me."

Nix took another step back and the automaton did not keep pace. Nix breathed easier with a little more space between them.

"I'll look elsewhere for the information I need," Nix said.

"You won't find it. And you're not leaving."

Nix did not like the sound of that. He glanced around briefly and caught sight of another automaton—noticeable for its height and voluminous cloak—striding briskly through the crowd toward him. A third burst through the line of tents, its face fixed on Nix. He had long suspected there might be more than one of Kerfallen's agents in the bazaar, but now he had confirmation.

"So," Nix said, drawing his falchion. "You're not just a wizard but also a thief?"

The two additional automatons closed. It didn't appear they could run, but their long strides approximated one and they ate up the distance. They plowed through passersby, knocked a wagon aside. One of them reached out a hand as it came, as if it could reach him from twenty paces. The first automaton advanced on him, too, a hand outstretched.

"Give me the plates, Nix," it said. "This instant. Now."

He'd faced Kerfallen's automatons once before, when he and Egil had run into the wizard's manse, thinking him in danger. Then, Nix and Egil had easily dispatched several of them. He crosscut with his blade, taking off the extended hand of the automaton near him.

"That's a no," he said, and followed up with a quick slash at the automaton's throat. The construct responded much faster than Nix would have thought possible, raised its remaining hand, and caught Nix's blade. The edge scraped against the metal under the automaton's flesh. The creature wrenched the weapon out of Nix's grasp, tossed it aside, and grabbed Nix's shirt, trying to pull him close, hold him maybe until the other two could assist.

Nix jerked back, the shirt tore, and several buttons went flying. He stumbled but kept his footing, drawing his dagger as he backed up against the fence. People had caught sight of the fight. A few pointed.

"I liked this shirt," Nix said, and flung his dagger at the creature's face. It sank half its length into the creature's eye but the automaton showed no response at all and instead lunged for him, hand grasping. Nix sidestepped its outstretched arms and kicked it in the knee—hurting his foot and doing nothing at all to the automaton.

The creature got hold of a fistful of Nix's cloak and used it to pull him clear off the ground. The other two were closing. The one holding him pawed at his satchel with the stump of its other arm. Kerfallen's voice cursed through the agent's mouth.

"Forgot that lost hand, yeah?" Nix said, and squirmed out of the cloak.

"Stop!" the automaton said.

Nix hit the ground, rolled to his feet, bounded over the fence, and ran.

"Nix!" Kerfallen called through the mouth of his creature, which cast his cloak aside. "Don't be a fool!"

"Stop!" shouted one of the other automatons, speeding toward Nix, its movement herky-jerky and awkward, but fast. It crashed through a section of the fence. So too did the other. They tried to cut him off.

Behind him, the one-armed automaton gave chase, too, likewise smashing through the fence and slowing only slightly as it snapped the wood.

Passersby shouted and pointed at the sight of the three towering creatures trying to close on Nix, one of them with a dagger protruding from its eye. Someone shouted for the Watch.

Nix ran through a gaggle of carts, past a donkey, an acrobat who almost flipped into him, and a score or more passersby. He had only small blades now, secreted about his person, so he kept running, wondering in passing where in the Pits he was supposed to buy his gewgaws now.

"Out of the way, out of the way!" Nix called, knifing through the crowd.

People scrambled aside, surprise or anger on their faces, their gazes not so much on him as on his pursuers. He ran a block, two, trying to open some space and thinking the automatons would not go far outside the bazaar. But he was wrong, and from the rising shouts and screams behind him, Nix assumed the automatons were simply plowing through the street traffic as they kept up the chase. Nix spotted an idle horse hitched to a wagon loaded with barrels and swatted it hard on the rump as he ran past.

"Hyah!" he shouted, and the startled horse jerked, whinnied, and started down the street at a gallop, taking the wagon with it, bleeding barrels as it went.

"Whoa! Whoa!" shouted a middle-aged man on the sidewalk, cursing as he chased after the wagon.

Nix hoped it would cause enough commotion to at least slow the automatons. He leaped over a fruit vendor's cart, snatching a peach as he went, and darted down an alley.

"Hey!" shouted the vendor.

Nix heard a crash from behind and turned to see one of the automatons shoving the cart out of its way, spilling peaches and summoning curses from the vendor.

"You are stubborn creatures," Nix muttered.

Ahead, the alley split left and right. Nix started to head right, out to Tanner's Street, but the towering form of another automaton filled the far end of the alley mouth. He spun and looked left, and the third automaton stood there. He was hemmed in. He cursed, checked the wall.

The automatons saw what he was doing and hurried after him, closing from three sides.

He put the peach in his mouth and ran his hands over the face of the rough bricks, found purchase for his hands and feet, and started up. He'd gotten halfway up the wall by the time the first of the automatons, the one he'd maimed and stabbed in the eye, reached him. The construct did not bother to try to climb—Nix presumed it must be very heavy and it looked nowhere near agile enough to manage a vertical surface—but instead reached for his foot and barely missed. Nix almost laughed but the thing jumped as best as it was able and got ahold of his boot heel.

Nix spit out the peach and cursed, grabbing a protruding wood joist with both hands as the creature yanked on his heel. The other two were almost upon him, too.

"Just give me the plates," one of the other automatons called in Kerfallen's voice.

"You should've asked more nicely, bunghole!" Nix said. He shook his foot, trying to loose the creature's grip. He kicked down with his free foot and caught the hilt of the knife he'd thrown earlier, driving it deeper into the creature's face. It did not so much as ease its grip, even as Nix's grasp on the joist started to slip. His hands and forearms ached with the strain. He kicked down with his free foot again, again, his hold on the joist slipping as another of the automatons reached him, stepped beside its twin, and snatched for his free foot.

Desperate, Nix wriggled his foot in his boot, loosened it just enough, and slipped free of it just as the other automaton snatched at him, its fingertips grazing his free foot. He used the joist to pull himself up out of their reach.

"A shirt, my cloak, and now a fakking boot? You slubbers are hard on attire!"

"You don't know what you're doing, Nix. Give me those plates!"

Figures appeared at the end of the alley mouths, curious pedestrians trying to figure out what had happened. The Watch would be coming soon. The automatons looked up at him, dead eyes fixed on his satchel.

"Tell me what they are," Nix demanded. He burped and winced—Gadd's fakkin' stew was a ghost that would haunt him forever.

"I can't," said Kerfallen through the mouth of the maimed automaton. "And you wouldn't understand anyway."

"Then I'll keep them and you owe me a boot and a shirt," Nix said, and started climbing. "And a cloak. And whatever else I decide to extract in payment for the damned inconvenience of running down the street! Where am I supposed to buy my enchanted items now?"

The automatons watched him ascend for a moment, then spread out in either direction, perhaps hoping to cut him off or perhaps returning to their master's manse or the bazaar. Nix had no idea how Kerfallen could control all three of them simultaneously. It had to be taxing the wizard's abilities. In any event, Nix knew he was free of them for the moment. They couldn't climb and he knew the Thieves' Highway as well as anyone in Dur Follin.

And now he knew another thing: The plates were valuable and a wizard wanted them.

He and Egil had their adventure.

The distant whistles of the Watch sounded from the street below.

He took off his other boot, finding it too awkward to have one and not the other, grinning as he traversed the rooftops on his way back to Shoddy Way and the Slippery Tunnel. He periodically checked the streets below to ensure he wasn't followed by the automatons. If Kerfallen didn't already know that he and Egil lodged at the Tunnel, the wizard would find out soon enough; he and Egil didn't keep their ownership of the brothel a secret. Nix didn't think the wizard would send his minions after them at the Tunnel in the broad light of day, but then no such scruples had kept him from attacking Nix in the Low Bazaar and pursuing him down the street. And of course night would be another thing altogether.

Nix figured he and Egil would have some time, but perhaps not much. They'd need a place to hole up. And then he needed to figure out what in the Pits the plates actually were.

Nix turned his mind to it as he scaled down the wall into an alley near Shoddy Way, cursing the wizard anew when the coarse bricks scraped the skin of his toes.

CHAPTER FOUR

When Nix reached the Tunnel—barefoot, in a torn shirt, and without his cloak—the working day was well under way. Gadd stood behind the bar, a priest of tankards and ale. A dozen or more patrons sat at the tables or milled about the room. Two serving girls carried trays and Tesha's working men and women stood their posts on the stairs or moved suggestively through the room, wooing those who showed interest. Gadd took in Nix's missing boots and torn shirt and looked a question at him as Nix went past the bar and into the back.

"All's well," Nix said to him. "Or maybe not. I'll let you know in a bit."

He went down the back stairs to the room Egil typically used at the Tunnel and rapped on the door.

It had been only an hour or two since Egil had gone for some sleep and a growl answered Nix's knock.

"I see you're speaking with your usual articulateness," Nix called. "Time to wake."

"No. Go away."

Nix looked down the hall both ways to ensure no one was near enough to overhear. He leaned in and said, "The minions of a wizard are coming after us."

Some rustling from through the door. "*After us,* after us?"

"Aye."

"What time is it?" Egil asked.

"What? I don't know. Still morning."

"Gods, Nix. It's still morning and you already got us sideways of a wizard? That seems unlikely even for you."

"Well . . . it's late morning," Nix said defensively. "Almost afternoon, really. And I can get us sideways of anyone with great speed."

"That's true enough," the priest said. More rustling. The creak of the floor.

"Get dressed and meet me in the common room," Nix said. "I'll fill you in. And bring your hammers."

"Aye, that," Egil called.

Nix turned to go and saw Gadd's towering silhouette at the top of the stairs.

"Trouble?" Gadd asked as Nix ascended the stairs.

"Maybe," Nix said. "Wizard shite, is what. I don't think it'll come here, but keep that tulwar handy. And I need to get some boots and blades, a new cloak, and a few needful things from my room."

"Gewgaws!" Egil shouted from the other side of the door.

"How could he even hear that?" Nix said to Gadd, who shrugged. "Listen, Gadd, whatever you heard, keep it between the three of us for now, yeah?"

Gadd gave him a long look but nodded.

"Good man."

Later, rearmed and fitted with a spare pair of boots and a new shirt, Nix sat at the bar with Egil. He'd rewrapped the plates in the concealing blanket and bore them in his satchel. The business of the Tunnel went on as normal. Nix knew Kerfallen was capable of crafting constructs that were almost indistinguishable from a person, so he closely watched the patrons who came and went—not many, since the Tunnel's business picked up in late afternoon and early evening. All seemed in order.

Nix caught the priest up on the morning's events. Gadd listened, too, though he made as though he were just tending his cups.

After listening to Nix's story, Egil ran a hand over the eye of Ebenor. "I don't think he'll come at us here. You?"

"He might, but if he does I don't think it'll be soon."

Egil nodded. "What are you thinking, then? That we go at him first?"

Nix shook his head. "I wasn't thinking that, no. He *is* a wizard."

"So? We're a priest of a one-man faith and a wizard school dropout."

"Ha! And I was expelled."

Egil leaned forward in his stool, cracking his knuckles, visibly warming to the thought of violence. "I'm serious. You wanted to get our reputations back. Let's go burn his fakking mansion down, drag his small-statured self into the street, and make him apologize for chasing you up a roof."

Gadd poured them both an ale, giving Nix a moment to gather his thoughts. Nix nodded at the Easterner in gratitude.

"That's one idea," Nix said carefully. "And sounds appealing, I'll grant. But—"

"But?" Egil asked, and slammed the entirety of the ale Gadd had just given him. He signaled for another.

"But we should consider—"

Something crashed through the leaded glass windows on the Shoddy Way side of the Tunnel, spraying glass and eliciting a shout and curse from the patrons at the table nearby. One of the working girls exclaimed in surprise. Heads turned. A few patrons stood. A chair toppled. One of the patrons near the

window lurched over and looked out on the street for the cul-
prit, cursing the vandal prophylactically.

"Don't see anyone," the man said.

Nix slipped off his stool, his hand on the hilt of his blade.
Egil did the same, hand on one of his hammers.

"What the fak was that?" one of the patrons called. "A
stone?"

Another window on the other side of the building shattered
as something flew through it, too. The serving girl screamed
again. Everyone stood or looked about in alarm. Behind Nix,
Gadd growled.

"What is that?" said a man, standing from his chair and
leaning over to look at the fist-sized round object that had broken the window. "It's metal."

"What is going on?" Tesha called from the landing at the
top of the stairs. "Nix?"

"Patrons outside, right now!" Nix said, drawing his sword
and pointing at the doors with its tip. "All my people get upstairs to your rooms and stay there!"

No one moved. Several looked at him as if he were mad.

"What is this, Nix?" Tesha asked.

"Tesha, tell them to do as I said!" Nix said.

She glared at him but did as he asked. She must have heard
the urgency in his tone. "Everyone upstairs!" she shouted. "You,
too, Gadd. Right now. To your rooms. No one comes down
until Nix says so."

"Move!" Egil bellowed, and thumped his hammer on a
table. That broke the dam.

The working girls and men rushed upstairs, crowding the
staircase as they went. As Lis passed one of the objects, she said,
"This thing is vibrating, Nix."

"Don't touch it," Nix said. "Go!"

Something flew through another window, another. The objects landed on the floor and rolled until they hit a wall or table

leg. They looked like fist-sized metal balls lined with gouges or seams. Nix had an idea of what they might be.

"Out!" Nix said to the patrons. "Hurry!"

The spheres on the ground began to buzz, to rock slightly back and forth. Chairs spilled as the last dawdlers hurried for the doors.

Gadd was last up the stairs, tulwar in hand. He glanced back at Nix. Nix waved him on.

"Watch over Tesha and the rest. This is for Egil and me. Go, Gadd."

"Gofti," Gadd cursed, but heeded Nix's words and continued upstairs, hurrying the Tunnel's workers along.

"They could explode," Egil observed.

Nix shook his head. "Not Kerfallen's style. These are constructs."

"These tiny little things? I'll just throw them back outside."

Before the priest took three steps toward the nearest of the metal spheres, their vibrations reached a crescendo and they began to open, unfolding like flowers in rain.

By then the patrons were almost all through the doors, their exit disorderly and chaotic. One of the last of them, a potbellied man with long wild hair, stopped near the door to look at one of the unfolding spheres. He stood frozen, watching it.

"Get away from it, man!" Egil shouted.

The ball unfolded fully, taking the form of a fist-sized insect. At its core was a large blue gemstone, and attached to the stone by wires or filaments or sorcery was a sharp stinger, thin legs, and parchment-thin metal wings that fluttered rapidly, giving off an odd metallic hum. It buzzed into the air, its movement sharp and quick. The potbellied man who'd stopped to look backed off toward the door, eyes wide, staring at the magical metal insect hovering near him.

"Don't move," Nix said, but the man did not heed him and instead turned suddenly, trying to bolt.

The mechanical insect buzzed toward him like a shot arrow

and drove its stinger into his back. The man arched, screamed, shuddered, then stiffened as his flesh—and only his flesh—turned to a dull gray. The magical insect pulled free before the transformation was complete. It took Nix only a moment to register that the man had been turned to stone.

"Go ahead and throw them outside, would you?" he said to Egil.

Meanwhile, the rest of the metal spheres had already twisted and transformed into similar insectoid constructs, six in total, and took to the air, wings buzzing. Each had a different-colored gemstone for a body. Nix knew each would be lethal in its own way.

"Of course it leaves his clothing and possessions unaffected," Egil said.

Nix nodded. "That's because Kerfallen already owes me some clothes. Probably doesn't want to get further in the hole."

"Or because he wants the plates and cares shite for our skins."

"Possibly that, too," Nix conceded with a tilt of his head. "My blade's shite for this work. Hammers will do for a kill, but too slow for much else. Each one of these things will kill in a different way. Don't get stung."

"Sound advice," the priest said sarcastically. He kept one hammer in hand, put the other in its thong on his belt.

"I don't have anything to finish them," Nix said, his heart beating fast. "So you'll have to smash anything I bring down."

"Done," Egil said.

The creatures gathered together into a swarm above one of the tables. They were going to come at them all at once.

An idea struck Nix, but he couldn't act on it before the creatures buzzed toward them, a cluster of glittering, flying knives. Nix grabbed a chair and hurled it at them as he darted toward a window. The chair split the flock, catching one of the creatures—a wasplike thing constructed around a ruby—and sent it spinning to the floor, where it buzzed and skittered along the ground. A black substance leaked from its stinger, no doubt a poison.

"What are you doing?" Egil called after him, upending a table.

"Just don't get fakkin' petrified, yeah?" Nix called back.

Two of the creatures buzzed after Nix. When he reached the window, he yanked down the heavy curtains. Through the glass, he caught a glimpse of two tall, cloaked figures moving quickly through the crowd outside, making their way toward the door—two of the automatons from the bazaar, probably coming to finish what the insectoid constructs started. Nix flung the curtains at the two creatures flying toward him.

"Constructs outside on the way in!" he called to Egil.

Egil heaved up the table he'd tipped and flung it at the three creatures flying at him. They veered, darting to either side and avoiding the table, but Egil had already grabbed a chair. He spun as he picked it up, swung it, and struck one of the creatures flush. Its stinger sank through the wood of the chair's seat, and it stuck there, buzzing angrily, the stinger emitting a shower of sparks. Egil slammed the chair to the floor and crushed the damaged construct with a blow from his hammer, hurriedly taking a wild swing at the other two as they flew at him. He dove under another table to avoid their attack, rolled out, and leaped back to his feet as the creatures came back around for another pass.

Nix's curtains had enveloped the other two constructs. He hurriedly grabbed for the ends of the fabric and pulled them together, forming a makeshift bag to hold them. They buzzed and squirmed under the heavy folds but he soon had them. Stingers poked through the fabric, one barely missing his palm. He cursed, heaved the bag up, and swung it hard into the floor. Stingers poked through anew, an angry buzzing. One of the construct's stingers was edged and knifelike, and the creature used it to start slitting the fabric. Nix cursed, hefted the bag, and slammed it down again, again, the weight of the curtain's fabric working against him and cushioning the impact. The creatures would squirm or cut themselves free soon enough.

"Egil!"

But the priest had troubles of his own. Egil had dropped his hammer and now had a chair in each hand, spinning like an awkward dancer as he swung first one and then another at the two creatures, one built around a yellow gem, and one built around an emerald. They darted in and around, feinting, looking for an opening. Egil caught one with the chair and sent it flying into the wall behind the bar, where it broke into several pieces. He dropped one of the chairs and swung the other two-handed at the last construct, missing it.

It reared back and then darted in for Egil's chest, stinger first. In desperation, Egil let go of the chair and grabbed at the construct with his hands. At first Nix thought Egil had somehow caught it around the middle of its body without getting stung, but then he saw. The stinger had gone through Egil's palm. Blood poured down the priest's arm.

"Egil!"

The priest grimaced, grabbed the creature around the body with his other hand, and pulled it out of his skin, grunting at the pain. It squirmed in his grasp, buzzing, its motion causing his arm to wheel left and right and up and down. Holding it tightly and mindful of getting stung again, Egil slammed it into the petrified body of the patron, shattering the creature.

One of the creatures wriggled free of the curtain but before it could take flight Nix stepped on it with his boot. It wriggled and buzzed angrily under his weight.

"I could use a priest with a fakkin' hammer!" Nix called.

Egil bounded across the room, crushing under his boot as he came the construct they'd downed earlier. He drew the hammer at his belt. Nix could see his flesh was darkening.

"Don't crush my foot, yeah?" Nix said. "What are you feeling? What did the stinger do?"

"I'm warm," Egil said, raising his hammer. "Getting warmer by the moment."

The priest smashed the exposed head of the creature with

his hammer and it went still, then he methodically located and smashed the remaining one through the fabric of the curtains.

"It's a fever toxin. You'll be dead in half an hour."

"What?" Egil said.

"Or you could drink this," Nix said, hurriedly fishing a healing elixir from his satchel of needful things. Once, Egil had been poisoned in the Demon Wastes east of the city and Nix had barely been able to save him. He'd carried healing elixirs in his satchel ever since. He tossed one to Egil and the priest popped the seal with his thumb and drank it down. Immediately the wound in his hand closed and the redness in his skin lightened.

"I only have a few more," Nix said. "So maybe do better next time? Didn't I say not to get stung?"

"Fak you."

Nix drew his blade and nodded at the Tunnel's double doors, just as two automatons from the bazaar walked through. "Ironically I bought those healing elixirs from one of those fakkers in the bazaar a few months back."

The automatons paused in the doorway, took in the scene.

"I want the plates, Nix," Kerfallen's voice said from the mouth of the one foremost.

"Come get them then, wizard," Egil answered. He tossed aside the empty elixir vial and strode across the common room floor, hammer at the ready.

A third automaton appeared behind the first two, smaller and hard to see. The two foremost started forward and one of them abruptly halted as a blade sprouted from its chest. It started to turn and the person behind it—not an automaton, as Nix had first supposed—kicked it to the ground, pulled his blade free, and slashed the automaton in the head, splitting the skull. Some kind of a dark ichor flowed from the gash.

The second lurched at Egil, hands extended, but Egil slammed his hammer into its head before it could get a hold on him. The blow knocked the head clean from the body and sent it flying against the wall. The headless body fell to its knees, then flat on the floor.

"What the fak are these things?" said the man who'd ambushed the first automaton. He looked up and Nix recognized the thin face and beard.

"Jyme!"

They hadn't seen Jyme since they'd left him behind in the Afirion desert, after defeating the servant creatures of Rose and Mere's devil-worshipping brother. Then, Jyme had reluctantly been in the employ of the brother, but he'd come around by the end of things. The former watchman and mercenary wore a sun-faded tan cloak, a leather vest, stained breeches, high boots, and his steel. He had a different look in his eye than the last time Nix had seen him, a harder look, like maybe he'd lived through some things. Nix glanced out the window to see if any more of Kerfallen's agents were en route, but he saw nothing other than the street traffic and the patrons who'd fled through the doors milling about.

"Jyme?" Egil said. He peered more closely. "Shite, it is. That's a well-timed arrival, Jyme. Like you fell out of the sky, almost."

Nix thought maybe a bit too well timed. He and Egil shared a knowing look.

Egil hurried to the doors of the Tunnel and shouted, "All's well, but we're closed for a bit to clean up." He shut the doors, turned, and said to Jyme, "What brings you back?"

"That's a bit of a story," Jyme said, sheathing his blade. He looked wide-eyed at the petrified patron standing in the center of the common room, his body and expression frozen in a position of agony.

"That just happen?" Jyme asked. "He gonna stay like that?"

Egil shrugged.

Jyme looked at Egil, then at Nix, then nodded at the automatons. "I have to ask again though. What the fak are those?"

Nix walked over and kneeled down. Jyme's blade had opened

the head of one of the humanoid constructs and through the black ichor or grease or whatever it was, Nix made out hair-thin lines of spun metal, tiny clusters of gears, shafts, and rods. The work was intricate and Nix had never seen anything like it.

"It's the work of a wizard," he said, standing. "One that's none too happy with us at the moment."

"Gewgaws," Egil snarled. He stayed close to Jyme as the three of them, without saying anything, walked toward the bar.

A voice called from the rooms upstairs, Tesha's voice. "Did you say all was well?"

"Not just yet," Nix answered. "Give us a moment more."

Jyme was smiling. "You boys are a welcome sight. I was—"

The moment they reached the bar, Egil grabbed Jyme with both hands, twisted an arm behind him, and bent him over until he was cheek down on the bar's surface.

Jyme struggled for a moment, but he was no match for Egil's strength. He might as well have been trying to lift a mountain.

"What the fak's going on?" Jyme snapped over his shoulder, teeth gritted in pain. "I just helped you. Let me up, Egil."

Nix leaned in near Jyme's ear. "This is what's going on, Jyme. We just got sideways of a wizard today, got attacked in our own place, and you show up right then after . . . How long's it been, Egil?"

"Been a while since we've seen Jyme," Egil said, giving Jyme's arm an added twist.

"Ow," Jyme exclaimed.

"A while," Nix echoed. "The timing's improbable, wouldn't you say?"

"No, I wouldn't," Jyme protested, trying to maneuver free but failing in the face of Egil's strength. "Damn it, Egil! That hurts! Listen, you two are always sideways of a wizard, ain't you? I could show up anytime and the story'd be the same."

Nix stood up and looked over Jyme at Egil, eyebrows raised.

Egil shrugged and tilted the bucket of his head. "He's got a point."

"He does," Nix said. "Maybe."

"Then let me the fak up," Jyme said. "I ain't here for no wizard."

Nix nodded at Egil and the priest released Jyme, though Egil kept a hand on his back.

"Ale?" Nix said to Jyme, taking the seat beside him at the bar. "It's good."

Jyme, rubbing his shoulder, snapped, "I've had it before and I know it's good. Pits, I'd been looking forward to seeing you two and I get . . . fakking grappled."

"Grappled, he said," Nix said to Egil, and chuckled. "Look at Jyme with the words, now."

Egil went around to the back of the bar and started drawing ales. "He grew himself a beard, too, instead of that boy scruff he used to wear."

"You two are just the same, I see," Jyme said, massaging his shoulder. When Egil put a tankard before him, Jyme took a long drink, staring ahead at Mung's picture.

"We don't have a lot of time for conversation, Jyme," Nix said.

"Wizard and all," Jyme said, setting the tankard down.

"Time enough for an ale, though," Egil said.

Nix wasn't so sure, but decided not to press.

"Last we saw you," Nix said, "you were going in the opposite direction as us."

Jyme colored, hid behind his tankard while he took a quaff. "I've no pride in that."

"No shame in it, either," Egil said, filling himself a tankard. "I said as much then."

"You did, but it hung on me, still," Jyme said. "Anyways, I spent some time in Afirion after that. Sessket. You know it? Did some things, made some coin." He shrugged.

"And now here you are," Nix said. "Right at this moment."

Jyme turned to look into Nix's face. "Coincidence, Nix. Like I said."

"Not to worry," Nix said. "I can see you're the Jyme we knew and not some wizard's pawn. You picked a bad time to show, though."

"That wizard isn't going to stop coming, I'm thinking," Egil said.

"Agreed. Even so . . ." Nix raised his tankard. "To old traveling companions returned."

Jyme brightened at that.

Egil asked, "Should we call Tesha and the rest down now?"

"Gadd sees you behind his bar, he'll have your head," Nix said. "He's still got that tulwar in hand, remember. Best we finish these ales first, then be on our way."

Egil nodded. "Watch'll be coming."

"Who knows with those slubbers," Nix said.

Egil came around the bar. He didn't sit, but leaned on the bar near Jyme. "So what are you doing here, Jyme?"

Jyme opened his mouth a couple of times, searching for the words. Finally he shook his head and said, "I don't even want to tell you now. It doesn't matter anyway. You got things to handle."

"And we don't have time for guessing," Nix said, standing. "Owing to that wizard I mentioned and us being sideways of him. So, it was good to see you Jyme, but . . ."

Egil didn't budge. "I want to hear it. You said it hung on you, yeah? Not coming with us. That's the core of it, eh?"

"It's pointless now," Jyme said.

Egil simply stared at him.

"We are in a hurry," Nix said to the priest, or Jyme, whichever.

Again Tesha called from upstairs. "Is it clear or not, Nix?"

"Not quite," Nix called back. "Jyme, spill whatever you need to spill or Egil will stand here all day."

Jyme studied his hands. "Fine. So . . . I thought we'd become almost friends over that business in the desert. Am I wrong?"

Nix looked at Egil, then back at Jyme. "*Friends* might be a bit strong, Jyme, but you had our respect when we parted."

"Well I guess that's somethin'," Jyme said. "But like I said, not going with you when you went after that nobleman—"

"He was a wizard, too," Egil said.

"Damned if you weren't right, Jyme," Nix said, rapping the bar with his knuckles. "We *are* sideways of wizards more often than not."

"*Anyway,*" Jyme said. "That hung on me, yeah? So I carried that around until it got too heavy. Then I dragged it and me back here."

"To do what?" Egil asked. He took a drink of his ale, looking thoughtful.

"Fak's sake," Nix said. "The priest is getting philosophical now. I can see it in the furrowed brow. We really should not linger, Egil."

"Bah. To do what, Jyme?"

Jyme ignored Nix and gestured aimlessly with his hands. "I don't know, Egil. Make sure the two of you got out of that scrape in the desert with your skins, maybe? Make up for my not comin' with you back then?" He looked from Egil to Nix. "Look, I wanna go in with you two on something, an adventure like, is what I'm sayin'."

Egil looked over at Nix, shaking his head. "Even Jyme is looking for adventure now. The world is upside down."

"It's a sign," Nix said, drumming the bar impatiently with his fingers.

"A sign?" Egil said. "Aren't I the priest?"

Nix chuckled. "That, too, might be a bit strong of a word."

"Bah," Egil said, and took a drink of his ale.

"*Gofti,* you mean," Nix said. "This is Gadd's realm. Calls for his vernacular."

"Bah," Egil offered as retort. "And *gofti.*"

"Did you save them?" Jyme asked them. "Those girls?"

The question sobered Egil, and it was the priest's turn to look at his hands.

Nix answered for both of them. "That time, yeah. That brother got what was coming to him."

The moment stretched in silence. Finally Jyme cleared his throat and sat up straight. "Look here. I didn't come here beggin' with my cock dragging on the floor. I just felt like I owed you two something for how I acted. But I can see you got your own matters to see to and if you don't want me around, that's fine, too. I've got other things to look to."

He pushed back his stool and stood.

Nix could see the man was in earnest. "Don't go running off, Jyme. Fak, man. At least finish your ale."

"I thought you had to clear out," Jyme said to Nix.

"We do," Nix said. "But even so."

"Sit," Egil echoed. "Besides, I understand you."

Jyme hesitated a moment but sat back down. "Egil the priest understands being ashamed of his own cowardice? I don't credit that a bit."

Nix sighed. "It's not going to turn into a fakkin' confessorium in here, is it?"

Egil ignored Nix. He put his thick forearms on the bar and interlaced his fingers. "You did something that didn't square with how you see yourself, or how you want to see yourself, so you came back here to reconcile that."

Jyme pursed his lips in thought. "Yeah, I guess that's right."

"I know how *that* is," Egil said.

Nix put a hand on Jyme's shoulder. "You know what I think? I think it's even worse than all that. I think old Jyme here doesn't just want an adventure to square accounts. Listen to his tone. No, an adventure's not enough. Jyme here wants to be the hero of the story." Nix gave him a gentle shake. "Isn't that about the size of it?"

Jyme colored, squirmed in his seat. "I don't know about that. As you would say, *hero* is maybe a bit strong of a word. I just want to hold my own, is all. I know I ain't the two of you, robbing tombs and facing this and that, but I know my way with a blade and could likely be a help. And then . . ."

He trailed off but Egil finished for him.

"And then the Jyme you see in your head will match the Jyme that walks the world, yeah?"

Jyme studied his hands, nodded. "That's about it, yeah. I guess you *are* familiar with the feeling."

"I am," Egil said. He slammed the rest of his ale. "Never have squared the two, though. So best get used to the dissonance, Jyme."

"Hmm," Jyme said and cleared his throat. "Well."

"Well, indeed," Nix said. "Hells, maybe that's the point, eh? We're not supposed to meet our expectations for ourselves. We're supposed to just keep trying and failing and try again."

Neither Egil nor Jyme said anything.

"Come on now!" Nix said. "That could pass for profundity. Priest, what say you?"

"Bah."

"Jyme?"

"Eh," Jyme said.

"A pox on you both for not knowing that you sit beside a philosopher of note," Nix said. He finished his ale. "And with that it's about time we headed out, priest. We're going to have to stay clear of the Tunnel for a while."

"Agreed," Egil said.

Nix said, "Kerfallen will be regrouping already. He'll be at us again, next time with worse. I think these flying things and the automatons from the bazaar are just what he had to hand. He'll get something more suitable next time."

"Did you say 'Kerfallen'?" Jyme exclaimed. "Kerfallen the Grey?"

"He wants something we've got," Nix said, resting his hand on his satchel. "Badly, it seems."

"You stole something from a wizard?" Jyme asked, incredulous.

Nix glared at Jyme. "No. In fact he's trying to steal something from us. But if I told you how we came by that something—came by it *honestly*—you wouldn't believe me."

"I might," Jyme said.

Egil glanced around the room, at the torn curtains, shattered tables, the remains of the clockwork creatures and the petrified patron. "We need to find out what these fakking plates are."

"Plates?" Jyme asked. "What do you mean 'plates'? Eating plates?"

"True," Nix said to Egil. "And we will."

"Fakking gewgaws," Egil cursed. "Another ale, Jyme?"

"Uh, yeah. But I thought you two were leaving and—"

"How do we find out?" Egil asked Nix. "Ideas?"

Nix heard a door click open upstairs. Probably someone peeking out to see if it was safe to come out yet.

"Stay up there still!" Egil called, and the door slammed shut. He poured himself and Jyme another ale.

Nix frowned. "We need to clean up this mess and then we should move. I'm thinking on options."

"One more ale hurts nothing," Egil said. "And you were about to tell how we could find out what the plates are?"

"What are these fakkin' plates?" Jyme asked, exasperated.

Nix ignored him. "If I hadn't been expelled, I could make an inquiry at the Conclave. Kazmarek could tell us. The library there is comprehensive."

Egil said, "But you *were* expelled, so you won't, and therefore he won't, and so I ask anew: How do we find out?"

"You're sideways of a Conclave wizard, too?" Jyme asked Nix. "Fak, man. It's like you have a disease."

"Look at this," Nix said, thumping Jyme on the back hard enough to spill a bit of Jyme's ale. "We leave Jyme alone in the desert and he comes back funny. Everyone's funny now. It's as contagious as the crotch pox."

Jyme colored and his expression fell somewhat when Nix mentioned the desert, but he rallied enough to ask, "Why not just ask him? Pay him some coin, a donation to the school or something?"

Nix knew it would be futile. "They don't work that way. Kazmarek detests me personally and I'm not allowed on the premises. Possibly I insulted him. A few times. And, before you volunteer to try paying him yourself, Jyme, let me say that I don't want another wizard seeing these plates. Because whatever they are drove Kerfallen to attack me in the bazaar and then in here. And that's not normally his way. So I don't know why it would be any different for the High Wizard of the Conclave. And the last thing we want is the entire Conclave coming down on us."

Jyme shrugged. "Maybe just give them over then?"

"Bah," said Egil, slamming the rest of his ale.

"And that's the short of it," Nix said. "You're going to stumble out of here if you have another, priest. Anyway, the long of it is that it's the principle now. The plates are ours, hard come by, and I'm not giving them over to some wizard who tries to strong-arm us. He should've just asked to buy them."

Jyme looked puzzled. "But if you'd have sold them—"

"It's the *principle,* Jyme," Egil said.

"It is," Nix added.

Jyme took another drink of ale, then said, "Maybe it's not that wise a principle, is what I'm sayin'. Anyways, how *do* you plan to find out what these things are?"

Nix smiled. "As I said, I was thinking through options. Option one is that we're going to go to the Conclave."

"I like it," Egil said, raising his tankard in a toast.

"But you just said they wouldn't deal with you."

"They won't," Nix said. "Which is why we'll break in. I just need access to the library. The book sprites will help me find what I need there."

"Book sprites?" Jyme asked.

"Magical creatures. Fae," Nix answered.

Egil harrumphed. "I don't even ask, Jyme. Why bother is my thinking. He could tell me they were demons, or imprisoned souls, or anything else and I'd not know better. I just take him at his word."

Jyme leaned back in his chair. "So, are you both drunk? Because half of what you've said makes no sense. You have plates you might have sold to a wizard, but now that you know he really wants them, you won't give them over at any price. You won't use a proxy to make a request of the Conclave, but you'll risk breaking in to get what you need."

"That's about the size of it," Egil said.

Nix smiled smugly at Egil. "I told you I'd have an adventure for you."

Jyme looked from one to the other as if they were mad, then his face fell in resignation. He stood. "Well enough. So when do we start?"

"Ha! Didn't I say it?" Nix said. "Wants to be a hero."

"Aye," Egil said.

"Listen, now—" Jyme began.

Nix put a hand on Jyme's shoulder, a kindly gesture. "We don't doubt you. But Kerfallen is looking for us, not you. You want to help? We need someone here with Gadd to watch over the Tunnel while we're away. Wizard could take another run at the place."

Jyme shook his head. "I don't want fakkin' guard duty. I didn't come back for that. And he's not going to hit this place without you two in it."

"Maybe," Nix said. "Or maybe not. If he does, you and Gadd will be here to stop him."

Egil put one of his huge hands on Jyme's other shoulder.

"Place means a lot to us, as do the people in it. This isn't a small ask, Jyme."

"It ain't a big one, either," Jyme protested, but from his softened expression, Nix could already see he was won over.

Nix gave him another moment, then said, "We need to get clear of here, Jyme. More or less right now. Can we count on you?"

Jyme sighed, nodded, and sat. "You can. But once this wizard shite gets cleared up, I want in on whatever's next, yeah? *In* in, I mean, not guard duty."

"Done," Nix said, and clapped him on the back. He was vaguely surprised to find that he liked Jyme.

"Done and done," Egil echoed, then to Nix said, "If the Watch does come, we'll want to be gone. Let's get Gadd and Tesha down here, get the room cleaned up. You have the plates with you, yeah?"

Nix nodded. The plates would stay with him, in his satchel, until matters were settled.

"Let me get a look at them," Egil said. "So I'm reminded of what in the Hells we're talking about."

CHAPTER FIVE

Nix went upstairs and brought only Tesha and Gadd out from the rooms, deflecting questions from everyone else and instructing them to stay put for the time. The less they saw and knew, the better.

Gadd fell in behind him and Tesha.

"You're all right?" she asked, eyeing him for wounds. "Egil, too?" Wisps of her dark hair fell in curly lines across her face.

Nix was touched by the sincerity of her concern. "Of course we are. It's us."

"Stop saying it like you can't get hurt, Nix. You can. Both of you. Don't be stupid."

"Well enough," Nix said, chastened.

"Now," she said as they walked for the stairs, "tell me what just happened. I heard the ruckus."

Nix had rehearsed an answer in his head so he offered it. "We're in a hurry, so I'll have to be short. We didn't expect this. Not in the day, and not here or I wouldn't have come back. I hope you know that. We have something a wizard wants—"

"A wizard?" she asked.

"Gofti," Gadd swore.

Tesha stopped when they reached the top of the stairs. She looked down on the common room.

"It's not as bad as it looks," Nix hurriedly explained, his words put to the lie by the torn curtains, shattered windows, and the broken tables and chairs. She looked at Nix as if he were the stupidest man in Dur Follin, then looked back down on the room, her eyes tallying the damages, her mouth a fixed line.

Egil had already moved the two humanoid constructs and the insectoid creatures to the rear yard of the Tunnel. They'd burn them in a bonfire there, protected from watchful eyes by the tall fence that secured the Tunnel's expansive green space. Now the priest was straightening chairs, setting overturned tables back up. The priest pointedly did not look up. Jyme sat at the bar, looking uncomfortable, staring at his hands as if they were interesting.

Tesha licked her lips. "We need to get this cleaned up quickly so we can reopen. Will the Watch come?"

"Likely," Nix admitted. "And probably soon. But the story is that miscreants threw rocks through the window and that started a brawl that cleaned the place out. We kicked out the brawlers and the rock throwers are all long gone. The Watch won't work too hard to poke holes in that."

She ran a hand through her hair. "There were patrons inside. They saw those things come through the windows."

"What did they see, Tesha? Metal spheres cast through the window and then what? Most of them were out before anything happened and whatever the rest saw is nothing anyone will believe. They were mostly all gone before those things took form and flew at us."

Tesha looked at him, her dark eyes wide. "What things?"

He forgot that she hadn't seen the creatures, either. "Wizard shite," he explained. "They were constructs, mechanical creations animated by magical energy; it's hard to explain."

She frowned. "They can also be animated by bound spirits, and"—she put a finger on his chest—"I probably know as much about spellcraft as you."

Nix could not keep the surprise from his face. "Oh. So you . . . ?" He shook his head. "How do you know that?"

Behind them, Gadd chuckled, a rumble like thunder.

For the hundredth time, Nix reminded himself to figure out Gadd and Tesha's story.

"That's none of your business," Tesha said. She nodded down at Jyme. "Who is that?"

"That shifty-looking hiresword? That's Jyme. He's with us now." Nix called down to Jyme. "Jyme, this is Tesha. She runs the Tunnel. You know Gadd already. He runs the ale and cups."

Jyme stood from his stool and offered an awkward bow. "Milady. Gadd."

Tesha snorted at being called "milady." "Why is there a petrified man in the center of the room?" she asked Nix.

Nix cleared his throat. "Well, that was one of our patrons who moved too slowly. One of the constructs got him."

"The flying constructs?" she asked, and started down the stairs. Nix and Gadd fell in behind her.

"Yes," Nix said.

Tesha went to the petrified patron and Gadd went to his bar, frowning when he saw the tankards Nix, Egil, and Jyme had left atop it.

"Did you tap one of my kegs?" Gadd asked, incredulous.

"It was Jyme," Nix said, pointing.

"It was not!" Jyme protested.

"You'd think we committed a sacrilege," Nix said to Egil.

"He is particular about his cups," the priest said. "Let's stick with blaming Jyme."

"He's still got that tulwar to hand," Nix called over to Jyme.

"I'd maybe give him some space. And think more about it next time before you violate a man's bar. You'd do well to apologize."

Jyme laughed. When Gadd did not, Jyme cleared his throat, rose, and came over to Egil and Nix. Gadd grabbed Jyme's tankard, muttering.

Tesha walked a circle around the petrified patron. "I don't know him. Is he dead?"

Nix reminded himself to take his eyes off the curve of her hips. It took effort. "Sometimes the effect is permanent. Sometimes not. Depends on the whim of the wizard."

"How much did this one hate you?" she asked.

Egil guffawed.

"Now, who can really hate me?" Nix asked innocently.

The look she shot him was pointed enough to lance a boil.

"I think I'd rather be sideways of a wizard than her," Jyme said softly. "That alekeep and his pointed teeth, too."

"You're a wise man," Egil said to him, then to Tesha, "That statue is the only problem we'll have with the Watch. Someone comes looking for him, we may have to own up. But in the meanwhile, Gadd and I will move him out back. If the magic wears off, he'll wake up all right there. I've already taken care of the other . . . creatures. Which reminds me." He stuck a hand in his pocket and pulled out several gems, the main part of the bodies of the destroyed constructs. "Bribe the guards with those, if necessary."

Tesha placed them in the breast of her dress. She nodded at the petrified man. "And if he doesn't come back?" she asked.

Nix had no intention of leaving the man forever turned to stone. "Then Egil and I will fix him somehow. But we can't do it now."

"Because of the wizard," Tesha said.

"Because of the wizard," Nix affirmed. "And because of the Watch. And because we're leaving and we won't be back until this business is done."

She crossed her arms under her breasts. "And the business is what precisely?"

"Figure out what we have," Nix said, realizing how ridiculous the words sounded.

"And squaring accounts," Egil added.

"And that," Nix said. "Jyme will stay here and help you and Gadd keep the house in order. It's just business as usual after we leave, yeah?"

"Yes," Tesha said, but looked at Jyme skeptically. "I guess you know how to use that sword?"

Jyme stood up straight. "Not as well as those two, I'll own. But well enough, milady."

Egil shook his head. "See, Tesha, Jyme went away for a while and came back honest and polite. It's strange, yeah?"

"Nice change of pace, I'd say," Tesha said, looking at Nix meaningfully.

Nix made as though she'd stabbed him in the stomach.

"Don't be dramatic," she said. "Just make sure the two of you stay whole. I suggested you do something to get out of your doldrums, but this is not what I had in mind. And you," she said to Jyme, "stop calling me 'milady.'"

"Yes, of course," Jyme said.

"As for us," Egil said, "we're good at staying whole if little else."

Nix winked at her and she half-smiled, but the smile vanished when her eyes fell on the petrified patron.

"This feels a bit different," she said.

"I'll own it does," Egil agreed.

"Enough," Nix said. "Let's get to moving."

Egil and Gadd and Nix maneuvered the petrified patron out to the gated yard behind the Tunnel.

"Birds will shit all over him," Egil said afterward.

"Better to wake up covered in shit than not at all," Gadd said, and smiled a mouthful of pointed teeth. "And no, Nix, that is not a saying from my homeland."

"Wisdom in it anyway," Nix said, grinning.

They returned to the inside of the Tunnel, checked gear—Nix had put the quiescent talking key in his satchel with the plates and his other gewgaws and equipment—and started to head out. Before they did, Jyme pulled them aside.

"I'll keep things square here, but what if we need to find you?"

"Just follow the wizardly shite," Egil said, adjusting the hammers at his belt. "We're usually near to that."

Jyme smiled. "No, really."

Nix considered, then reached into his satchel. He sifted through the dozens of things he kept in it and withdrew a small cloth pouch. Inside was a single piece of enchanted parchment, a small vial of enspelled ink, and a stylus.

"You lettered? Be truthful, Jyme."

Jyme looked offended. "I'm no fakkin' poet, but I can string a few words."

Nix nodded. He spoke a word in the Language of Creation to activate the magic of the kit, then tore off two tiny pieces of the parchment. He handed one to Egil.

"Eat it," he said to the priest, and swallowed down the other piece.

Egil looked at the torn bit of paper, then handed it back to Nix without a word. Nix sighed.

"It's just you and me then, Jyme. You saw me eat a piece of that parchment, yeah? That linked me and it. Whatever you write on that larger piece, I'll hear it aloud in my ears. It only works for a sentence or two and then not again, so don't get wordy."

"Well, 'fak off' is only one sentence, so that'll leave me some room to say more."

Tesha, walking by, laughed aloud at that.

Nix chuckled, too. "Came back from Afirion funny and no doubt. Glad you're here, Jyme."

"Same," Jyme said.

Nix and Egil said their farewells to Gadd, and Tesha, and Jyme, then walked out of the Tunnel through the back exit. From behind, they heard Tesha call for everyone to come down. The Tunnel would be back in business within the hour.

Out back, Nix and Egil halted within the shelter of the Tunnel's high wooden fence. Chickens scrabbled in the grass and dirt. The Tunnel's dairy cow lowed within its pen. A bird had already shit on the petrified patron. Egil saw Nix eyeing the man.

"He's a problem for another day," the priest said.

"Aye. We'll fix you eventually," Nix said to the patron.

"Kerfallen will have eyes on the place if he can," Egil said.

Nix nodded. "He would, but I'm hoping he spent what he had on that attack and will need some time to get something else in place."

Egil ran a hand over his pate. "We shouldn't count on that, though. He could always divine our location. Should I assume you have a plan?"

"You may so assume."

"Would the assumption be correct?"

Nix smiled and thumped Egil on the shoulder. "Well, that's a different matter now. I'll add that I find you very suspicious for a priest."

"It's the company I keep," Egil said. "Breeds a suspicious nature."

Egil dug his ivory dice out of a pouch on his belt. He shook them in his fist, his habit when they faced uncertainty. "How far along are we in thinking this through?"

"Not that far," Nix said. "But then this all just started, so I say we're doing all right. We'll make the rest of it up as we go, same as always. That's the fun, yeah? At this point I'm thinking we sneak into the Conclave, get to the library, make the book sprites find information on the plates, sneak out, and then act on whatever information we have."

"The sneaking in and out part strikes me as problematic," Egil said doubtfully.

"Problematic, you say?" Nix said. "That word's as big as your hammers. You should read less, priest."

Egil went on as if Nix hadn't spoken. "A job like that normally would take planning. And for that we haven't time. Needs darkness at least, and that means we need a place to hole up, clear of Kerfallen's agents and spells. So that maybe leaves only one option."

Nix sighed. "Right. I was thinking the same."

"Not sure how that's going to work out, though," Egil said.

"I guess we might as well go find out."

"I guess."

Nix felt exposed the moment they got out of the lee of the fence. Out of habit, they checked rooftops and alleys as they melted into the street traffic of wagons, horses, donkeys, and pedestrians.

"What do you make of Jyme?" Nix asked Egil.

They cut down a narrow alley, positioned themselves in the shadows to either side of the wall, and waited. Nothing.

"I think he means exactly what he says," Egil said, double-checking a passerby who must have struck him as suspicious. "The man is not exactly opaque."

Nix nodded and they hustled through the alley out onto Butchers Way. Egil looked right and Nix left.

"All clear," Egil said.

"Good here," Nix said, and they stepped out into the street. "Anyway, I think likewise. So what in the Hells is wrong with him then?"

They eyed the street traffic with a wary eye as they moved briskly west—a man leading an old cow, a few wagons, half a dozen pedestrians. The air stank of butcher's offal.

Egil said, "A man leaves a little bit of himself behind with every act of cowardice he commits. I think he's just trying to pick up a piece or two he dropped back in the desert."

Nix stopped and faced his friend. "Listen to you, with the profound priestly observations."

A tall figure came around a corner ahead. Nix and Egil instinctively used nearby pedestrians as cover, put hands to hilts and hafts, but they relaxed when it hailed someone with a raised hand and called out.

They cut down another alley, repeated the process of waiting. Again, nothing.

"One of us needs to be profound, Nix," Egil said. "Else what's the point?"

"And he does it again!" Nix said, as they headed down the alley. "And even makes a sharp point in the process! I think all that drinking did you some good. Expanded your mind some. Or at least loosed your tongue so it gives voice to your thoughts. Anyway, looks like we don't have a tail."

"Aye. At least for now. Best hurry, then. Rusk may just say no and if he does we'll need to come up with something else. Maybe just stay on the move until nightfall."

"We can't let him say no. We need that safe house. Kerfallen will find us with a divination if we just stay on the street."

They headed west through the city while Ool's clock announced the hour, heading toward the Meander and the Squid, the guild house of Dur Follin's Thieves' Guild. They kept an especially sharp eye as they moved, as each block brought them closer to not only the Squid but also Kerfallen's abode. The wizard's manse was a walled fortress just this side of the Archbridge. Nix toyed with the idea of taking a run at Kerfallen then and there.

"I see you looking in the direction of the bridge," Egil said. "And I know what you're thinking. We go hard at Kerfallen right now. Figure out the plates afterward at our leisure."

"You're a mindmage now? Reading thoughts?"

"Well?" Egil pressed.

"That is what I was thinking. Ill-conceived?"

Egil nodded. "You said it was when I suggested doing just

that. And you're right. He'll be prepared. In fact, concern for that is probably why we haven't encountered any of his minions on the street yet. He's got them watching home for the moment in case we do what both our natures incline us to do."

Nix knew Egil was right. The last time, they cut with ease through Kerfallen's guards, but then the wizard had wanted them to get through the guards quickly. Nix knew it wouldn't be that way this time.

Egil went on: "I say we determine what the plates are and then figure things out. Too soon to go at a wizard in his own place. Might come to that, but not yet."

Nix thought of Tesha's admonition that he and Egil make it whole back to the Tunnel. "I'll agree for now, but observe that it galls, skulking around in our own town."

"Aye, that," Egil said with a nod.

In time they came to Mandin's Way, the wide, winding road that ran along the Meander and tracked the river's course. The ancient white, unmarred stone of the Archbridge rose to their left, reaching across the river to the west bank, where the rich of Dur Follin lived in their walled and gilded manses. To Nix the Archbridge and Ool's clock were of a piece, enormous architectural relics of some previous, more accomplished civilization, leftovers from another time.

Paper orbs of various colors hung from string from the bridge's side, bouncing in the breeze. Each represented the wish of the person who'd left it there. Superstition said the wish would come true if the wind pulled the orb from the bridge and it floated safely to either shore. A person could make good coin selling those lamps, and many did. Hopes were born and died every day in Dur Follin. The shallows were littered with waterlogged orbs, the hopes they represented sodden and unrealized. Only once, as a boy, had Nix put a lamp on the bridge. Time would tell if his secret hope would ever be realized.

"This is risky, Nix," Egil said. "The plates are on you. Guild boys could just try to take them, or try to kill us. We're counting a lot on Rusk being reasonable."

Nix knew, but he had little else. They needed a safe house. If they stayed on the street too long, Kerfallen would find them.

"We could head out of town," Egil said. "Come back tonight or some other night. Make a run at the Conclave library then."

Nix had considered that already. He shook his head. "Gives Kerfallen that much more time to prepare. And he'll track us or the plates or both and catch us out on the road. Or he and his minions will be waiting when we try to come back. He'd have agents at every gate. We could just hand the plates over to a messenger and have him take them to Kerfallen. Then this is all over."

Now it was Egil's turn to shake his head. "Fakker tried to turn us to stone. He's not getting these, not easily anyway."

Nix knew Egil would respond just so. "Agreed. So I'll summarize. We are sideways of a powerful wizard who wants something we have, wants it desperately enough to have twice attacked us in broad daylight. We're seeking help from the leader of a guild whose hall we not long ago assaulted, killing many guild men in the process. Assuming we can avail ourselves of the guild's safe house, we then plan to sneak into the Conclave during the night and figure out what is actually going on. We are doing these things because we eschew taking a simple way out, which is just to give the plates over to Kerfallen. Did I miss anything?"

"You did not," Egil said. "Points for 'eschewing.'"

"We ready?"

"We are."

Merchant guild halls and society clubs lined several blocks of Mandin's Way, gathering places for the various organizations and tradesmen of the city. Farther down, through the thicket of wagons and the groups of sailors and fishermen and horses and pedestrians that thronged Mandin's Way, Nix saw the Squid, once a tavern and club for fishermen, now home and temple for

Dur Follin's Thieves' Guild, which was equal parts criminal enterprise and Church of Aster, the god of rogues.

Nix and Egil eyed the street near the guild house, saw the spotters atop two nearby buildings, saw the two groups of muscle loitering across the street. The rogues guarding the door would have plenty of help if they needed it.

"If we went in through the sewers again," Egil said, "we could just kill our way to Rusk. Worked the once."

Nix chuckled. "Come on."

They started down the street, on the side opposite the guild house. Nix waited until he knew he'd caught the eye of the spotters, then hooked his left thumb on his belt and put his right hand in his trouser pocket. He kept them that way so no one would think it happenstance. Hand signals and a whistle went down from the spotters, to the muscle, to the doormen, and four of the muscle came strolling toward Egil and Nix.

"Maybe try not to beat them in public?" Nix said.

"No promises," Egil answered.

"We may need to emphasize the importance of our request, so watch my lead."

"Aye," Egil said.

Nix smiled at the four men as they approached. All of them wore boiled leather jerkins and sharp steel. Of course, all of them were bigger than Nix, but not one was bigger than Egil. They did not smile back.

"Calm now, boys," Nix said. "This is business and we intend no trouble."

The smallest of the four, bearded and with tattoos covering his bare arms, merely smirked. With practiced precision the four fell in around Egil and Nix, one of them putting a hand on Egil as though they were long-lost friends. Another did the same with Nix. One took position in front, and one in back. Signals came down to them from the spotters on the roofs, presumably indicating the all-clear.

The one in the rear did the talking.

"You know the signs but aren't of the faith," he said. "That's crime enough. But then it turns out I recognize the two of you and remember well the last time you walked the halls of our house. I was outside the door that time. You remember? One of you was running your mouth."

"That'd be me," Nix said. "Were you the dumb one or the dumber one?"

The man holding Nix gave him a rough shake.

"You tell me not to beat them, but then pick a fight," Egil said.

"I'm not picking a fight," Nix protested. "I asked in all sincerity."

The man behind said, "I see it was you indeed. And that you've a sharp tongue still. We get inside the hall, maybe I'll show you something sharper still."

"Not your wit, of that I'm sure," Nix said, unable to help himself.

"Shut up, Nix," Egil said. "Gods."

"Well, they shouldn't make it so fakkin' easy then," Nix said.

"Listen," Egil said, "we didn't come for trouble. We came to see Rusk, the Upright Man. You make sure he knows that. No trouble. Just talk."

"The Upright Man will decide if there's trouble or talk or both or neither. You just do as you're told."

The men steered them across the street, through the wagons and donkeys and horses, toward the guild house. The smell of fish hung heavy in the air. Nix burped up the taste of Gadd's stew.

"If you try to disarm me inside, I'll kill you all," Egil said. "Fair warning."

The men chuckled darkly.

Nix felt vindicated. "Now who's picking a fight, priest?"

"Bah," Egil said. "I offered it in all sincerity."

"You two blab like old birds," the one behind them said. "Is this supposed to be distracting because—"

Nix grabbed the dagger from the belt of the man in front of him, tripped him as he spun, and put the blade to the neck of the man with his hand on his back. Egil read his move, put an arm lock on the man with a hand on his back, spun, grabbed the man behind them—the one talking—by his cloak, and pulled him close.

"That's it," Nix said, and dropped the blade and held up his hands. Egil released the arm lock and turned his back to the guild thief who'd been talking.

"See," Nix said over his shoulder. "If we'd wanted to go hard, I'd have just slit a throat, Egil would have broken that one's arm and head-butted you hard enough to shatter your nose and probably kill you. Your spotters on the roof would have whistled up aid and crossbow quarrels would have flown, but Egil would have carried one of you as cover from the shots as we charged the front door. As we went we'd have stomped on the head or throat of the one I tripped. And those boys on the porch there, those ones looking questions at you right now, they would've had no chance with us. We all know that. Once we got inside we'd have locked the reinforced door behind us so the boys out here would've had to take the long way around. Not even a window to get in, since they're all grated. And Egil and me, we know the layout, so we'd have headed straight for the alternate way in. Probably killed a few of you on the way. Maybe a lot of you. It's happened before, yeah? Once there, we'd have either ambushed those boys as they came in or just locked them out and cleared out the house. I know you know we could do it. But like I said, we didn't come here to go hard at the guild. We came here to talk. Which I'm doing a lot of at the moment. So anyway, let's go."

"Shite," one of the muscle said.

A hand went to Nix's shoulder again, but not roughly and no one touched Egil, but they walked them toward the house. Questions came down from the spotters and the muscle signaled back that all was under control.

The guards on the guild house porch eyed them as the muscle took them through the reinforced front doors, through the foyer, and into a small, windowless room off to the side of the main hall.

"Don't cause no trouble in here," the same muscle said.

"Rusk and Trelgin," Nix said. "Just tell them we're here to see them, yeah?"

"Yeah," the man said, and closed the door. Locks clicked into place.

"This going about how you figured?" Egil asked him.

"About," Nix said. "You think you could take that door if you had to?"

Egil eyed the wooden slab. "I could. This is an outside wall. My hammers could make a window in it, too, if we had need. I don't think we will, though. I believe we made our point."

Nix didn't feel as certain, but he figured there was nothing to do but wait on Rusk. They didn't have to wait long.

The door soon opened and Rusk and Trelgin entered the room. Behind them, in the hall outside, Nix saw a dozen or more guild men milling around like a mob. Necks craned to see and lots of angry glares landed on Nix and Egil.

For his part, Rusk looked much as he had when they'd seen him last. Maybe his dark hair and beard were a bit grayer, and he sported a few more lines around his eyes and mouth. His jacket, vest, and trousers, too, were a bit nicer than last they'd seen him. Both he and Trelgin bore blades at their belts, of course, long and short. Trelgin had pulled his hair back into a tail, but its middling length made the tail a stub. Sweat stained the pits of his loose-fitting shirt, which was covered by a leather vest.

"Shut the door," Rusk said, staring at Egil and Nix, and Trelgin did.

"Because we two ain't worried about you two," Trelgin said in his sloppy tones.

Nix swallowed a quip and instead said to Rusk, "You look a

bit worse for wear. Heavy is the head that wears the crown, yeah?"

Rusk ignored the comment, looked them up and down, and ran a hand over his beard thoughtfully. "You attacked my people in the street? I thought we'd settled things after that bit with the witches in the swamp."

Nix feared that Rusk calling Rose and Mere "witches" would trigger Egil's temper, but the priest held his calm.

"We were just making a point," Egil said. "Your people were taking liberties with our persons. We didn't mean them harm and I think you know that."

"You look better'n you did last night at the Masquerade," Trelgin said to Egil, smirking.

"And you look just as shit as when I saw you on the street outside the Masquerade last night," Nix said. "So maybe we drop that whole line of discussion, yeah?"

Rusk put a hand in one of his trouser pockets, maybe just to look relaxed. "You know, I could've had you both clicked a ways back. Thought about it now and again. But like I said, I considered us past that."

"Lots of people have tried clicking us, Rusk," Nix said. "And none have succeeded yet. In fact, that was part of the point we made in the street, I thought. Egil, didn't we make that point?"

"We did, I thought," Egil added. "Among others. Could be it was lost on those boys. Not the sharpest of blades, I'd say."

"Didn't I say?" Trelgin said to Rusk. "Mouthy is what. And not just Nix."

Nix went on. "Hells, as I recall the last time someone from the guild took a run at us, it ended badly for the guild. But then, that wasn't your guild then, Rusk."

Trelgin's face trembled with anger. "Fak you, Nix, and your smart mouth! Some of them boys you clicked back then were friends." He looked at Rusk. "Maybe we ought to just click 'em here and now. Or let the boys outside have a go, even. It'd do them good."

"Maybe you should try not talking for a while," Egil said to Trelgin.

"Lots of people saw us come in," Nix said. "Some would know us. Might be bad for business you doing harm to us now."

"*Trying* to do us harm, anyway," Egil added, and put a hand to the haft of a hammer.

Nix said to Trelgin, "We know some of those men were your friends back then. But it never would have come to that if some of those other boys, *at Channis's direction,* hadn't tried to put a match to *our friends.* Done is done, though. We made recompense for all that, Rusk, yeah?"

Rusk stared at Nix, committing to nothing.

"Recompense, my arse," Trelgin said, spraying spittle as he said the words.

"And today we came to buy something from you," Nix said, ignoring Trelgin. "Business. You still do business?"

Trelgin started to say something but Egil pointed a finger at his face and said, "Don't talk."

Nix went on. "We pay and you provide a service. That's all we're asking."

"We don't owe them," Trelgin said.

"No," Nix said. "You don't, which is why we're looking to pay, not to ask a favor."

Rusk sucked his teeth for a moment, then finally said, "What's the service?"

"Time in the Vault," Nix said.

Trelgin scoffed.

Rusk's brow furrowed and he shook his head. "That's not possible."

Nix was pleased that Rusk hadn't denied the existence of the Vault. The guild had long been rumored to have a special room or rooms, immune to magical scrying, in which they kept particularly hot swag or kidnap victims. Nix had long assumed it must be true, else lots of activities of the guild would have been easily thwarted by a wizard-for-hire.

"Why not?" Egil asked.

"What the fak do you two have that needs to go in the Vault?" Trelgin asked.

Rusk stared at Egil. "Because the Vault's for guild use only."

Nix shifted on his feet, irritated. "Is that a rule or a religious edict or something else?"

Rusk said nothing.

"Because if it's just a rule and not handed down from some holy book of Aster, then it should be bendable. We can pay, Rusk."

Rusk ran a hand along his beard, affecting disinterest. "The guild doesn't need coin, Nix."

Nix had anticipated that. "I'm not talking about just coin. I'm going to reach into my satchel, yeah?"

Rusk nodded. Trelgin watched him carefully.

Nix withdrew the magic key. He'd packed a handful of various fruits and vegetables, too.

"What the fak is that?" Trelgin asked.

"It's a morphic key," Nix said.

"Fak you," Trelgin said, leaning forward to eye it more closely. "It is not."

Rusk looked skeptical but intrigued.

Nix spoke a word in the Language of Creation and the teeth of the key yawned.

"Give us an artichoke," it said.

Rusk inhaled audibly. Trelgin's sloppy mouth went still sloppier as it hung open.

"It's temperamental, yeah?" Nix said. "Always asking for this or that before being willing to work. But it opens any lock if you feed it what it asks. Useful to the guild, I would imagine?"

"Give us a carrot, then," the key said.

Nix took a carrot from his satchel and held it before the key's teeth. It took a few bites. To demonstrate its power, Nix walked past Trelgin and Rusk and placed the key in the key-hole on the door.

"This is a lock I've never seen before and I'm putting the key in from the wrong side."

He turned the key to lock the door, turned it again to unlock.

Nix took the key out and held it out to Rusk. "Any lock, Rusk. Just keep some fakkin' fruits and vegetables on hand."

"It's nice," Rusk said, nodding at the key but not taking it, obviously trying to play coy. "But even with coin added, it's not enough."

Nix smiled knowingly. "No, it's not."

"Of course it's not," Egil said.

"I do this for you and you owe me," Rusk said. "Not in a wise-arse Egil and Nix way, but a true debt. One you'll pay when I ask. A service. A task. I'll ask it, and you'll do it. Or I'll ask you not to do something, and you won't do it. You won't ask questions and try to subvert what I say. You'll just do as you're told."

Nix looked at Egil.

Egil looked to Rusk. "On condition whatever you ask doesn't harm our friends or an innocent. You agree to that, we have a deal."

"An innocent," Rusk said, and chuckled. "What're those?"

"Done or not?" Nix asked.

"Done," Rusk said. He spit on his hand, Egil and Nix did the same, and they shook on a deal closed.

"What is it that you need to store and for how long?" Rusk asked.

"We need to store us," Nix said.

"Just until nightfall," Egil added. "Then we'll be on our way."

At first Rusk did not understand, then his eyes showed that he did and he nodded. "Well, you two must be in some real shite to have wizards hunting for you."

"Shite deep and dark," Trelgin said, then chuckled. "For

you to put yourselves in the guild's pocket. I can't wait to see how you get spent."

"That's enough," Rusk said to him. "Clear the hall outside. Then call a meeting of the Committee. I'll get these two into the Vault and then explain to the others."

"Sooner is better," Nix said. "The deep and dark shite we're in and all."

"I'll get some bodyguards," Trelgin said, looking meaningfully at Egil and Nix.

"No need," Rusk said. "As Nix said, this is business. We're past that."

Rusk looked to Nix and Nix nodded.

Trelgin looked surprised, but did as Rusk bade.

After he'd gone, Rusk faced them and said, "Now, if I thought worse of you two, I might figure that your actual play here was, first, to confirm that there was a Vault, and second, to recover something that we keep there. Just so you know I'm not a fool."

"Look at you, scheming," Nix said with a grin. "No wonder you got the Eighth Blade."

"I don't think you'd be standing here alone if you thought that," Egil added. "Out of concern that we'd kill you."

Rusk smiled and echoed Egil's words back at him. "*Try* to kill me. But anyway, since I know what's in the Vault, and I know that nothing in there would be of interest to you two, I don't think you're running a play, though I know I've heard only that part of the truth you cared to share." He held up a scarred hand to stop their protestations. "I don't need to know more than that. Business is important to me, and good business is good business. I just want you to know that I'll collect on your promise to me. I consider that the most valuable thing to have changed hands here today. And I should be clear: Not holding up your end would be bad business." He looked them each in the face, his expression serious. "I don't like bad business."

Nix grinned. "Look at him now, Egil, with the implicit

threats even. I'm impressed. That crown fits you well indeed, Rusk."

"We'll hold up our end," Egil said.

"Assuming we survive the night," Nix added.

"I'll throw a pray to Aster asking for just so," Rusk said, and managed to mask most of the sarcasm. "Now come on. Walk with me."

He led them out of the room and through the guild house, taking them through two cleverly concealed doors under stairways that Rusk unlocked with a small key. As they went, he took from his pouch a long glass vial filled with a yellow substance. As he held it, it began to glow and soon shone as bright as a large candle. He took them down several flights of stairs into a series of narrow, low-ceilinged, curving hallways. They saw no one else the entire time. Nix made a point to remember the route.

"We're under the Meander," Egil observed, looking up at the ceiling.

Rusk said nothing.

Nix tried to visualize the layout of the hallways they'd traversed since passing through the first concealed door. He realized they formed a figure.

"The halls form the shape of a warding glyph," he said. "Clever."

Rusk raised his eyebrows, apparently impressed.

Nix understood why Rusk had brought them alone. "You didn't know about any of this until that Eighth Blade showed up on your arm, did you?"

"No," Rusk admitted. "Knowledge comes with the title."

"What's that like?" Egil asked. "Having all that pop into your head all of sudden?"

Rusk looked back at the priest, as though wondering if the question was serious. Apparently determining that it was, he said, "Unnerving at first. Like being born again. But then it just seems like you've known it all along."

Egil grunted.

Rusk stopped at the end of a long corridor, before a metal door, the slab engraved with glyphs, the symbol of Aster in relief, and fitted with an elaborate lock and lever.

"Give me the key," Rusk said, holding out his hand. "If it can dub this jigger, I'll be truly impressed."

Nix took the key from his satchel and handed it over.

"Just say some—"

"I know how to make it work," Rusk said.

Nix held up his hands and backed off. "All that knowledge, I guess, huh?"

Rusk spoke a word in the Language of Creation to animate the key, then held it before the door. Nix imagined the spirit within the key studying the lock and contemplating its payment.

"Give us some celery," it said.

Rusk looked back to Nix.

Nix had packed a stalk, among the other produce, in his satchel. He handed it to Rusk and said, "You're getting by easy. Thing was always asking me for obscure shite."

"Didn't like you, maybe," Rusk said, as he fed the celery to the key.

"That's not possible," Nix answered.

After the key had taken a few bites, Rusk placed the key into the lock and turned. Tumblers clicked and the lock opened. Rusk nodded and put the magical key in his vest pocket. He turned the lever on the door and swung it open.

Several bottles filled with the glowing yellow substance cast the room in light. Nix was pleased to see that it looked more like a bedroom than a storeroom or true vault. Several overstuffed chairs, a divan, tables, and a thick carpet covered the stone floor, though it smelled of stale must. A row of chests lined one wall, all of them closed and presumably locked. Thick wooden beams set at even intervals reinforced the ceiling.

"A bit too nicely outfitted for just swag," Nix observed.

Rusk chuckled. "You're not the first seeking refuge from wizards."

"Must work well for kidnappings, too," Egil said.

To that, Rusk said nothing.

Before walking in, Nix said, "If we thought less of you, we might figure your actual play here is that, first, you'd lock us in here, and second, you'd find out who was looking for us then sell us out for more than we paid to hole up here."

Rusk tilted his head to concede the point. "I'd have been a fool not to consider it."

"You'd be a fool to try it," Egil said darkly.

"There is that," Rusk said.

"And having considered it?" Nix pressed.

"Having considered it," Rusk said, "it's not a good play because first, I don't care for wizards or witches and their ilk, owing in part to what happened in the swamp. And second, an open-ended promise from you two is worth more to me than anything a wizard could pay. And third, at some point, those doing business together have to trust each other. Take precautions, but trust. You're free to leave. Just me here. No one is stopping you."

Nix looked to Egil, who shrugged.

"In for a dram," Nix said.

"In for a drink," Rusk finished.

With that, Egil and Nix entered the vault. Rusk lingered in the doorway.

"You'll be safe here. Good business, as I said. I'll return after nightfall."

"Make it Kulven's setting, yeah?" Nix said. "Don't want to get started too early."

"Start what?" Rusk asked, grinning.

Nix grinned in return, but said nothing.

"Well enough," Rusk said. "See you soon."

He shut the door and the lock clicked into place.

Egil exhaled loudly and took a seat in one of the chairs. He took his ivory dice from the pouch at his belt, absently shook them.

For his part Nix paced the room, examined the furniture. He did not try to open the chests, though he found them tempting.

"Gonna be a while," Egil said. "Sit. There's nothing for it now but to wait. And your pacing irritates."

"Your calmness irritates," Nix said. "And I think he's got something in mind for us already. Rusk, I mean."

"You think, perhaps?" Egil said sarcastically.

Nix stopped pacing and glared at him. "We wanted adventure. Not only do we have some right now, we're also storing some up. If he didn't have something in mind, he'd sell us to Kerfallen. I didn't read that on him."

Egil smiled and pocketed his dice. "Nor I. Now sit, for fak's sake."

Nix nodded and fell into another of the chairs. He was ill-suited to sitting and soon fidgeted, dithering with his knives and daggers, checking the inventory of items magical and mundane in his satchel. He soon grew bored of it.

"I've got a few healing elixirs in here," he said to Egil. "Be so advised."

"I'm so advised," Egil said.

"Gods, we don't even have a way to track time in here," Nix said. "Fak."

"Been about an hour now," Egil said. "And I think we can say with certainty Rusk isn't selling us out. If he were, Kerfallen's minions would already have come. Given that, why don't you start figuring how we'll get into the Conclave. That'll keep the boredom at bay. I don't know it as you do, so I'm of little help. I presume you've got some more things in that satchel that will be of help?"

"A thing or two more," Nix said, nodding absently. "But not as much as I'd like."

"That bodes ill," Egil said. He crossed his arms over his chest, stretched out his legs, and closed his eyes.

"Key would've been handy," Nix said.

"Maybe next time think of that *before* giving something away?"

"Aye, but I needed to buy us some time in this room," Nix said. "I knew they'd find the key tempting."

"Aye," Egil said, never opening his eyes. "And anyway, done is done. We'll figure it out. We always do."

"Aye," Nix said.

Egil was soon snoring.

Nix turned his mind to the problem of sneaking into the Conclave. He had scant idea of how to do it, other than find a way in, watch for traps, don't trigger the spell wards, and get out fast. He went through his satchel again, thinking how he might use the items he had to get them in and out of the Conclave. He soon had the beginnings of a plan.

In time, the Afterbirth reached the edge of the ruined land and climbed to the top of a windswept ridge and the morning light put long shadows on the terrain and he looked out toward the far horizon and saw the brown line of a wide river that snaked its way toward a large walled city. The breeze picked up, carried on its current the scent of the Great Spell, and he knew it came from somewhere within that city. He had only to find a way in and a time to walk among them without being trapped. He feared no weapons no blows but he feared confinement. Walking the world in despair even if it wasn't his world was preferable to an eternity spent in a cage so he could not simply force his way through the gates and find and take what he wished. At least not yet.

His eyes went to the river to the fishing boats some of which already plied its shallows the docks and piers of the city jutting like accusations out into the slow-moving water. He watched the boats a long time their comings and goings thinking planning as day turned to dusk to night and soon knew what he would do.

When the moons set, he headed off for the river. He felt exposed as he crossed the open plains between him and the water, seen, watched by the stars and gods and sky of a world not his. Buildings stood to either side of the road up near the walls of the city, roadhouses and inns, and he kept well away from them. A line of wagons awaited entrance before the city's closed gates. The last time he'd encountered a camp of wagons it had ended in slaughter and screams.

He was downwind of the city and could smell the horses and the donkeys and the food and the fires and the humans, their sweat and waste. The city, too, carried a smell, mostly of decay, but also of something familiar, something different from the rest of the world, and it only reinforced his conviction that the faint tang of the Great Spell that he'd smelled so many leagues ago had to have come from somewhere within its walls.

He stayed far from the people and buildings, moving hunched through the unoccupied area distant from the city's walls. Lumbering across the grasslands, mumbling and grunting, he eventually reached the road and hurried across it without slowing.

The breeze carried a sharp whistle from his left, laughter, the whinny of a horse and a raised voice. He sped up, mumbling in nervous spurts, hoping he'd not been seen. He'd never before dared enter a city but to find the Great Spell he had to risk it.

The ground sank gradually toward the river until at last the grassland gave way and he found himself standing on the gently sloped, muddy bank, looking across the wide, smooth expanse of the slow-flowing water. The snaking river cut a meandering north-south path through the plains, a winding dirty line drawn through the grass.

Downriver the city lined both banks, the two sides connected by a soaring stone bridge decorated with dangling lights that swayed in the breeze. He stopped when he saw the bridge, seeing in its curves and stone and immensity something of his own lost world. People were on the bridge, people born to this world, and wagons, too, and he heard music and chanting and laughter and smelled incense and smoke.

Grunting, he moved down the bank, his eyes still fixed on the bridge, perplexed by what its otherworldly nature might imply, and he lost his footing and slipped and tumbled the rest of the way down the bank, feet over head, his mouths exclaiming in surprise until he hit the cool water with a large splash and his weight sank him a hand span into the muddy bottom. He came up, gasping, and heard a distant voice from the darkness off to his right.

"What's that now?"

"All well?" called another. "Sounded like someone went in the drink, din't it."

"Aye. Pull up that net. Uncover the lantern. Here we go."

Oars splashed, a beam of light cut through the night, and the Afterbirth hurriedly moved away from the boat, heading for deeper water, but he was slow, a poor, loud swimmer.

"Ho, someone there?"

As the light neared him he dove under though he still was in fairly shallow water and imagined by day he would have been easily seen. He hoped the darkness would shield him. He heard an exclamation but the water muffled the words. The splash of oars grew closer. He could hear the voices even through the water. They were coming, coming for him, to catch him and hold him maybe.

He could not allow himself to be seen they would raise a hue and cry and find a way to hold him contain him and he could take no risks before getting into the city. He tensed and looked up through the murky water, saw the shadow of the boat framed against the lighter darkness of the sky, the glow of the lantern. . . .

He tensed and propelled himself out of the water.

The two men in the boat, one older and one younger, had only a moment to respond to his attack. Their faces registered surprise, terror, and they reared back, mouths open, and they had nowhere to go but shrank away from him as best they could. He crashed into them and the boat, his weight causing some of the boat's wooden planks to shriek and crack. He snatched a man in each hand and rolled off the boat and dragged them underwater. They screamed, the sound muted by the water, a flurry of bubbles pouring out of their mouths. They struggled, kicked, punched, and finally went still.

He lifted his head out of the water and listened. He heard nothing. No one had heard.

He released them and let the river's ponderous current take the corpses. If they were seen at all before floating past the city in the dark, they would appear to be nothing more than an accidental drowning. He left their boat where it was, crooked and broken on the surface, and swam out into the river, keeping only his head above water and watching for more late-night fishermen.

He saw none near him and swam closer to the city, to the bridge.

A sound carried through the night, a deep gong, repeating, perhaps tolling the hour, and the sound, like the bridge, carried the promise of another world. He felt it on his skin, in his bones, in his soul, the tingling energy of something he'd thought long gone, something as alien as him. He felt dizzy for a moment, as though he had stumbled onto some secret place, some dreamscape where worlds collided and he wondered if he had gone fully mad at last and if his perceptions were lies and if he would soon awaken in one of the dank caves he had called home since the birth of the world and he wanted to weep but he could not weep because his anger held back tears and his hope kept him buoyant.

The gonging sound ended and he felt its absence. He floated out in the center of the river, staring at the lines of the city's buildings, watching the piers, waiting for stillness, picking a place from which he could emerge from the water and walk among the alleys and dark places. A few men worked on the docks still, loading barrels or crates. A few other men stumbled along the night-shrouded streets, and now and then a carriage or wagon moved slowly along the road. He let the current take him some, looking for a likely place to exit the river.

The clock tolled another hour, energizing him with its sound, as he waited and watched and hoped.

Soon the activity on the docks and piers ended, and most of the torches and candles on the streets and in buildings went out or burned low. The city was dark, mostly asleep. He saw no one. He'd have to move quickly and quietly, hunched and cloaked, sticking to alleys and sewers and trash heaps.

The unseen currents that bore the world's magic carried to him another taste of the Great Spell, coming from somewhere within the tangled nest of the city's buildings.

Unable to resist, unable to wait any longer, he swam for shore.

CHAPTER SIX

Hours later, the heavy clicks of the lock on the Vault's door presaged its opening. Nix leaped to his feet and drew his falchion. He kicked Egil's boot to wake him.

"Huh? What?" Egil said, but took in the situation in a blink and clambered to his feet, hand on a hammer haft.

The metal slab swung silently open. Rusk stood alone in the doorway, a glowing glass globe in his hand. "Minnear and Kulven are both down and that's all the time you boys bought. Let's go."

"No trouble for you and yours owing to our trouble?" Nix asked.

"None as of yet," Rusk said.

As they walked past him, Nix said, "I bet you took no end of shite from the rest of the Committee for sheltering us here."

Rusk closed the Vault door and fell in with them. "They do what I say and they see the value in your promise. Just remember that you owe me."

"Not the guild, but you?" Egil asked.

Rusk smiled. "It's the same thing."

Having committed the way to memory, Nix led them out back through the series of concealed doors and into the guild house proper. Trelgin awaited them there in a candlelit room, standing near a table. Circles painted the skin under Trelgin's eyes. He hadn't slept in a while.

Seventh Blade's a shite job, Nix thought.

Rusk squared up to them. He looked tired, too, Nix thought.

"Trelgin will see you out," Rusk said. "I've got other things to see to tonight. Whatever you're up to, don't die, yeah? I'll need you for something later."

"That is deep and abiding affection for us right there, Egil," Nix said.

Egil said, "I think I may swoon."

Rusk smiled and went off into an adjacent room, where Nix caught sight of a few gathered men, all of them olive-skinned foreigners in unusual dress.

"What's he up to in there?" Nix asked Trelgin, just to irritate him.

Trelgin's droopy face twisted with contempt. "Front door or sewers, slubbers?"

"Front door and we know the way," Egil said, and walked past him.

"Suit yourself," said Trelgin, who despite the words fell in behind them.

The interior door guards tensed at their approach, but Trelgin put them at ease.

"They're leaving," Trelgin said to them as Egil and Nix neared the front foyer.

The guards slid the series of bolts and bars that unlocked the door.

To Egil and Nix, Trelgin said, "I ain't as worried about the two of you dying; you want to, you go ahead. But if you don't, we'll see you soon to collect on that debt."

Nix didn't turn around, but raised his hand in an obscene gesture as they walked through the door.

"Likewise to you," Trelgin called after. "And good eve."

Egil and Nix pulled up their cloak hoods and headed off briskly onto Mandin's Way. Blocks of charcoal burned in the streetlamps and a few pedestrians and fishermen's wagons dotted the streets. Guild spotters watched them from rooftops, grumbling.

"Something important going on in there," Nix said. "You see those foreigners?"

"I did," Egil said. "Rusk and Trelgin were on edge, too. Not our worry, though."

"Not yet, anyway," Nix said. "You know, seems like just yesterday I was walking the streets looking to head off your nightly drunk. No, wait. It literally was just yesterday."

Egil harrumphed. "Should I interpret your mention of a point entirely sideways of our current situation to mean that you have no fakkin' idea how to get into the Conclave?"

"Incorrect," Nix said, holding up a finger. They cut down an alley, immersing themselves in the darkness. "I have an idea. But you might want to take your dice out and give them a few shakes, because it's not a *good* idea."

They stepped past a drunk snoring in a heap against the wall and continued through the alley until they reached the cobblestone paved way beyond. Again, a few pedestrians and carts moved along the street. Candlelight and voices and sometimes music carried out of the windows of inns and eateries and taphouses.

"I'm not sure I want you to tell me," Egil said.

"But since you asked—" Nix began.

"I didn't."

"Since you asked," Nix continued. "I'll tell you: We're going in the front door."

They picked up their pace, avoiding the main thoroughfares, moving through alleys and side streets, all of which smelled of decay and urine and occasionally vomit. They moved quickly across Dur Follin.

"The front door, you say?" Egil asked. "Agreed that may warrant the dice. Elaborate."

Nix grinned while looking up and down the street and into the sky for any sign of Kerfallen's constructs. Seeing none, they crossed the thoroughfare and went down another alley, one that stank of dead fish. Probably a fishmonger had dumped his unsold spoiled catch there. A cat hissed at them from a pile of refuse.

Nix stomped his foot at the feline, then elaborated as Egil had asked. "The doors are closed at all times, to keep the students in and to keep everyone else out. Not that anyone would want to sneak *into* the Conclave."

"No one smart, anyway," Egil interjected.

"Right. Anyway, the wizards don't trust the doors to human eyes or human weakness, so a pair of animated iron statues guards the doors."

"Iron statues give me pause," Egil said, running a hand over his head. "Why not go over the walls?"

Nix said, "Because the walls are warded with alarm spells. Learned that the hard way when I was enrolled there. Those get set off, most doors in the Conclave get magically locked, some hallways get fogged with a mist that confuses, more statues animate, and the Masters all get alerted. Things get tricky then."

"We don't want tricky," Egil said.

"Aye," Nix said. "We don't want tricky."

They hurried through the night-shrouded streets as fast as prudence allowed, eyeing every pedestrian with suspicion, but seeing no sign of Kerfallen's constructs. Nix knew it was only a matter of time, though. He could not imagine Kerfallen giving up just because he'd lost them while they'd sheltered in the Vault.

Ool's clock was chiming a small hour when they reached their destination—a vast public expanse of grass and trees and scrub and benches known formally as Erilton's Park, after the lord mayor who'd established it long ago, but which everyone simply called the Sward.

The Sward covered several acres within the city's walls and at its far southern end butted against the walls of the Conclave. By day the Sward would be filled with people taking their ease, by night with people satisfying their vices, but in the very small hours, as now, there was no one save a few sleeping drunks or homeless.

Egil and Nix hurried along the walking paths, past the central bronze statue of Lord Mayor Erilton, and toward the low, gently sloped hill on which stood the Conclave, perched like a buzzard over the body of the city.

Popular wisdom said the land on which the Conclave sat had been ceded to the school by an unnamed lord mayor generations earlier, but like Ool's clock, like the Archbridge, the Conclave seemed to have always been there, a thing apart. Nix sometimes thought the whole history of Dur Follin was built on rumor and tales and little else.

They stopped and sheltered in a copse of trees on the Sward, a bow shot from the Conclave. The wind rustled the leaves. Nix scratched at the stubble on his cheeks.

Smooth walls of basalt, perhaps twice as tall as Egil, formed a polygon around the grounds. When Minnear, the green Moon of Mages, rode full in the sky, its light suffused the walls, so that they looked like a deep, green pool lit from below. Small crowds sometimes gathered on the Sward to watch the otherworldly show. When Nix had first come to the Conclave, he'd marveled the first time he'd seen the walls light up.

But the glowing walls were the only architectural marvel of the Conclave, which otherwise gave an impression more of a jail or barracks than a college. And Nix supposed it was as much jail as anything. Students with an affinity for magic came from all of the Seven Cities of the Meander, and some from farther away than that, and all of them spent their days locked inside, immersed in study, classroom instruction, and practicum. They were seldom allowed to leave the grounds, and then only under the eyes of a Master.

Nix had found the classroom instruction mostly tedious and the rules unbearable, but the practicum he'd loved. He'd been born with a sense for magic that his fellow students had envied. He had no idea where it came from—his unknown father, he supposed—but Mamabird had noticed it somehow and arranged to have him plucked from the Warrens in his teens and sent to the Conclave. He'd lasted only a year before getting expelled.

"Can't see why you'd quit that place," Egil said sarcastically. "It's quite inviting."

"It's a fakking jail," Nix said. "And I was expelled."

"So you say, but never why."

"So I say," Nix agreed. "And the why is my own."

A wide, tiered walkway of polished stones led up out of the Sward to the elaborately carved stone façade and oversize double doors that allowed entry onto the Conclave's grounds. Two towering statues of iron, half again as tall as Egil, stood to either side of the large, metal doors. Each looked like a helmed warrior of old, complete with breastplate and a spear. Nix had seen them animate once, when a panicked horse had ventured across the Sward and come too near the gates. Responding to the commands that guided them, the statues had animated and skewered the poor animal in their ruthless, mechanical fashion.

Egil reached into his pouch, presumably for his dice, but must have thought better of it.

"The gates will be warded with an alarm spell," Nix said, and reached into his satchel. "I'll handle that."

Egil stared at him, waiting, then, "There are two giant statues there. Did you notice those?"

"You've found your wit, I see. And yes, I did notice them. But they won't notice us." He unwrapped the golden plates and lifted the cloaking shroud from his satchel.

Egil waited, eyebrows raised. Nix let him hang on the silence for a moment before he went on.

"Human guards can be bribed, incapacitated, or killed. Bound spirits are angry at being bound and can be bargained with or dismissed. The Masters take no chances with such things." Nix looked out on the statues, still and dark in the night. "The statues are dumb, deliberately so. Magic animates them and nothing more. The Masters gave them no discretion. If they see something approach and that something isn't invited or expected or doesn't know the pass phrase, they kill it. But because they are what they are, they don't see like we see. Their sight is itself nothing more than a spell." He held the shroud up before him. "Behind this, they won't see us at all."

Skepticism furrowed Egil's brow. "We're going to walk up to those two metal men hiding behind a piece of enchanted cloth?"

Nix grinned and nodded. "Aye."

Egil looked from Nix to the statues, then back again. He eyed the thin fabric of the shroud, measuring with his eyes whether he thought it large enough to shield them both from the eyes of the statues.

Nix waited for it.

"Fakkin' gewgaws," Egil said.

There it was.

"You ready?" he asked the priest.

"No other way in?" Egil said.

Nix scratched the stubble of his cheeks. "There were always rumors of secret tunnels that led out, exiting at various places around the city. But I never saw them. So this is the only way."

Egil put a hand on the haft of each hammer. "We'll barely be able to fit the two of us under that, when it comes to it."

"And whose fault is that for being bizarrely large?"

"Bah."

Nix smiled, the banter his and Egil's usual method of dealing with tense situations. "We have to move fast. The statues will be linked to a Master, a different one every other month. Even the Grandmaster takes a turn."

"Shite, man. You're telling me this Master will know when the statues animate?"

Nix nodded. "If they animate. The point of the exercise is to keep them just as still as they are now. But if they happen to animate and we're fast, it won't matter. Everyone in the Conclave knows they do so if animals get too close, or a drunk wanders near, or sometimes without any reason at all. Hells, street urchins sometimes run at them in the day to animate them, then dart away. Like a game of dares. The Master, who'll be sleeping anyway, will at first assume it's nothing and won't come right away. So if we get through the gates and they deactivate before the Master comes, he'll assume something inadvertent triggered them."

"Hold on," Egil said. "They'll deactivate after we've activated them?"

"Right. Remember that they're dumb. They stay animated only so long as they see or hear a threat. That said, if we take too long and leave them animated for a while, the Master will show up. And then . . ."

"And then," Egil said. He sniffed, rolled his head on the stump of his neck. "Wizard shite."

"Aye. Ready?"

Egil eyed the shroud, inhaled deeply. "Aye."

"Stay close now," Nix said.

Nix held the shroud up before them, arms held high and spread wide, as though holding up laundry to dry. They eased out of the copse of trees and moved toward the gates. Nix felt ridiculous sheltering behind a piece of enchanted cloth as though it were a shield wall. The sheer fabric allowed him to see through it and he kept his eyes on the statues' eyes, trying to gauge the angle of their line of sight. He stopped well before he thought that angle would allow them to see behind the shroud. Egil bumped into him and whispered a curse.

The head on one of the statues turned in their direction, the metal creaking with the motion.

They both remained still and said nothing. Long moments passed and the statue did not move again.

"Why stop?" the priest whispered.

Nix tucked his chin into his shoulder and whispered back, "We need to lift the shroud over us as we hunch. The angle of their sight changes as we get closer. They'll be looking down on us, so I can't just hold it before us. They'll see. We need it over us. And nothing can stick out or they'll see it, yeah?"

"Yeah."

"Ready?"

"No, but as we're standing in the road hiding behind a sheet," Egil said, "I guess we should continue."

"Do *not* make me laugh, priest. Hunch over, I'll lift and hand the end back to you. Draw it back until it covers us. Slowly. I don't want to lose the other end. We want to be like a turtle."

Moving deliberately, Nix lifted the shroud high and back, and Egil took it. The priest started to draw it back. Nix hunched, took the bottom of the shroud in his hands, and lowered himself onto all fours, holding his end tight against the paving stones. Behind him, Egil did the same, though he had to have been reaching back and just bent at the waist. Soon they were bunched together under the shroud.

"We never tell anyone about this, yeah?" Nix whispered.

"You're not to make me laugh, either," Egil said. "But agreed. No one hears of this."

Slowly, awkwardly, taking care to stay completely covered by the shroud, they crawled forward toward the statues and the doors. Nix braced for the grating, metal-on-metal screech of the statues that would indicate that he and Egil had been seen, but they closed the distance and the statues remained still.

Soon they were directly between the statues, the only thing protecting them a sheer piece of enchanted cloth. The doors, huge metal slabs, were directly ahead. The statues loomed like titans on either side. Nix eyed their feet—cast as though wearing sandals—through the shroud. He could have reached out and touched their spears, the butts pressed to the ground.

Neither he nor Egil said anything as they silently crawled toward the doors. Working under the shroud, Nix held his palms near them—not touching them for fear of triggering the wards—and felt for the enchantment. He had a tool in his satchel that would enable him to bypass them but—

Metal grated on metal, the sound like the movement of a huge, rusty hinge. He turned to whisper to Egil to remain silent and perfectly still but before he could, the priest exclaimed as he was jerked out from under the shroud. Nix barely kept the fabric over himself.

"Fak!" Egil said. "My boot must've poked out! Don't say anything, Nix! They're dumb, as you said. Fak!"

It took everything Nix had not to throw the shroud off and attempt to help his friend.

A clamor sounded, the deep ring of Egil's hammer striking one of the metal men. Nix heard a thud and whump, and imagined Egil being dropped to the ground by the statue. A different sound followed, like a weapon being sheathed—the spear of one of the statues sinking into something, but Nix could not tell if it was flesh or soil.

He had his answer when Egil's hammer rang off one of the creatures again.

"I can't hurt them!" the priest said, through the screech and grate of the statues' movements. "Get the doors open, Nix, then I'll get back—"

A huge thud sounded and Egil cursed.

"Fakkin' thing tried to stomp me!"

Egil's hammer sounded again, gonging futilely against a statue.

Nix knew what Egil intended. He'd keep the statues occupied while Nix got the doors open, then hurriedly get out of sight or under the shroud.

Another ring of Egil's hammer. Another curse and grunt. "Hurry the fak up!"

"Get back under," Nix hissed, looking back. His voice drew the attention of one of the statues, which left off Egil and turned. Nix imagined its eyes scouring the ground for him. He held still, the shroud held above him like a tent, while Egil side-stepped another stab of the spear.

"Get the fakking things open!" the priest shouted. "A wizard will be coming!"

Nix turned and put his palms back near the door, trying to move as little as possible. Behind him the movement of the statues sounded like the turning of great, rusty gears. Now and again he heard the shuffle of Egil's feet between the grates and creaks of the statue's movement, heard the priest's breathing and whispered curses, heard a sudden, sharp creak, and felt the ground tremble slightly, probably as the statue drove its spear down at Egil and hopefully hit only earth. Nix flashed on the horse he'd seen the statues impale years before.

"Egil?"

"Work!"

Egil's hammer rang off the metal of the statue, the chime an echo of Ool's clock.

Nix closed his eyes and forced himself to concentrate. The magic of the door's ward caused the hairs on his forearms to rise. He let the nature of the ward sink into his skin, made sure he had a good feel for it, then took from his satchel a thin silver rod tipped with a tiny turquoise. He tuned the wand by putting it between his palms and spinning it rapidly, as if he were using a stick to start a fire, transferring the feel of the ward from his palms to the wand. The residuum of the ward still left in Nix's skin sank into the rod and the turquoise started to glow. When it did, Nix gently touched it to the door.

A snap sounded, like a twig breaking, and the turquoise flashed brightly and turned black. Nix held still as one of the statues, apparently having heard the sound, turned and stepped near him, its sandaled foot on the corner of the enchanted shroud. Egil still labored behind him, but Nix had to remain still until the statue turned back to the priest.

In moments it did, taking its foot off the shroud as it turned, and Nix held hands to the door. No tingle. The ward was gone. He turned the large lever in the center of the doors, felt the vibration as the mechanism released.

Behind him, he heard a statue turn toward him, drawn by the turn of the gate mechanism. Nix pushed the doors open and crawled through. He turned around, still shielded by the shroud, and saw one of statues staring at the open doors, the other stabbing and stomping at Egil.

"Now, Egil!" Nix shouted.

The priest leaped aside as the statue stabbed at him with the spear. He sidestepped a stomp as he ran past the other. The moment Egil was through the doors, he turned to close them, but the statues were already in pursuit. Two steps brought them to the doorframe. Egil cursed, but before he could do anything more, before the statues could attack him again, Nix dove at the priest and tackled him.

"Be still, be still, be still," Nix said, covering both of them with the shroud. "Don't fakkin' move!"

"What the fak are you doing?" Egil hissed, starting to rise.

"They don't think, Egil," Nix whispered. "They're like animals but dumber. They don't sense us now. Quiet. Quiet."

His words reached the priest, for Egil stopped struggling. They lay on the ground under the shroud entirely still. The statues moved through the doors and looked about. Nix was facing the ground and could not see them, but he could hear them, and he felt Egil hold his breath, presumably as the statues looked at the place where they lay.

One of them stepped forward, its foot sinking into the turf beside Nix's face. If it took another step forward with its other foot, it would likely step on them. Nix tensed; Egil, too.

The statue's leg ground and creaked and Nix prepared to

bound up, but instead of stepping forward the statue turned back.

He exhaled silently, listening to the sound of the statues taking their ordinary positions just outside the door.

"Fak," Egil whispered.

"A moment longer," Nix said.

"You're not going to try to kiss me, are you?" Egil said.

"Your breath is too foul," Nix answered. "Listen now. The statues will have their backs to us. I'm going to get up, taking the shroud with me against the possibility of them turning around. I'll shut the doors under its cover. You're going to roll away out of their field of view as soon as I rise, yeah?"

"Yeah."

Holding the shroud aloft as he rose, a fabric wall between him and the statues, Nix stood and hustled to the doors. Behind him, Egil scurried off to the side.

The statues stood their posts just as he had expected. He put a hand to the gate and swung the first one closed. It swung silently, easily, and clicked into place. When it did, the statues creaked, starting to turn around. Still shielded behind the shroud, Nix darted to the other door and swung it closed, too. He breathed easier once it clicked into place. They'd gotten past the guardian statues without alerting the entire Conclave.

He donned a smug smile and turned to face Egil, but the smile faded and the words stuck in his throat when he found himself face-to-face with Kazmarek the Grandmaster. Tattooed glyphs decorated the wizard's clean-shaven cheeks and the outer corners of his gray eyes. He wore embroidered velvet robes thrown over his nightclothes. Short, steel gray hair framed his stern, wrinkled face. His eyes, the dark circles under them like stains, widened in surprise but briefly; he overcame his shock before Nix.

"Nix Fall," he said, half question, half statement, and held aloft his right hand, the back of it facing Nix. Nix started to reach for his blade but the blue gem set in the silver ring on the wizard's index finger sparkled, drew Nix's eye, held it, and froze him.

"I knew you'd return someday," Kazmarek said, the sound of his voice summoning memories of Nix's time at the Conclave. "But I didn't think like this."

Jyme sat on the floor of the Tunnel with his back to the bar, his blade drawn and lying on the floor beside him. Gadd sat on the floor near him, the big Easterner's breathing as regular as the hourly chime of Ool's clock.

Jyme had slept on the road often but couldn't get comfortable on the floor so he shifted and sighed, unable to sleep. He was still irritable at having been left behind, though he admitted to himself that Egil had pegged him correctly. Jyme had spent months in Sessket, trying to forget the moment in the desert when he'd had a chance to show bravery but hadn't. He'd even met a woman in Afirion, an ebon-skinned beauty named Ziza, who'd had a voice and manner so soft and delicate that she had reminded Jyme of a gentle rain.

Thinking of her, her laugh, reopened the wound of her death. It'd been for nothing. There'd been no meaning to it, no heroic buildup and sacrifice, just ridiculous chance.

She'd been trampled with five others when a crocodile had attacked one of a crowd of hundreds of religious bathers celebrating a rite of harvest in the water's shallows. And that was it. She'd died for nothing in an absurd accident.

Her death had emptied him out, of emotion, of meaning, of caring. It had taken him a long time to decide that doing anything was worthwhile. But when he did, he'd decided that his days of doing nothing notable were done. He'd realized that he wanted to make a mark on the world and he'd do it in honor of Ziza. And he'd realized, too, that he had amends to make, to Egil and Nix, and to himself.

So he'd returned to Dur Follin, coming around the long

way to avoid the Demon Wastes, determined to make up for his cowardice in the desert. But instead he found himself sitting watch in a whorehouse that Kerfallen would ignore now that Egil and Nix were gone. Worse, he couldn't sleep. Even worse still, he needed to piss.

He heaved himself up, groaning at the effort, and looked around in the dark for a pisspot. Though they'd left a night wick burning atop the bar, the moons had set long before, the fire in the hearth had burned down to nothing, and he could see little in the dark.

He resolved that he'd relieve himself and then find somewhere more comfortable than the floor to sleep. Kerfallen was not coming, nor were his creatures.

Halfway through his piss a creak on the porch outside stilled him. He stopped his flow, wincing at the effort, and listened. A sniffing or chuffing sound carried under the double doors in front, another creak, prolonged, as of something heavy trying to quietly shift its weight. He laced up his breeches half-assed and moved quietly back to the bar. He reached down to awaken Gadd, but the big Easterner spoke before Jyme touched him, his voice quiet.

"I am awake."

"Did you hear that?" Jyme said. "By the door? What is that? A dog?"

Gadd stood, unrolling his towering frame, both hands on the hilt of his tulwar, eyes on the rectangles of the doors. "That is not a dog."

Jyme's heart picked up speed. He kneeled and grabbed up his sword, his breeches, poorly laced, trying to slip down his hips. He'd get his chance at redemption, after all.

"Wizard shite, then," he whispered. "Nothing gets up the stairs, yeah?"

Tesha and the working women and men of the Tunnel were sleeping in their rooms upstairs. Jyme had no intention of allowing harm to come to them.

"Yes," Gadd answered.

They moved furtively but quickly across the common room, navigating through the tables and chairs, toward the doors. Jyme, trying to better tie off his breeches as he went, peeked out a window on the way, but the angle was bad and he could make out nothing but a very large form hunched near the doors.

"Definitely not a dog," he whispered. "It's big."

Gadd nodded, his eyes wide and white in the dark oval of his face.

The chuffing outside grew louder, more urgent, as if whatever it was had caught a scent. Jyme pictured the thing bent all the way down, its nose down by the bottom of the doors.

"You think it can smell us?" he whispered to Gadd. He had his breeches tight enough now.

"It smells something," Gadd said, his eyes on the doorway.

Jyme gestured Gadd to one side of the doorway while he moved to the other.

"I'll open it," Jyme whispered. "Stand ready."

Gadd nodded and readied his blade.

As Jyme reached for the lock, something huge slammed into the door, cracking wood and causing the floor to vibrate. Tankards fell from their pegs behind Gadd's bar.

Jyme cursed, bounded back away from the doors, and readied himself. Gadd did the same, snarling to show his filed teeth. Another powerful impact struck one of the doors and it gave way entirely, the hinges pulling free of the jambs with a squeal, splintered wood showering into the room. A huge form filled the opening.

Though hunched, the creature still stood a few hand spans taller than even Gadd, and appeared wider than a barrel. An overlarge, filthy, wet cloak covered its lumpy form, and rags and straps wrapped the trunks of its legs. Its breath came in loud, wet heaves and it stank like decay and fish. Jyme winced at the reek. A hood and more wraps shielded most of its face from view. Jyme could see only the rapid blink of eyes, the pair of them oddly close together and fixing on no point for more than a moment.

Gadd growled and rushed it from one side, tulwar raised high in a two-handed grip, while Jyme rushed it from the other.

The creature turned and lurched at Gadd, snarling as the Easterner's blade chopped it in its shoulder beside its neck. The blow should have felled it, but seemed to have no effect. Blood flowed, but not enough. The creature grabbed Gadd by the arm and flung him away. Gadd crashed into a table, into the chair beyond, and fell to the floor groaning. Jyme lunged forward and stabbed the hulking thing through its back and out its stomach. Again blood sprayed but the creature did not buckle. Instead it growled and whirled to face him, wrenching Jyme's blade from his hand.

Jyme stood before it, looking up dumbfounded into its rage-filled eyes. It slammed a palm into Jyme's chest, driving the wind from him, maybe cracking his sternum, and propelling him across the room. Careening backward, he tripped on a chair, went heels over head, and slammed the back of his skull against the floor. Things went black for a moment, then sparks, but he stayed conscious. He was blinking, staring up at the beamed ceiling, trying to breathe.

A scream sounded from the upstairs landing—one of Tesha's girls must have come out of her room at the sounds of the combat. Jyme heard the tread of footsteps from above. He lifted his head to see the creature looking up the stairs, its chest heaving under the robes. It looked back at Jyme and spoke, but its voice was like many voices, raspy and gravelly and high-pitched and deep all at once. It held out a hand, huge and mis-shapen, the skin filthy and creased but looking like melted candlewax.

"ThegreatspellthespellgiveittomeImusthavehaveit."

Jyme clambered to his feet, wincing at the pain in his chest, feeling dizzy for a moment, trying to catch his breath, and otherwise having no idea what the creature was babbling about.

He drew a dagger from his belt, a paltry weapon against so large a creature.

A roar came from behind the monster as Gadd rose up and leaped over a table, swinging the thick blade of his tulwar at the creature's throat. It raised an arm to defend itself and Gadd's blade sank deep into flesh and bone. Gadd snarled into its face and the creature responded only by slamming the hammer of its fist against the side of Gadd's head, a blow that sent Gadd reeling to the floor. His tulwar skittered away.

More screams from up the stairs, Tesha calling out, herding the girls away. They'd have to jump out one of the second-floor balconies if the creature headed upstairs. Jyme would buy them as much time as he could.

He dropped the dagger, grabbed a chair, and slammed it over the creature's head and shoulders. The chair broke and splintered, and Jyme might as well have struck a tree, for all the good it did. He thought quickly enough to grab his blade and jerk it clean of the creature's body as it turned to face him.

"What the fak are you?" he said. If it hadn't been for the blood, he would have assumed the hulking thing to be one of Kerfallen's constructs.

"GivemethespellIsmellithere!"

"I don't know what the Hells you're talking about," Jyme said, but then he did.

The plates Egil and Nix had, the plates Kerfallen wanted, the writing on them. The creature must want them, too.

"ThespellthespelltheGreatSpell."

Jyme backed up a step, blade ready. Gadd was unmoving on the floor. Jyme maneuvered himself around so that he stood between the creature and the stairs.

"Go out the balcony if you have to," he called over his shoulder, but had no idea if anyone heard him.

The creature clenched its fists and roared, its body rippling with its rage, and Jyme tensed, ready to die fighting. More screams sounded from the landing, followed by the twang and whistle of a crossbow quarrel. The creature sprouted a bolt from its side, the missile sinking deep into its flesh. It snarled and looked up the stairs. Jyme glanced back, too.

Tesha stood at the top along with several of the working girls. She was already reloading the crossbow she held. Jyme took the opportunity. He bounded forward, desperation lending him speed, and stabbed the creature through the face. His blade sank deep and it felt to Jyme like he'd stabbed a melon. The creature took a step back, but only that. It tore the blade loose, again jerking it from Jyme's grasp. Blood poured from the gash in its face, but only for a moment before the wound seemed to close.

Jyme stared wide-eyed, mouth hanging open, knowing he was going to die.

The creature, stinking and bloody and huge, raised a fist high to crack Jyme's skull. As it did the crossbow sang again and another bolt slammed into it, this time in its chest. It didn't seem to notice.

"Get out of here!" one of the girls screamed from the top of the stairs. "Leave us alone!"

"You aren't possible," Jyme said softly.

The creature tensed to strike and . . . stopped.

It raised its nose and sniffed, inhaled deeply. A low growl sounded from somewhere deep in its chest. It glared at Jyme through bloodshot eyes, lowered its fist, turned, and lumbered out of the Tunnel.

A spike of pain flashed in the back of Jyme's head. A wave of dizziness made the room spin. He sagged to the floor and the world went dark.

Nix tried to pull his eyes from the enchanted ring, from its dark blue depths, its swirling, infinite cerulean currents, but it transfixed him. He fell deeper into the blue, was swimming in it. Part of him knew what was happening but could not stop it because stopping it would mean removing his gaze from the gem and it was too fascinating, its pull too strong.

Kazmarek looked past him at the closed gates. "You bypassed the iron guards? How did you—"

Egil rose up behind Kazmarek and punched the wizard in the side of the head. The old man fell without a sound, collapsing at Nix's feet. The ring lost its glow and its hold and Nix blinked dumbly at Egil.

"You all right?" the priest asked, prodding the wizard with his toe. "What was that, you standing there slack-jawed? That ring?"

Nix shook his head to clear it, blinked away the blue fog. "Aye. A fixation stone. Got me before I could arrange my thoughts against it."

"Fakkin' gewgaws at every turn," Egil said, glancing about. He dug his toe into the wizard's ribs again. No response.

Nix looked around, wondering if anyone else had noted their presence. With the moons down, the meager starlight cast the vast grounds in grays and blacks and deeper blacks. Nix's memory filled in what he couldn't actually see.

The dome of the teaching college rose up into the night sky, the narrow tower of the calling gong sticking out of it like a raised finger. The low, unremarkable cluster of buildings that served as the students' quarters hugged the walls to their left, and the more elaborate, multistory buildings that housed the Masters and their laboratories crowded the grounds to the right. Between them was the gathering plaza, decorated with the statues of old Masters, carved topiary, the pool of memories. Behind the teaching college were the vast gardens and livestock pens that provided the Conclave with much of its food. The Master Herbalist tended the animals and kept the harvest rich year after year. What couldn't be prepared on the grounds was purchased in the city by way of hirelings, many of them enspelled to obey. The Conclave kept dozens of agents under spell or contract or both, and they acquired all the other materials the school might need, including corpses for experimentation.

"It's like a fakkin' cemetery in here," Egil said, taking in the topiary and statues. "Small wonder you quit."

Nix knelt, removed the fixation ring from Kazmarek's finger, and dropped it into his satchel along with the enchanted shroud. He rifled the pockets of the wizard's robes, tossing everything onto the grass except for the master key, a metal rod topped with a fleck of pearl, which he kept to hand. He put his ear to the Grandmaster's mouth and listened for breath.

"Still alive," he said to Egil, and stood. "You losing your touch?"

"Seeing as you didn't slit his throat, I assume we're not going to kill him?"

"No," Nix said. "We have a bit of a history, he and I. And he might be useful. So we're going to bring him."

Egil nodded. He heaved the unconscious wizard over his shoulders as though he were little more than a child. "I reserve the right to hit him in the head again. Meantime, let's get out of plain sight, yeah?"

"Yeah," Nix said, and walked at the double quick toward the teaching college. Picking his way through the statues and topiary reminded him of younger days, when he'd imagined a different course for his life than tomb robbing and owning a brothel.

But then, he couldn't imagine a life he wanted more than the one he had.

Stone dragons stood on pedestals at the base of the grand, sweeping stone staircase that led up to the closed doors of the college. They hurried up them until they stood before the double doors. Nix knew they'd be locked, as they always were after instruction ended for the day. Holding the master key he'd taken from Kazmarek, he placed the pearl against a shallow indentation under the door handle. An illusory mouth formed on the door and said, "Good evening, Grand Master."

The doors clicked and swung open. The air in the hall and foyer beyond smelled as Nix remembered—stale but aromatic, like a dried onion. That smell would forever remind him of the theaters in the round he'd stood in during classroom instruction, watching demonstrations of spells, item use, listening to lectures on alchemy.

He missed it. A little. Maybe.

Huge portraits covered the walls, old Masters and famous wizards, and magical symbols were engraved in the floor. Carved in an ancient tongue above one archway were the words:

Knowledge is both power and peril.

Nix had always found it trite.

Veins of glowing minerals lined the stone of the walls and floor, providing dim yellow light, the pattern of them reminiscent of a luminous spiderweb.

"Nightlights," Nix said, by way of explanation. "Follow me."

The college's massive library occupied essentially the entire floor belowground. Nix led them down a staircase, down another hall, to the far side of the college, then down a triple-wide stone staircase that descended deep into the earth before giving way to a wide, carved archway that opened onto the vast, vaulted room of the Conclave's library.

"Gods," Egil said, standing in the doorway.

"Aye," Nix agreed. He hadn't seen the Conclave library in years, and he'd forgotten its grandeur. The glowing veins of minerals lined walls and ceilings and provided light, testifying to the size of the chamber.

The room was larger than the entire footprint of the college above. The floor was tiered, with short individual flights of stone steps leading to this section and that. Tables and chairs and divans stood here and there, all of them ancient and ornate. Shelves ran floor to ceiling along the walls and in free-standing bookcases, all of them stocked with leather-bound tomes, thick grimoires, scrolls, engraved metal plates, centuries of accumulated knowledge on subjects arcane and mundane. The Conclave library was often proclaimed to be the single greatest depository of knowledge on Ellerth, and Nix had never doubted it. The books and writings collected in the huge room numbered in the hundreds of thousands. No one could read them all, not in multiple lifetimes. No one could catalog them all. No one except the book sprites, swarming, obsessive little fae with a fixation on the written word.

Even at the late hour the book sprites flitted through the room, their tiny wings trailing glowing motes of various colors. They were like a swarm of sparkling insects, darting about the shelves and tables. Hundreds of them, maybe thousands. Two score candles on tall candelabra burned on various tiers, the flames at the end of their wicks a deep green.

"Open flame in here seems a risk," Egil said.

"The candles are enspelled," Nix said. "They're everburning but never burn down. And the flames won't burn paper, parchment, or wood or the like."

Egil frowned, no doubt irritated to be in the presence of more gewgaws.

Kazmarek groaned. Egil laid him on the floor. Nix kneeled down and pried open one of his eyes. No focus yet. Nix dug a length of thin cordage from his satchel and handed it to Egil.

"Bind him. If he talks and we don't fancy his words, we'll gag him, too."

"Aye, that," Egil said. The priest expertly bound the Grand Master at wrists and ankles. The wizard groaned throughout, slowly working his way back to his senses.

"Come on," Nix said, and hustled up the stairs of one tier and then another. Egil heaved Kazmarek over his shoulder and followed.

Book sprites flitted around them as they went, curious, their high-pitched voices discernible to Nix only as a kind of rising and falling whine. He stopped when he reached the highest, central tier of the library.

The Block, as the students had called it, featured eight long tables with accompanying high-backed chairs, all neatly arranged. It offered a view of the rest of the library. Students studied and researched there. One of the candelabra with three everburning candles stood to one side of the table.

As they stood there, more of the book sprites gathered around them, the beat of their wings a faint, soothing buzz, while others flew off. It was like standing in a shower of embers.

Egil placed Kazmarek in one of the chairs, where the Grandmaster slumped. Book sprites buzzed about him for a moment, no doubt curious, then flew off. The wizard groaned again and his finger twitched.

"Coming around," Nix said.

"Aye," Egil agreed. He put a hand on the haft of one of his hammers. "Where do you start in here? These little pyrotechnics can help, you said?"

"They can."

Kazmarek straightened, looked around blearily. "Are we in the . . . ? What are we doing here? What are you doing?"

"Nothing I care to share with you just yet," Nix said. He grabbed a summoning candle from a small drawer built into the underside of the table.

"You could've killed me," Kazmarek said to Egil. "Striking me like that."

"If I'd wanted you dead, I wouldn't have used my hand," Egil said, patting the haft of his hammer.

"You should talk less," Nix said. "This isn't one of your lectures."

Kazmarek took in the summoning candle. "Whatever you're planning, it's not too late to stop. You can still just leave."

Nix ignored him. He removed the plates from his satchel.

The Grandmaster squirmed in his chair to get a better look at them. "What do you have there?"

"He said shut up," Egil admonished.

The Grandmaster ignored him. "Show me those. Nix, show me those."

A few of the book sprites darted over, too, hovering near the plates for a moment. The plates caught the sprites' light, cast it back in a rainbow of green and orange and red.

"Nix," Kazmarek said, his voice different, quieter. "Please let me see those. I'm bound. I'm not dangerous. Maybe I can . . . help you."

Nix raised an eyebrow. "I think you can see them just fine from there. Do you know what they are? That's why we're here."

"I can't see them well from here," Kazmarek said. "Bring them over. I need to see them close up."

Nix could not quite read his expression or tone, but if he'd been forced to put a name to it, he'd have called it fear. Nix took one of the plates and slid it across the table until it was before the Grandmaster.

"Don't try to touch it, even with your nose." He drew a dagger and held it at the ready. "And if I even think you're starting a syllable in the Language of Creation I'll cut out your tongue."

Kazmarek, sitting very still, merely stared at the plate. He licked his lips and leaned forward, probably studying the script. Nix tensed, ready to stab him if he touched the plate. He didn't touch it, and despite the green glow of the candles, he seemed to go pale.

"Well?" Egil asked.

Kazmarek seemed not to have heard him. He leaned back and looked up at the ceiling, his brow furrowed in thought or worry. He swallowed hard, looked again at the plate, then at Nix.

"You don't know what you have?" he said.

"If we fakkin' knew," Egil said, "we wouldn't be here."

"As the priest said," Nix said, "it's a long story. Anyway, you know what they are. I can tell from your face. So?"

Kazmarek cleared his throat. Nix could tell he was measuring out every word, trying to keep his tone of voice level, trying to reveal nothing.

"How many of these plates do you have?" the Grandmaster asked. "Just those two? Where did you find them? Who else knows you have them?"

Nix took the plate from before the wizard and for the briefest moment it seemed Kazmarek might try to leap out of his seat to stay close to it. He watched the plate go as if his eyes were attached to it.

"Where we found them doesn't matter," Nix said.

"It does!" Kazmarek said, his voice loud and echoing in the library. At the sound, book sprites flew from the shelves like startled birds. "It does matter!"

His earnestness took Nix aback. He shared a look with Egil, who raised his thick eyebrows in the equivalent of a shrug.

"We've got just the two," Nix said to the Grandmaster, seeing no harm in offering a bit of truth. "And almost no one knows what we have."

"You and another wizard," Egil added. "He's a bit more irritating than you, in that he keeps trying to kill us. But only a *bit* more."

"Jyme, too," Nix added.

Kazmarek leaned forward in his chair. "Which wizard? Never mind. Listen to me. Both of you. What you have here is bigger than you. You won't understand it. And you could do . . . profound harm. You must stop."

"We'll take all that into consideration," Nix said somberly. "Egil, have you considered?"

The priest nodded, his expression serious. "I have and I've reached a decision. I do not give a fak. Nor would I trust the word of a wizard, much less this one."

"Seconded in all respects," Nix said. Then to Kazmarek, "Drop all the wizardly 'our doom is upon us' shite. Just tell us what they are and we'll move along."

"Nix," Kazmarek said, his eyes fixed on Nix's face, almost febrile in their intensity, "please hear me. Please. You must not learn what these are. Once you know, you can't unknow. For your own well-being, don't. Just leave them with me and go. That's the best thing you can do now. I'll take care of it all."

Nix gave Egil a knowing look. "And there it is. Angling for our swag."

"Aye," Egil said, but it was halfhearted and he looked unsure.

"Ah," Nix said, seeing Egil's hesitation. "The priest wavers but shouldn't. Egil, this man is a liar. A skilled one. He appears earnest, sincere, yeah? He's neither. I know him better than you. He wants the plates for himself, the same as Kerfallen, but his motivation isn't our well-being."

"Kerfallen," the Grandmaster said, the word coming out like a curse. "That stunted little fool." He looked not at Nix but at Egil. "Nix is right. I lie when necessary. But I'm not lying about this. The plates are dangerous. For you. For all of us. Just leave them here and forget you ever saw them. That's all you have to do. There won't be any repercussions for trespassing here or attacking me."

"They're just pieces of metal," Egil said. "Gewgaws and naught more. Dangerous for all of us seems a stretch, indeed."

"No," Kazmarek said, shaking his head. "You're not hearing me. They're much more."

"Then tell us or shut up," Nix said.

When the Grandmaster said nothing, Nix turned away. He imagined he could feel Kazmarek's eyes on him, the heat of their regard two smoking points on his back. He placed the summoning candles before him. Threads of gold and silver swirled through the gray wax of the candle. It smelled of cinnamon and cardamom. He lit it with a match from his satchel. Like the other candles in the library, the wick burned a soft green.

"Nix," Kazmarek said, shifting in his chair, his tone carrying a hint of desperation, "you would've made a fine Master. That's what I always had in mind for you. Did you know that? It's not too late."

"As you said," Nix said, "you lie when needed. And now you turn to flattering lies. You never thought anything of the kind. You considered me a warren rat and begrudged every moment I spent here. You lie now because you're afraid."

"Yes!" Kazmarek said, nodding, his eagerness to agree nearly toppling him in the chair. "Yes! I am afraid! You don't know what you're doing. For me to explain it would . . ."

"Would what?" Egil asked.

"Be beyond us?" Nix said. "We've already heard that."

"No," Kazmarek said. "To explain it is to name it. Nix, this is something you should not know, must not know. Priest, make him understand."

"He already understands," Egil said.

Indeed, the more the wizard protested, the more determined Nix became to learn the nature of the plates. He watched the smoke from the summoning candle spiral up toward the vaulted ceiling. Glowing lines veined the smoke, igniting for a moment like little lightning bolts. A few of the nearest book sprites caught the scent, flew over, and gathered in the smoke, pleased by the smell.

Egil stepped beside Nix and spoke in a quiet voice so Kazmarek would not easily hear. "Are you sure about this? His fear seems real."

"The only thing I'm sure of is that I don't trust him. Do you?"

A bit of a pause before Egil said, "No."

"You want to give him the plates and walk away?"

"Fak no."

"Nor I," Nix said. "I concede he seems in earnest. But *seems* is the critical word there."

"Maybe," Egil said doubtfully.

"We're here," Nix said. "Let's just see it through, yeah? Knowing what they are can't hurt."

"Yeah."

Book sprites swarmed overhead, so many they looked like a

glowing cloud of sparks. They glowed in various colors—green, orange, violet, and red, changing as they flitted about.

Nix arranged the two metal plates to either side of the candle. A score of the sprites flitted down, hovered over them.

"Do not obey this man," Kazmarek said to them, in the commanding voice Nix had come to know so well when he'd attended the Conclave. "I am commanding you. You answer to me. Do not obey him."

Nix brandished Kazmarek's master key and showed it to the sprites. "He doesn't hold the key, I do. So, you will answer to whoever lights the summoning candle. You'll do as I bid."

"You are forbidden!" Kazmarek shouted at them, and the sprites darted about in agitation, their colors changing rapidly from green to orange to violet and back again. Several more flew down from the ceiling, as though to investigate.

"Do not obey this man," the Grandmaster said again to the sprites.

"Nix . . ." Egil said.

"He can end it himself by telling us what they are," Nix snapped. "Tell us, old man."

"No! Never!" To the sprites, Kazmarek said, "And you are to show him nothing."

"And now I know what I want is here," Nix said. Before the Grandmaster could reply, Nix said, "Another word and we gag you."

Kazmarek ground his teeth and stared rage at Nix.

Nix tapped the plates with his finger and spoke to the sprites. "There are books here that identify these. Find them and bring them to me."

"No!" Kazmarek said, and struggled against his bonds.

Egil cuffed the wizard in the back of his head. A bit half-heartedly, Nix thought.

The sprites hesitated, flew around Nix, around Kazmarek, over the plates.

"Do as I've commanded," Nix said, and the sprites, bound

by the magic of the candle, driven by their fae need, darted off. They spread out across the library, delving into its hidden, forgotten corners, seeking to fulfill Nix's command.

Kazmarek was wide-eyed, tense. "There's no book here that will answer your question."

"I already know that's a lie," Nix said, watching the sprites about their work. "Something's here."

Kazmarek shifted in his chair. "I never should have brought you out of the Warrens. The Art was always beyond you."

"If it was, that's because the teaching here was so poor," Nix said.

"Poor, you say? Why—"

"Shut up," Egil said, cuffing the wizard a second time, not so halfheartedly this time.

Nix watched the swarm of sprites as they checked books and scrolls, from time to time coming back to eyeball the plates, as if to remind themselves what it was they were looking for.

Egil stepped close to him. He put his fingers near one of the plates, but didn't touch it. "Maybe there's nothing here?"

Nix shook his head. "Look around. That's not possible. Gotta be something here."

As though on cue, the pitch and rhythm of the sprites' chatter changed, getting higher and faster. They flew across the library from all the directions, gathering in a distant corner of the room that Nix had not noticed before.

Behind him, Kazmarek's intake of breath was sharp enough to cut skin.

"They found something," Nix said to Egil.

"Aye," the priest said softly.

The sprites clustered together, a congregation of colors, and as one removed something from the shelf. They flew it over to Nix, all of them glowing violet as they worked together, and set it on the table. Their work done, the sprites dispersed into a multicolored spark shower, and each returned to its perch on its favorite shelf or table.

In their wake they left a slim grimoire, the thin, beaten metal covers stained dark with age. The vellum pages bound within looked stiff, wrinkled, and dry, obviously old. The tome was not labeled. Nothing on its cover suggested what might be within.

"Doesn't look like much," Egil said.

"If you open that book there's no going back," Kazmarek said.

Nix shared a look with Egil. The priest said, "Your decision. I'm with you, as ever. I'll own up to some . . . concern, though."

"Yeah," Nix said. "But even so."

He sat down, put his hands to the cover, and opened the book.

CHAPTER SEVEN

The Afterbirth ran out of the building that smelled of sweat and urine and sex and vomit and lurched through the dark streets. He left a trail of his blood in his wake like a line of crimson thread stretching out behind him, but he soon felt the pinch in his skin as the wounds he'd suffered stitched closed. He knew he was taking a great risk moving openly through the street but he could smell the Great Spell in the air, smell it as sharply as ever and he could accept no delay no none. He'd rely on the dark to conceal his appearance, to hide the truth of him.

At his passage dogs barked and growled from out of the night, cats hissed and darted down alleys, and horses and mules whinnied with fear, bucking in their stalls and pens. His weight cracked cobblestones underfoot and he hunched low, knuckles sometimes scraping the street. The hour left the avenues mostly empty but he saw or smelled a few people, most of them rife with the stink of alcohol and unwashed bodies. He could feel their eyes on him as he passed, could guess at the questions his form raised he figured they'd assume the night or their drink or drugs had played tricks with their vision and that they'd mistook what they saw.

The spoor of the Great Spell was rich in the air, more powerful than he'd ever sensed since . . . since as far back as he could remember, and what he could remember he could not trust as his own. He drooled and muttered as he ran, following his noses, sometimes needing to double back and circle around because he hit a dead end, but moving ever south through the city. The sun would rise before too long. Already the sky to the east had gone from black to gray, the stars fading into the background. He had to hurry.

"Fasterfasterfaster."

In time the roads gave way to a large park or plaza, a swath of grass and trees and statues. The Afterbirth did not slow and hurried across the park, muttering with excitement and hope, moving toward a large walled compound at the park's far end. The Great Spell was behind the walls, he could smell it, could almost taste it, and spit dripped from his malformed mouths, mingled with the blood to further wet his cloak.

Somewhere in the minds that inhabited his numb malformed body was the knowledge of how to cast the Great Spell. He would use it to end his existence, end his pain, for a word rose out of the murky depths of his memories, hit him hard enough to temporarily slow his stride.

Palimpsest.

He could not remember what it meant but the word stuck, a splinter in his memory, irritating, needing to be pulled out. He knew that it had to do with the Great Spell, with an error in the casting, but . . .

It struck him and he remembered that in the casting there were leftovers, always leftovers, like him, the Afterbirth, that was it, that was what he wanted to recall.

He shook his head, trying to remember more but failing, the voices in his mind clamoring, the cacophony maddening. He couldn't remember or they couldn't remember or maybe he could maybe the spell could be cast differently, to account for the leftovers, he didn't know, and . . .

He put a big fist to his temple, thumped it against his skull, his anger growing.

Ahead, the walls of the compound rose tall and dark and even he would never be able to climb them or break them down. But he saw a gate, saw the two large metal statues that flanked it, towering metal men cast to look like warriors. He smelled magic on them and without hesitation he rushed up the paved walkway toward the gate.

"Thespellthespellthespell."

As he neared, the two statues came unexpectedly to life, the metal of their bodies screaming as they lurched into motion. They pointed their spears and stepped before the gates to block him and the Afterbirth leaned toward them and sped up his approach, intending to push through them, and one of the statues stabbed its spear into his torso and out his back and still he did not slow. Muttering, drooling, bleeding, he pulled himself along the spear's length until he was within reach of the statue, staring at its unmoving, emotionless face. He heaved himself at it and he was as big as the metal man and his weight toppled it. It held on to its spear and he fell atop it, bleeding, still impaled, the gore-coated spear pointing skyward.

He reared back and pummeled the statue in the head, his fists landing with great dull thuds, but the blows doing the statue no more harm than its spear had done him. The second statue, the metal of its form grinding as it moved, stabbed him from behind. The second spear pierced his back, went through his body, and sank deep into the dirt, pinning him to the ground.

Unable to move, stuck to the earth, an unadulterated bout of panic seized him. He moaned, whined, seeing in his mind's eye the terrible possibility of living his life constrained, an eternal existence of pain and purposelessness with no hope of an end.

The panic gave way to rage, a rage that filled him, saturated him, anger at any delay in finding the Great Spell. He wrenched his body and half-turned, the two spears' shafts bending under his effort, the hafts grating against his bones and flesh and gouging open his body. Blood and gore rushed from the wounds but he did not care. He reached back, his hands slick with his blood, got a hand on the spear of the statue standing behind him, and wrenched it from the statue's grasp. He tore himself free of the statue on the ground and rose to face the other, gore pouring from him in a crimson shower, the two spears still stuck in him and jutting from him like pennons. His body already was re-sealing wounds and he pulled both spears out of him and they came free with a wet slurp.

The statue behind him started to stand and the one before him advanced on him, arms reaching. He had no more time to waste and roaring and screaming and shouting from his mouths, many of them ruined for the moment by the spears, he launched himself at the statue in front of him, ducking under its grasp, and wrapping it around the middle, match-ing his strength against its weight. It slammed its fists down on his back, cracking bone and splitting flesh, but he grunted and lifted it from the earth and flung it into the other statue before the second one had fully risen and the two collided with a great metallic clang.

His anger was not sated nor his work done so he jumped atop them, raging, took the head of one in both hands and slammed it into the head of the other, again and again and again. Their hands closed on his arms, clutched handfuls of his flesh and squeezed but they could harm him only for a moment. The blood pouring from him made his grip slippery but he held on and smashed until the statues' faces deformed under the impact of his beating, their visages becoming odd reflections of his own deformed mien. They seemed to be slowing, the magic that ani-mated them beginning to fail.

He reared back and stood and took one of them by the leg, spun, and swung it hard into the wall. It struck with a loud, hollow boom, its metal body snapping apart at the shoulder and waist. A puff of glowing smoke exited the hollow body and the statue went still. He turned to face the other statue, his fists clenching reflexively. The statue was trying to rise in its slow, awkward way. He lunged forward and grabbed it by the mid-section and lifted it fully over his head and threw it against the gates. The gate mountings broke under the force of the impact and the doors flew open, the left one losing a large hinge and hanging askew. One of the statue's legs snapped off and again a puff of glowing red smoke flew from the hole, the magic animating the creature dissipating into the air. The Afterbirth, soaked in his own gore, chest heaving, stepped over the metal man and through the ruined gates and roared.

A few people had gathered outside buildings some distance away to the left and right. Probably they'd heard the melee at the gates. More of them ran out of the buildings to see what was happening, or poked their heads from windows, some of them young, some of them old. They froze when they saw the Afterbirth and even across the grassy expanse he smelled their growing fear. A few pointed; several shouted. The Afterbirth heard words spoken in the Language of Creation but all of them fled back inside, the younger ushered along by the older. He resisted the impulse to crush them all. His senses were attuned to the Great Spell, on fire with the scent of it, and he would endure no further delays. He ran toward the large building with the wide staircase and domed tower, his feet putting deep divots in the soft soil.

A tap on his cheek and a woman's voice brought Jyme back. He blinked open his eyes, found himself looking into Tesha's face. Her eyes crinkled with concern, putting a deep divot over the bridge of her nose.

"Jyme!" She shook him by the shoulder. "Jyme!"

"Did I—?" He tried to get his bearings. He must have

passed out for a moment. He put his fingers to the robin-egg-sized lump on the back of his head and winced. "Shite. How long was I out?"

"Moments only," Tesha said. "What in the Hells was that?"

"We should call the Watch," another of the girls said.

"No Watch," Tesha said. "Everyone, back to your rooms. No, just . . . stay in the building but do whatever you must. Jyme?" she asked, and started down the stairs.

Jyme recovered himself enough to check on Gadd. He crawled over. The big Easterner was breathing.

"He's alive," Tesha said to him.

Jyme nodded. A lump the size of a stone fruit was forming on the side of Gadd's head. "He needs a healer."

"Lis, Gretta, go get a priest of Orella," Tesha ordered. "Hurry now. Tell her she'll be paid well if she's quick."

"I don't want to go out there," one of the two girls said.

"Gretta—" Tesha said.

"I'll go," Lis said. Jyme saw she was a petite redhead, maybe twenty winters old. "Let me get a cloak."

Tesha came over and knelt near Gadd, alongside Jyme. She ran her fingers along his jawline, said something that sounded like a prayer in a language Jyme didn't know.

"A healer can save him," Jyme said. He felt around his chest where the creature had stuck him. Nothing broken, but breathing hurt. The knot on the back of his head ached. Tesha nodded. No tears, Jyme saw. The woman was tough.

"Are you all right?" she asked. "I thought you were dead when you fell over. I checked you for wounds, but—"

"I'm all right. That creature is after the enchanted plates Egil and Nix have. I think it senses them somehow, smells them." He stood, felt all right. "You see the way that it chuffed? Like an animal."

"I saw. Do you know where they are?"

He nodded. "I think so."

"Go warn them, then. I have this. Go on, Jyme. They can't

harm that thing any more than you and Gadd could but they won't know that and they'll ... do something foolish. Go."

Jyme nodded and hurried out of the Tunnel.

He'd head to the Conclave, hoping to catch Egil and Nix before they tried to get inside. He assumed he knew the city better than the creature, and he knew where he was going. It was just following a scent. He should be able to beat it there.

He ignored the pain in his chest and head as best he could and ran through Dur Follin's dark streets.

Halfway to the Conclave he remembered the enspelled parchment Nix had given him. He cursed himself for a fool, stopped in the street in front of a cobbler's shop, and took out the parchment and a chalk stylus. He composed his thoughts and started to write with a shaking hand.

Nix read, the script swirling under his gaze, and as he did his heart began to race, his head to ache. He could feel a vein pulsing behind his eye.

Your script is probably not mine. Small things change in the casting no matter the will of the speaker. The creation is not entirely our own. But the writing in this tome is magical and will change to allow you to read it and hopefully understand. It's possible that what you're reading now isn't even from the latest casting, but is from one much earlier. Many things carry over, even across multiple castings.

Be warned. At first you will not believe what you read. You'll think me mad. Possibly you've heard me described so already. I will leave that behind again, to amuse myself. But soon enough you will come to believe. It is always thus, I think, cycle after cycle. I'm not certain why I'm leaving this book for someone to find. Perhaps that, too, is always the case. Perhaps I don't want knowledge to disappear. The speaker of the Great Spell leaves an imprint of himself in the wake of the casting,

a deep mark on the world. I was mighty in my history, or
in a history. That is the very point of the casting, or at least is
often so. My name is Ool, and I will tell you what I know,
though it will mean you can undo what I've done.

"You can stop," Kazmarek pleaded. "Nix, you can stop
right now."

But Nix couldn't stop. He felt connected to the writing, immersed in it. He ignored the Grandmaster and pored over the
book, the words soaking into him. Some trick of the magic in
them not only made them decipherable but also allowed him to
read them more quickly, to understand them more thoroughly.
As he read, his disbelief grew, just as Ool had warned.

"This can't be true," he said, shaking his head. "It can't."

"What?" Egil asked, stepping closer. "What does it say?"

The priest made no attempt to read over his shoulder. Nix
knew that Egil had no appetite for magical tomes.

Nix made no reply and instead looked up and over at
Kazmarek. "Do you know what this says?"

Kazmarek's pained expression told Nix the answer before
he spoke it. He looked every bit the frail old man he probably
was. "Much of it. Not the words. Reading the words is too
much. I started once, but stopped. But I grasped the meaning.
All Grandmasters know of it. It's heavy, Nix. And the weight,
once placed, is never lifted."

"But this isn't possible," Nix said, his voice higher than he
liked. "No."

"What does it say?" Egil asked again, this time a note of
tension creeping into his voice.

Nix looked up at his friend, stricken. "I don't . . . I can't,
Egil. It's . . . not possible. This is some wizard trick."

Egil's expression turned questioning. "You're pale."

"I'm all right," Nix lied.

"No you're not," Kazmarek said. "And what you read is not
only possible, Nix, it is the truth, insofar as we've been able to

determine. For generations it's been nothing but knowledge, a thought experiment, more an article of faith than a subject for study. But that changed the moment you brought those thrice-damned plates here."

"I don't even know what they are yet!" Nix said.

"Yes you do! Or you soon will! And that's why you must leave them with me. I'll keep them safe. Hidden. No one else need ever know. No one else *can* ever know."

"Other people already know," Egil reminded them.

Nix didn't seem to hear him, instead said to Kazmarek, "Then the plates are . . . ?"

"Yes," Kazmarek said. "I surmised it the moment I saw the script on them. They're the spell, Nix. The Great Spell. The One Spell. The Original Act. It's all there on the plates."

Nix found it hard to breathe. He stared at his hands, the table, the library, the Grandmaster. "But he's implying . . . worlds. How many?"

Kazmarek responded to Nix. "No one knows for certain. How could we? The knowledge could be implanted when—"

"Implanted? Worlds? What is this?" Egil said.

Kazmarek suddenly went rigid, his eyes wide. He blinked, sagged in the chair.

"What is it?" Nix asked, half-rising from his seat, thinking it a ruse.

"If this is a trick . . ." Egil warned, and let the threat dangle.

"It's not," Kazmarek said, his voice hoarse. "Someone is attacking the statues at the gate. Someone . . . destroyed them."

"Kerfallen," Egil said. "Shite."

"Kerfallen would never attack the Conclave," Kazmarek said. "No, this is . . . something else." He looked at Nix, franticness in his eyes. "It's coming for the plates."

"It?" Egil asked.

Kazmarek ignored the priest and looked at Nix, his eyes intense. "Nix, there are things you don't know yet. And you don't need to learn them. You shouldn't. Don't burden yourself further. Just leave me the plates. Leave them right where they are and go. The Conclave will handle whatever attacked the gates and there will be no more castings of the Great Spell. Grandmasters take that oath."

Nix pushed back his chair, his thoughts bouncing around, his body weak. He felt outside himself. He thought about standing, but wasn't sure his legs would support him.

"No," he said. "No one can keep them safe. And I'm not leaving them in the possession of some fakkin' wizard. Your oath is worth shite."

Egil put a hammer in each hand. "Whatever came through those gates is going to be here soon. We need to get ready or get clear."

Nix stood, his hands on the table for support. He stared at the plates. He'd taken them on a whim, a lark, nothing more. "We never should have brought them out of the swamp, Egil. We should've left them at the bottom of that bog, guarded by that fakkin' thing, and never known any better. Shite, shite, shite."

"Are you gonna tell me what they are?" Egil asked. He sounded tentative, as if he didn't really want to know.

"Tell him," Kazmarek said, in the superior tone of voice Nix had always hated. "Tell the *hillman* what they are. Or maybe I should?"

"Fak off, wizard," Egil said, pointing the head of one of his hammers at Kazmarek. "For all your spells and training, you're still the one in bindings who got punched in the face. By the hillman."

"Punched twice," Nix said, standing under his own power. "And even now you can't resist being a smug bunghole. I should give you a third punch. Third time being lucky and all."

"I tried to warn you," Kazmarek said. "Didn't I? *Didn't I?* But you always have to know, always have to prod, always have to learn things you can barely understand."

"In fairness he seems to know you pretty well," Egil said.

Egil poking at him made him feel more normal. "Fak off," he said, and half-grinned.

Kazmarek went on: "You still speak the Language, don't you? Don't you? But you barely understand it. It's just a tool you use to impress the fools you associate with. You just—"

Egil stepped beside Kazmarek and punched him in the face. His nose broke and blood sprayed. He groaned and sagged in his chair, semiconscious.

"I'd heard about enough," Egil said. "You?"

"Third time was lucky," Nix said. "In that it shut him the fak up. He can drown in his own snot for all I care."

Nix looked down at the book and felt a new wave of dizziness. He wobbled. Egil's hand on his biceps steadied him.

"That bad?" Egil asked.

Nix nodded. "That bad. Shite, Egil. Shite."

"We going to get around to you telling me or . . . ?"

The words rose up, eager to be spoken, but Nix swallowed them down. He couldn't tell Egil, at least not yet, and maybe not ever. Kazmarek had called the knowledge a weight, and he'd been right. Nix could not imagine anything heavier. He wasn't ready to put it on Egil's shoulders, too.

"I barely scratched the surface," Nix said, which was true, but worked as well as a lie to deflect Egil's question. "Let me learn more, understand it better."

"He told you not to," Egil said, nodding at the Grandmaster.

"Fak him," Nix said.

"Fair point," Egil said.

A buzzing sounded in Nix's ear, an itch, a sharp pain. He put a hand to his ear and exclaimed.

Egil tensed, hefted his hammers, and looked around. "What is it?"

"It's all right," Nix said, realizing what was coming. "It's Jyme."

"Jyme? What?"

"Shh," Nix said, as a monotone voice sounded in his ear.

Something big attacked the Tunnel searching for the plates and I think it can track them and is coming for you and it cannot be hurt with weapons run you fakkers.

Egil must have read his expression. "Now, what?"

"Something is coming for the plates. Jyme says we can't hurt it with weapons. He says to run. Oh, and he also called us fakkers."

Egil looked back at the archway that led into the library. "Being called fakkers I'm used to, but I'm getting a bit tired of running. You?"

Ordinarily Nix would have agreed with Egil, but given what he'd just learned, given what the plates were, he thought differently.

"Yes," he said. "But we run anyway. For now. Trust me on this, yeah? I need some time with this book. Besides, Jyme said the thing can't be hurt. He wouldn't make light about it."

"Maybe it just can't be hurt by Jyme," the priest said, raising his eyebrows and hefting his hammers.

"Maybe, but now's not the time. I need to think and plan. So let's get clear, yeah?"

Egil looked him in the face, looked over at Kazmarek, then back at Nix. "You have something in mind? Because if that thing came through the gates, we need another way out."

"Get him sensible," Nix said, indicating Kazmarek. Meanwhile, he grabbed up the book and the plates and placed them in his satchel.

A roar came from the first floor somewhere above them.

Egil pinched Kazmarek's nose, eliciting a squeal of pain and a shake of his head. He opened his eyes. His split lips parted in a pained grimace and he glared at Egil.

"You had it coming," Egil said. "All three times."

Nix bent down and put his face in the wizard's. "Whatever attacked the gates is big and can't be harmed with weapons, or so we're told. It's here and, as you said, it wants the plates. There are tunnels out of here. Where are they?"

"No," Kazmarek said. "You're not leaving."

"It's after us," Nix said. "Not you. We stay here and it will get us all. And I'll leave you tied to the chair the whole time. Maybe it will overlook you, but I'm doubtful. I heard it roar. It sounded angry. Egil?"

"Very angry."

The wizard clamped his mouth shut.

"Maybe I should break one of his knees?" Egil asked.

Another roar sounded from somewhere on the ground floor, closer this time, savage, the rumble echoing down the stairway and reverberating around the library. The book sprites flew from their perches and flitted about in fear or agitation.

"Getting close," Egil said, and laid one of his hammers over his shoulder. "And I'm getting impatient."

"I will fix this," Nix said to Kazmarek.

Kazmarek looked at him as if he'd gone mad. "You're a warren rat, Nix Fall. You'll fix what the most powerful people in history could not? You?"

"The difference is that I don't want to use them," Nix said. "I want to destroy them."

"I don't believe you. And even if I did, your understanding is that of a child. . . ."

Another roar, yet closer. Kazmarek struggled against his bonds, but Egil knew knots, and there'd be no escape unless Nix freed him.

"Time is getting short," Nix said.

Kazmarek was sweating. "For you, too."

"We're used to it," Nix said.

"Aye, that," Egil said with a sigh.

Kazmarek gritted his teeth. "They can't be destroyed. The plates, the Great Spell. They're fundamental to creation."

Nix hadn't thought of that, and he heard no lie in the Grandmaster's tone. He bit his lip, thinking. "Then I'll figure out something else. But we have to get out of here first. I have a place I can go. Where are the tunnels?"

"Let me come with you," the Grandmaster said. "We'll figure it out together. Like we should have long ago, master and student."

Egil guffawed. "No chance. No wizards. Much less you, for fak's sake."

"As the priest said," Nix said, using a tone that left no room for negotiation, "your role in this is done except to tell us where the tunnels are."

Kazmarek ground his teeth, bunched his fists, glanced back at the stairway that led down into the library, then back at Nix.

"Free me first."

Nix stared. "A way out first."

Kazmarek stared at Nix a long while. Nix saw the walls crumble. "Behind the shelves on necromancy. The smallest of the shelves pivots out. The tunnel is there. It lets out into a safe house just outside the Sward. There's no one in it. Free me now."

Nix pointed Egil to the section on necromancy, down a few tiers against the far wall. He waited while Egil sprinted over there.

"Don't use them, Nix," Kazmarek said.

Nix looked him in the face. "I won't."

"You'll be tempted."

"No, I won't." He gestured to indicate the library, the academy, all of the Conclave. "None of this ever drew me. I don't want power. I don't want anything other than . . . Hells, I don't even know. But I do know that I like who I am, what I am. I won't use it."

Kazmarek studied his face, as if looking for a lie. "I believe you, or at least believe that you believe what you're saying. So listen to me. You know now that the world is made and unmade with words. Those plates . . . those plates are a tongue of their own. The Language of Creation is just their echo."

"The tunnel's here!" Egil called from across the library. "Tight fit but it'll serve."

Nix went about loosening but not fully releasing Kazmarek's

bonds. "Work at the rope some and you'll get yourself the rest of the way."

The snarl sounded from above, a crash, as though a door were smashed in.

"I'd be quick," Nix said. He held up the cloaking shroud. "You know what this is?"

Kazmarek eyed it while he worked at the rope. "A cloaking shroud."

"Right," Nix said. "So none of your spells will get through it. So even though you spouted some pretty words, don't try anything or I'll have Egil come back here and have a conversation with you that ends in blood."

"You're making a mistake, Nix. But you don't see it, yet. I hope you do eventually."

"Goodbye, Grandmaster," Nix said, and ran for the stairs.

Before he'd gotten halfway, Kazmarek called out, "The stakes are too high for me to let you take the plates. I'm sorry, Nix."

Nix cursed himself for not killing the bastard while the Grandmaster shouted a phrase in the Language of Creation, the syntax, cadence, and some of the vocabulary beyond Nix's ability to understand clearly. The purpose, however, became immediately clear.

The book sprites flew from their shelves and tables in their multitudes. They looked like pyrotechnics going off. There had to be thousands, far more than Nix would have suspected. They gathered in a cloud and flew fast for Nix.

Nix bounded down the stairs.

"Come on!" Egil said.

"Just drop the plates, Nix!" Kazmarek called, grunting as he struggled with the knots. "I'll call them off."

"Fak you!" Nix shouted, as the book sprites swarmed him, all around, colored lights, buzzing. He could barely see through the fog of them, shining before his eyes, changing colors rapidly to confuse and blind him. He kept moving toward Egil but stumbled on the stairs, fell to his knees. Cursing, he swung the cloaking shroud in an arc before him, caught a bunch of them within its folds and at its touch their light went out for a moment and they fell to the ground. Nix jumped to his feet and kept going. He avoided stepping on them as best he could, though more than a couple crunched under his boots.

The rest continued to buzz and flit all around him, the beat of their wings a metallic buzz in his ears. Scores of them clutched at his satchel and tried to lift its flap. He smothered them in the shroud, temporarily extinguishing their glow, but the moment he did that, a dozen more pulled at his hair, poked his ears, jabbed his eyes. It was as though he were being stung by a swarm of bees. He swung the shroud around him wildly, taking the stairs as fast as he could, keeping one hand over the satchel flap to hold it closed, cursing at the sprites as he went.

"Nix!" Kazmarek shouted. He sounded like he'd moved, like maybe he'd gotten out of the bindings.

Nix swung the shroud around before him wildly, scattering sprites, downing others, but in the process the shroud got caught on something. He stumbled but held on to it, tore it free, but in the process he pulled it across the flames on one of the candelabra.

The candles were enspelled to not ignite parchment or wood, but the magic did not reach fabric and the shroud caught instantly, the flames racing along its folds.

Nix tried to shake it to put it out but that only made it worse and he almost burned himself. Several of the sprites were caught within the flames, their magic extinguished, their burned bodies falling to the ground like ash. In moments Nix was holding nothing more than a curtain of flame.

"Damn it," he said, and dropped it.

"Nix!" Kazmarek said. "Stop!"

"Come on!" Egil said.

A roar sounded from within the library, the sound deep and full of frustrated rage.

The sound startled the sprites, and they left off their attack on Nix for a moment. Nix spared a glance back, saw a hulking silhouette of a creature filling the archway that opened onto the library.

"What have you done, Nix?" Kazmarek said, and started to incant in the Language of Creation.

The sprites scattered.

The creature in the archway audibly chuffed the air, and the angle of its huge head told Nix it was looking at him. It roared and rushed into the library, toppling tables and chairs, shouting in a slobbery tone as it came.

"Thespellthespellgiveusthespell!"

"Nix!" Egil called.

Nix turned and ran the rest of the way down to Egil and the escape tunnel.

"Go," Egil said.

The tunnel, carved out of the limestone that served as the foundation for the academy, was small enough that Nix had to crawl in. For Egil it would be tight, but the priest squeezed in behind him and pulled the bookcase closed after them.

Egil said, "I think that thing is too big to fit in here after us, but let's not count on it."

"Aye," Nix said. "If that thing can get in, we're dead."

"Not without a fight," Egil said.

Veins of phosphorescent ore lit the way down the tunnel, which extended out as far as Nix could see before turning slightly. He scoot-crawled along, trying to put some distance between them and the tunnel's opening.

Behind them a thump and a crash told them that the bookcase had been torn away.

"Can you see it?" Nix said. He could turn his head but Egil blocked his view.

Egil grunted, trying to position himself to see behind them. The creature roared, a prolonged wet, slobbery growl that

Nix imagined sprayed the walls with spittle. The creature seemed able to roar and mumble and shout all at once.

"Giveusthespellthegreatspellgiveitgiveitgiveit!"

Nix kept moving, Egil right behind him.

"Move, Nix," Egil said, tension in his voice. "Faster."

The creature growled and Nix heard it slam itself into the tunnel, as if trying to squeeze its otherwise too large form into the opening. Nix heard fabric rip, something pop and snap.

"Gods," Egil said. "It's trying to shove itself through. Keep going. Keep going."

Nix did, crawling as fast as he could.

The creature's wet breathing and frustrated roars echoed off the stone. It sounded as much like a trapped animal as anything.

"Talk to me," Nix said.

"It's stuck, I think," Egil said.

"Giveitgiveitgiveit!" it screamed.

The creature's wet exhalations went silent.

"It's gone," Egil said.

"Aye," Nix said, but remembered what Jyme had told him through the enspelled parchment. "But if Jyme was right and it can sense the plates somehow, we need to hurry."

"We get out of here and what? What's next, Nix?"

"I don't know. I don't know. I need to think."

"The guild house, then," Egil said.

"Rusk isn't going to shelter us again," Nix said.

"He will," Egil said. "Or we'll burn the fakkin' place down, yeah?"

"Yeah," Nix agreed. They had nothing else. They had to get back in the guild's Vault, where presumably the creature would not be able to sense the plates. That would give Nix some time and a few moments of peace to read the rest of the book and figure out what to do next.

The Afterbirth could almost taste the remnants of the Great Spell, the spoor of it a tangible line trailing down the tunnel after the two men. The proximity of it drove him mad and his inability to pursue them drove him madder still so he stood, growling, his mouths mumbling frustrated exclamations. His body was already rebuilding itself from the damage he'd done to it trying to squeeze into the tunnel.

"Gods," said a voice, that of a man who stood near one of the tables across the library. He wore elaborate robes and tattoos colored his flesh.

The Afterbirth could smell the fear on him, the stink of it pungent even over the smell of parchment and leather and burning fabric. He took a step toward the man, another, starting up a short staircase that led toward the upper tier upon which the man stood.

"Icomecomeforthespellspell."

"The Great Spell," the man said, coiled, prepared. "Are you . . . ? What are you?"

The question halted the Afterbirth for a moment and he stared at the man, then lowered his hood, revealing his visage. The man winced and the stink of his fear intensified.

"TheAfterbirthIamtheAfterbirth."

The man took a step back, shielding himself behind the sturdy wooden table near him as though it could somehow slow the Afterbirth's approach.

"You're the leftover? From the most recent casting or an earlier one?"

The Afterbirth did not understand the question and he had delayed too long. He bounded forward, intending to leave, pick up the scent of the Great Spell, and find the two men who bore it.

"Do you remember your name?" the man asked. "You had one once, yes? Or is it many names now? I'm very curious about you. Do you understand me?"

The mention of his namenamesname stopped him again

and a word rose up out of the cacophony of voices screaming in his skull.

Ebenor.

The name rose unbidden but as quickly as he heard it the screaming drowned it out once more.

"I can't allow you to leave," the man said. "*This* is the world and it must stay that way."

The man's words made him feel a pressure inside and he screamed from all his mouths in unison. "No! Aworldaworlda-worldonlyaword."

The man swallowed, nodded knowingly, raised his hands, intertwined his fingers, and spoke words in the Language of Creation.

The Afterbirth saw how things must go, snorted, and charged at him, leaping up the short stairway, plowing through chairs and tables while the man shouted the final words of his incantation and a spiraling column of blue energy exploded outward from his palms and entwined the Afterbirth. The energy sparkled and spun around him, a cage of blue lines.

But it was a cage built of the magic of a world to which he did not belong and which could not hold him, could not damage him any more than could the weapons of this world. He lumbered through the blue lines toward the wizard, fists clenched, mouths twisted in anger.

The man retreated, eyes wide, but speaking anew the Language of Creation, his voice strained. He stumbled over a chair as he backtracked and lost the thread of this speech and fell to his rump. The stink of fear on him intensified and the Afterbirth threw aside the table that separated them, heard it crash into another table nearby, scattering a few of the glowing mote creatures that inhabited this place. He stood over the prone man and glared down, his breath a bellows, his anger a storm.

"You shouldn't *be*," the wizard said.

"IamtheAfterbirth," he said, and stomped the wizard's chest, cracking bone and crushing organs. Unsated, he stomped the corpse and stomped and stomped, all while shouting, his cries sending the glowing creatures into a frenetic swirl near the ceiling. "Thisisnotmyworldnotmyworldworldnotmine!"

By the time he was done, the wizard was a slurry of sticky cloths, bone shards, and gore. The Afterbirth hurried out of the library and out of the building and onto the grounds, his bloody footprints marking the floor as he went.

The moment he stepped outside the doors of the building, a score of voices started reciting in the Language of Creation all at once and he saw that they had been waiting for him, that they stood on the stairs that led down to the grounds, half a dozen robed figures, two holding wooden staffs, one holding a thin golden wand, all of them with their hands making arcane gestures. A curtain of flames enveloped him, a shower of magical green darts shot toward him, a triangle-in-circle formed at his feet, to what purpose he didn't know and didn't care. None of it affected him and he stormed down the stairs, pummeling the wizards as he went. His fists felled one, sent another head over heels, his head hitting pavement with a loud crack. He grabbed another before she could run and threw her into another one of the wizards farther down the stairway. They all cursed and exclaimed and tried more of their futile magic while retreating from his advance and stinking of terror. Other people clustered in huddled groups across the grounds, near the buildings, pointing, murmuring, terrified. He resisted the urge to slaughter them all because the scent of the Great Spell was fading and he needed to find the two men who carried it.

Muttering and grunting, he lurched down the rest of the stairs and lumbered across the grounds. The people cursed and shouted after him and lines of magical energy struck him and did nothing and he fled past the metal men he'd destroyed earlier and out into the park.

He had little time. The sun would rise soon. He was covered in blood and stink and soon everyone would see him and he didn't know if he'd made a mistake in daring the city but he'd been desperate and so he had come.

Nix put a dagger between his teeth and climbed a sturdy metal ladder affixed to the stone wall. At the top he listened for a moment, heard nothing, and pushed open the trapdoor. It creaked open and he poked his head up into an old root cellar lit with a glow bottle. The cellar smelled of onion and stale herbs. Shelves lined the walls, empty but for a few small tins.

"No large roaring creature," he whispered down to Egil, and hurriedly climbed the rest of the way into the cellar.

"Better than the alternative," Egil said, following after.

A short stairwell led up out of the cellar to a door. Nix drew his falchion.

Egil hefted his hammers and softly said, "Could be a wizard up there, though. Would've been nice to still have that shroud you burned, yeah?"

"It would," Nix agreed. "And I didn't burn it intentionally. And also, fak you."

Egil tried to look innocent. "I'm saying only that you traded that enspelled key to Rusk, then burned up the shroud, and I can't help but wonder if maybe you're making things harder on purpose."

"Bah," Nix said, doing his best Egil imitation. "Partnering with you makes it hard enough and that's truth. And also fak you."

"You already said as much."

"It warranted repetition."

"Fair enough," Egil said with a grin. "You ready?"

"Aye."

The priest led the way up. He checked the latch, nodded to indicate that the door was not locked. They shared another nod and Egil threw it open and burst through.

They rushed up into a small dark room, found it empty save for some entirely ordinary-looking furniture—a cabinet, a couple of wooden chairs. The fireplace was dark and cold, though a small pile of wood was stacked near it. Another two small rooms adjoined the central room, both likewise dark. Nix checked them both quickly and found only pallets for sleeping. There was no one there and it looked like there hadn't been anyone there in a long while.

"Just a safe house," he said.

"Wizard hidey-hole, anyway," Egil said.

Nix opened the shutters on one of the small windows. It opened onto a narrow, deserted street that could barely have accommodated a wagon. Nix surmised they were in the cluster of buildings northwest of the Sward. Nix saw no candles or lanterns burning in any of the nearby buildings and all the shutters were closed. Probably the Conclave, through agents, owned most if not all of the buildings around and used them as a buffer for the safe house.

Nix looked out on the dark, knowing the creature would be after them, knowing Kerfallen's agents would be after them, too. For the first time, Dur Follin felt very small to Nix.

"We should go," he said to Egil.

"Aye," Egil said. "Let's hope Rusk is in a good mood."

"Hells, I hope he's awake."

Before they exited the building, Egil took Nix by the shoulder and pulled him to a stop.

"You going to tell me? What's in that book? What you meant by 'worlds'?"

Nix had, for just a moment, forgotten the plates, the Great Spell, and what it all meant. Egil's question brought the weight of the knowledge back down on him. He shook his head and did not look his friend in the face. "No."

"No?"

"No."

"Why?"

Nix considered lying, but thought better of it. Egil was his brother. "Because I'm concerned about what it might do to you. Because at this point you don't need to know."

Egil's eyebrows almost touched as he frowned. "How do you mean?"

"I mean . . ." Nix made a gesture of futility with his hand. "Egil, I don't know how to handle this myself. I'm still working on it. But you, with your penchant for brooding and melancholy . . ."

"Fak you," Egil said. "Tell me right now."

Nix could think of no way to tell Egil that everything the priest believed was wrong, was built on a lie, so he delayed.

"When we get to the Vault, if you still want to know, I'll tell you. I need to read more, like I said before, to make sure I understand everything, yeah?"

Skepticism narrowed Egil's eyes. "Yeah."

"Let's get moving," Nix said, turning his mind to the immediate matter.

They exited the building to the street and headed for Mandin's Way and the guild house. They were going as beggars to Rusk but Nix could think of no other place to go. He needed some time in a secure place.

Since they had enemies before and behind, they opted for speed over stealth, sprinting along the street while there was still enough darkness to hide them. They kept alert for any sign of Kerfallen's automatons or the creature.

With every block they covered, it seemed the burgeoning dawn ate more stars, lifting night's shroud and exposing them to discovery. Nix imagined the hulking creature somewhere behind them, sniffing the air, lumbering down the streets after them. Distracted, he came around a corner too fast and nearly crashed into a surprised-looking dungsweeper who pulled his donkey to a halt. The sweeper's eyes went to the blade Nix had in hand.

"I got no coin," he said.

Nix tried to look harmless. "Sorry for the start," he said, and they hurried on. Nix's mind was on the creature, a creature seemingly impervious to weapons, and it wanted the plates.

Why?

It would use them, he supposed. The same as they'd been used before. But to what end? What would a creature like that want with the most powerful magic in the world?

Lost in thought, he failed to realize that Egil had stopped and was peering around a corner. The priest stopped him with a raised arm before he went past.

"What are—"

"Shh," Egil said, and nodded down the street.

Nix glanced around the corner. Two blocks down he saw it—a cloaked figure too tall and too stiff in its movements to be a man. One of Kerfallen's constructs, and it was coming toward them.

"Wizard must have divined our general location," Egil said.

"Aye," Nix said. "We keep moving and at least he won't be able to pin us down. Those things can't climb. We should go up."

"Aye," Egil said.

They retreated a bit down the block, ducked down an alley, and started up the wall of a two-story building. Both were skilled climbers and they'd soon gained the roof, a flat, tiled affair. Their presence startled a few terns that nested near one of the building's chimneys. They cawed but didn't fly off—stubborn creatures. The night's wind stirred Nix's hair.

Nix dropped to his belly and scooted to the edge of the roof. The automaton stood on the street below, looking about in its deliberate, mechanical fashion. Nix glanced up and down the street, saw a horse-drawn wagon a block down. He looked back toward the Sward and the Conclave, but saw nothing except a jagged skyline of roofs and chimneys. No sign of the creature. He slipped back away from the edge.

"Automaton's right down there," he said to Egil.

"And where there's one . . ." Egil said.

"Aye. Let's put another block or two behind us and take another look."

Moving quietly and quickly, they traversed the Thieves' Highway: controlled slides down steeply pitched roofs, leaps across alleys, sprints across flat roofs.

Twice the gaps between buildings proved too far and they had to descend to street level before climbing again and renewing their trek. Nix did not like how long it was taking to get across town.

They jumped an alley, hit the tiled roof of the building on the other side, and got low. They moved to the edge of the roof and looked down. The sound of someone running carried up from the street, the sound loud in the predawn silence.

"There," Egil said, nodding up the street.

A figure turned the corner and ran down the street at a full sprint. The blade at his belt bounced with each stride.

"Is that . . . Jyme?" Nix asked, leaning out a bit and squinting.

The figure got closer, but it was hard to tell if it was actually Jyme or just some slubber.

Egil craned his neck. "I think it is."

"Came to save us," Nix said. "On his way to the Conclave, no doubt."

"Best hold him up lest he bump into the creature."

Nix cupped a hand over his mouth. "Jyme!"

He showed no sign of having heard so Egil whistled, the sound sharp and piercing in the night's quiet.

Jyme skidded to a halt, gasping, and glanced all around, his body tense, his hand on his blade.

"Up here," Egil said.

Jyme looked at the roofs on the other side of the street.

"Over here, Jyme," Nix said. "Gods, man. Listen, just turn around and run the other fakkin' way."

Jyme looked up, peering at the roof. He spoke between breaths. "What? No, I was looking for you two. You got my message, yeah? Did you see that creature? Gadd and me hacked it to pieces but off it strolled still. Did it get the plates?"

"Quiet," Nix said, looking up and down the street. "Both that creature and Kerfallen's agents are still after us. Like I said, you turn around and head back. We have somewhere to be. No, wait! You and Gadd fought that thing? Anyone get hurt at the Tunnel? Tesha?"

Jyme walked toward the base of the building. "Gadd got a beating put on him. But I think he'll be all right. Tesha sent for a healer. And I ain't going back."

Nix was relieved to know Tesha was all right. He went on: "Jyme, we credit you for coming to help, especially after you faced that creature. But we have a plan—"

"We do?" Egil said. "Since when?"

"We do," Nix continued. "So go back to the Tunnel as fast as you can and just lay low. Keep an eye on things as before."

Jyme shook his head and his tone sharpened. "No. I ain't running and guard duty is past and done. I'm coming with you two, now. We had a deal and I kept my end."

"He has a point," Egil said.

"No, he doesn't," Nix said. "And you're not thinking sensibly, priest. Nor you, Jyme. Now go back. We don't have time for this."

Jyme pointed his blade up at them. "Fak you, Nix Fall. I already told you I'm coming. I'll walk along down here if that's what I have to do. You think you could lose me?"

"I'm certain of it," Nix said.

"Well, you're wrong," Jyme answered. "And maybe I'll bump into that creature or a construct and then what?"

Nix blew out a frustrated sigh. He thought about the Great Spell. "You don't know what you'd be getting into here, Jyme."

"Neither do you, I'd wager," Jyme said. "The past bein' any teacher."

"He makes another point," Egil said.

Nix glared at the priest. "Will you shut up? You don't know what you're talking about."

"Because you won't tell me, is why."

"For good reason," Nix snapped, then said softly, "This will get very serious very soon, Egil. Even more than it is right now. We want Jyme in for that? Can he handle it?"

"I don't know," Egil said, looking Nix in the eyes. "Can we?"

"And now *you* make a point. Well enough, then." He looked down at the street. "Can you fakkin' climb, Jyme?"

Jyme sheathed his blade. "Can I climb? Better'n you, likely."

Jyme put his hands on the side of the building, felt for purchase, and started to ascend. He used a windowsill, protruding stone, a shutter, and soon reached the roof. Nix allowed he'd climbed with skill.

Egil said, "Where'd you learn that?"

Jyme's thin face was red with the effort of running and climbing. He had a wheeze, too, Nix thought.

"I had a life before the Watch and before going hiresword," Jyme said. "I climbed the Shelf once on a drinking dare. You two don't have the sum of me. You just think you do."

"Well, we don't think that anymore," Nix said, and thumped him on the shoulder. "Or if we do, we think you sum to more than we once thought. Let's go. Try to keep up."

"Where are we going?"

"The guild house," Nix said.

"As in the Thieves' guild? Channis's guild?"

"Rusk's guild now," Egil said.

"I'm gonna ask why," Jyme said. "Knowing a clear answer won't be had."

"Safe haven," Nix said.

Jyme sniffed, rubbed at his chest as though he were hurt there. "That's not the first place I think of when I think of safe havens."

"Look there, Egil," Nix said. "Jyme's still funny."

Egil nodded. "And he can climb. Like he said, we don't have the sum of him."

"That's right," Jyme said, a hint of defiance in his tone. "You don't."

CHAPTER EIGHT

Half a dozen times as they moved toward the Dock Ward they caught sight of Kerfallen's automatons on the street below, the creatures moving in silent pairs or threes, their lurching gait easy to spot from afar. The constructs moved along, heads swiveling side to side as they followed whatever instructions Kerfallen had given them for scouring the city. Nix, periodically checking the street below, diverted around the creatures.

After a few more encounters, they sheltered behind a double chimney atop some merchant's shop and took stock. They weren't far from Mandin's Way.

Jyme wiped sweat from his brow with the bottom of his shirt. When he did, Nix saw the ugly discoloration on his chest.

"Those ribs broken, Jyme?" Nix asked. "I've got healing elixirs."

"What? No," Jyme said. "Just badly bruised. Creature gave me a blow. I'm fine." He nodded down at the street. "Wizard got an army of those automatons? How many have we seen now?"

"Plenty," Nix said, thinking.

Egil tapped a finger on the brick of the chimney. "You seeing it?" he said to Nix. "Thinking what I am?"

Jyme looked puzzled. "Seeing what?"

Nix nodded. He'd been thinking as much the last few blocks. "I see it. Shite."

"Seeing *what*?" Jyme asked again.

Nix pointed down at the street with his chin. "We're *supposed* to see those automatons. Kerfallen knows they can't catch us, not unless we're cornered, which isn't going to happen. And that's why they aren't really looking for us. They're there to be seen. They're steering us."

Jyme cursed. "Like fakkin' pigs to slaughter?"

"Aye," Egil said, lips pursed. "That'll be an apt analogy if the wizard has his way."

"Apt for you and Jyme, maybe," Nix said, looking up at the stars and thinking. "I'm too pretty to be likened to a pig."

"So you say," Egil said.

Nix grinned. "I'm thinking Kerfallen must have figured that we holed up at the guild house the first time. He probably had us by way of a divination, then lost us while we sat in the Vault."

"Makes sense he would," Egil said. "Little fakker is clever. Remember that bit with the Night Blade?"

Nix nodded. He remembered quite well.

"He'll be waiting for us, then," Egil said.

"Aye," Nix agreed.

Jyme looked from Egil to Nix. "Wait, so the wizard is waiting for us?"

Nix sighed ruefully, more for effect than out of conviction. "You've gotta stop asking so many questions, Jyme. Makes you sound slow. Just nod, like you're following along, and things will come to you."

"Fak you," Jyme said, rubbing his whiskers with the back of his hand.

"That'll do as well," Nix said, grinning at him. "I'm jesting anyway. Egil and I have been doing this so long I usually know what he's thinking and him likewise as to me. You'll catch on."

Egil exhaled and ran his palm over the tattoo of Ebenor on his head. "Well, the creature's behind us, no doubt hard on the scent of those plates. And the wizard stands between us and the guild house."

"Staying awhile next to a chimney is starting to sound good," Jyme said.

"Still funny," Egil said to him. "I like it."

Nix said, "No, Kerfallen fakked up. He should have just let us get to the Vault and came at us then. But now we know he knows."

"So we deal with him before we hole up," Jyme said.

"That's following along," Nix said, pointing a finger at Jyme. "We have to. We get in the Vault without handling him first and he'll come at the guild house while we're locked up."

"And Rusk's boys can't stop a wizard," Egil said.

"And we'll be a gift in a box," Jyme said.

"No choice, then," Egil said, putting a hand on the head of one of his hammers.

"Aye. Only one thing to do," Nix said. He looked at Jyme expectantly, eyebrows raised.

Jyme cleared his throat, visibly thinking things through. "We go at the wizard right now?"

Nix smiled and nodded. "Get rid of that questioning tone, Jyme. Aye. We go at the wizard right now. We clear him, then we hole up from the creature as planned."

"Shite," Jyme said, blowing out a long breath. "Going at a wizard."

Egil thumped him hard on the back. "This is when it gets fun, Jyme."

"Fun is what you call it?" Jyme said. "You didn't see that creature back at the Tunnel."

"No," Nix said. "We saw it at the Conclave. And we've seen a few other things in our day."

Jyme looked sheepish. "Aye, I just . . ."

"Forget it," Nix said with a chuckle. He knew they had little time to spare, not with the creature coming up from behind. "So here's what we do. Instead of avoiding the automatons and getting steered into an ambush, we instead follow them the rest of the way to Mandin's Way. That'll bring us out somewhere other than where Kerfallen wants us to come out."

"Then we ambush *him*," Jyme said.

Nix shook his head. "Would be nice, but no. Likely he'll find us soon after and come for us."

Jyme scratched his head. "I thought we were coming for him?"

"Either, or," Egil said, his tone casual. "The point is to not walk into his ambush. But he's a wizard and a clever one, and he'll realize his plan went sidewise. Then he'll find us, and then we'll fight."

Jyme digested the words. "Think he has more of those flying creatures you mentioned, from back in the Tunnel?"

Nix had wondered the same thing. He figured it was possible the flying constructs could only function for a short time before consuming the magic that powered them, which might explain why they'd been thrown into the Tunnel in ball form rather than flying in. It would also explain why the three of them hadn't yet been attacked from above.

"Likely he does," Nix said. "And we may see them yet. You get turned to stone and we'll make you part of a nice fountain, yeah? Stand you next to that other slubber behind the Tunnel. The girls will tsk over you."

Jyme grinned. "Just don't let the birds shit on me."

"That's the spirit," Egil said.

"You want to pray or something?" Nix said to Egil, and winked.

Egil made his face grow somber.

Jyme closed his eyes. Nix tried not to laugh.

"Momentary God, we pray that we kill this fakking wizard

before that creature catches up with us and we pray that Jyme doesn't get shit on by birds after he's turned to stone."

Jyme opened an eye and guffawed.

"Well prayed," Nix said, hoping their jests helped put Jyme at ease. "Let's go."

They moved across Dur Follin's rooftops at a rapid pace, jumping, climbing, balancing, hoping to outrun any premature realization by Kerfallen that they wouldn't fall into his trap. As they went, Nix poked his head over the side of buildings and surveyed the street below for Kerfallen's creatures. He spotted them regularly and easily and used them as stepping-stones for their path.

"We could destroy a few as we go," Jyme said.

Crouched near the end of a flat roof, with a balcony right below them, Egil said, "He's connected to them somehow. We kill one and he'll know where we are."

"And then he'll know that we're not following his path," Nix said. "Keep moving."

The river put its smell in the air as they closed on Mandin's Way. Ool's clock rose high into the sky to their right. From the roofs they could see the Archbridge, the dark line of the river. They bounded across an alley onto the steeply pitched roof of a decrepit, two-story alehouse called the Dark Hole. Nix knew that the proprietor, a one-armed former sailor named Cobert Black, was a deadeye with a hand crossbow and had the reputation of shooting first and cleaning up the mess after.

"Soft tread and quiet voices here," Nix said to Jyme and Egil.

Egil nodded. "Cobert keeps late hours and if he found us on his roof he'd shoot us by way of a hail."

"We're past late and on into early," Jyme said.

Nix said to Egil, "You know, I looked for you here not a night past."

"Don't know why you would," Egil said. "Cobert's ale is shite and I don't drink shite ale. Also, that seems not a night past but a life ago."

"Aye, that," Nix said, thinking of all that happened and what he'd learned from the plates. He pushed it from his mind. Time for that later.

"We going or talking?" Jyme asked.

"Going," Nix said. They were just a few blocks from Mandin's Way. "Listen, both of you. No one can get these plates. Understood?"

Jyme nodded. Egil nodded, too, but absently. He was looking off into the sky. His heavy brow furrowed. "You've better eyes than me. What is that?"

Nix followed Egil's gaze. "That's a wizard," he said. "A flying wizard."

Kerfallen was flying toward them, bobbing through the night sky like some ridiculous bird. He wore a vestlike apparatus from which sprouted straps and harnesses by which a dozen or so of his flying metallic constructs held him aloft. Another score or two of the flying metal creatures buzzed in the air around him in a cloud. He held a short, gnarled wooden staff in his hand. He looked like a puppet.

Egil put his hands to his hammers. "We need to get down from here."

The wizard was closing fast. He'd seen them. The constructs whirled around him, as though in excitement or agitation.

"Here we go, Jyme," Nix said. He pulled out his sling and dropped a lead bullet into the pouch.

Kerfallen shouted at them, his voice strikingly deep for a man of his stature. "I credit you for cleverness in avoiding my ambush. But this is over now. Give me the plates."

While Nix formulated a reply, Jyme unslung his crossbow, cocked, and fired at Kerfallen with impressive rapidity. The bolt flew true and would have struck the wizard in the chest, but one of the creatures in the cloud of constructs flitting about his person intercepted it, allowing the bolt to strike it instead and falling from the sky.

Nix followed Jyme's lead, spun his sling, and let fly with a sling bullet and another one of the creatures interposed itself in the path of the ball, took the impact, and fell to earth. Kerfallen, carried aloft like a marionette by his creatures, his feet dangling, looked like he was hopping across the sky.

"Like Egil said, we should get down," Nix said. "Move."

But they were too slow. Kerfallen pointed his staff, shouted a single word in the Language of Creation, and a swirling, twisting column of green-veined black energy flew from its end toward them, the column shaped like a serpent, jaws wide, fangs tipped in a radiant, sickly green.

They cursed as one and dove over the peak of the roof, sliding down the far side, their boots knocking free tiles, as above them the energy struck the roof, exploding tiles and splintering the bricks of the chimney. The force of the blast accelerated their slide into a fall and Nix careened toward the far edge of the roof. He spun as he fell, unable to arrest his descent, and reached out blindly as he went over the edge.

His hand closed on Egil, catching the priest by the forearm, even as Jyme, likewise going over the side of the building, reached out and grabbed hold of Nix by the wrist and shirt. Buttons sprang loose and fell down to the alley below but the two of them jarred to a stop, hanging in space, the abrupt halt wrenching Nix's arm. The priest gripped the edge of the roof with one hand and held the two of them in the other. Egil growled with the effort to hang on. Nix did the same with Jyme.

"My grip's slipping!" Jyme said, gripping more tightly on Nix's shirt.

Nix could hear the buzz of the wizard's constructs. They were coming.

"Egil!" he said, his words strained, his arms stretched between Jyme and the priest.

"Right," Egil said. "Like a pendulum now."

Without waiting for a response, Egil grunted with effort and swung his arm to one side, then back again, then forward once more, all the while the three of them struggling to keep their holds. The swing of Egil's arm got Jyme close enough to the roof's edge that he let go of Nix, caught himself on the edge, and started to pull himself back onto the roof. Nix planted his feet on a windowsill and flattened himself against the wall. Egil, no longer bearing the weight of his two companions, slid over the side of the roof and started to move down the building. Nix couldn't see Kerfallen and couldn't have done anything even if he did. He needed to get to the ground.

"Shite," Jyme said, seeing something Nix couldn't. Jyme scrabbled over the side of the roof just as another blast from the wizard's staff sent a shower of tiles and debris over the side. Chunks of tiles struck Nix in the head and hands but he held his grip. The blast caused Jyme's boots to slip off the wall and he started to slide down the face of the building, between Egil and Nix, shouting, but he somehow caught himself on a shutter after only a short distance. The shutter opened and came off its top hinge but Jyme held on and swung back onto the wall to get a better grip.

"Gods!" Jyme exclaimed.

"The man said he could climb," Egil said, moving down the face of the building as fast as he could.

"Move!" Nix said, his own descent more like a controlled fall than a climb.

A voice carried from the alley below and Nix looked down to see Cobert standing there in a long, ratty nightshirt. He held a small crossbow in one hand and had it aimed up at them.

"What's this now but three bastards climbing my establishment and wrecking my place and needing a shot of this crossbow is what."

Nix didn't slow his descent and neither did Jyme or Egil. Jyme was almost down.

As he descended, the priest half-shouted, half-growled, "If you fire that fakkin' crossbow, Cobert, I will shove it so far up your arse that the only thing you'll say for the rest of your fakkin' days is 'twang'! You hear me?"

Nix added his own shout. "Also a wizard is about to appear over your roofline and it's him who's actually ruining your place! We would not take it amiss were you to shoot him in the face. Oh, and those are his creatures lurking up the alley there."

Cobert turned to look at the mouth of the alley, where eight or so of Kerfallen's tall, lumbering automatons had gathered. The constructs stood there, still and ominous, as if awaiting instructions.

Jyme hit the ground a few strides away from Cobert but the old pirate barely seemed to notice him. He looked down the alley at the automatons and back up at Nix. "Fak you boys, is what. I ain't even ate breakfast yet. Don't destroy my place no more!"

With that he darted back inside his building, no doubt barring the door behind him. Jyme unslung his crossbow again and nocked a bolt.

"You can end all this without harm," Kerfallen called down from above.

"Harm to whom, fakker," Nix muttered, and let himself drop the rest of the way to the alley. Egil did the same. Jyme fired at the automatons, striking one in the chest, but doing it no noticeable harm. It did not respond.

Kerfallen came into view against the slit of night sky visible through the gap in the buildings that formed the alley. They flattened themselves against the walls.

"We need to get him down here," Nix said.

"Yeah," Egil said.

"Look," Jyme said, and pointed. They saw movement at the opposite end of the alley, automatons gathering on that side, too. They were blocked in on either side and couldn't go up. But Nix saw something else. Down the alley toward the automatons they'd just spotted, the buildings leaned so closely together that they almost created a tunnel, and it went on for twenty paces. They'd have some shelter from Kerfallen there.

"We need to pick a side and rush the creatures," Egil said. "Break out. Maybe hit the sewers."

"I have a better idea," Nix said, nodding. "Let's just get in the lee of those buildings and stop. He'll have to come down a bit, then I'll get him all the way down. Come on."

Without waiting for assent, Nix sprinted down the alley and Jyme and Egil followed. Kerfallen's voice carried down from the sky, shouting in the Language of Creation, and a wide cone of green-veined black energy flew down toward them, engulfed the entirety of the alley. The cloud stank of rot, and voices whispered in it, repeating a phrase over and over, the words mumbles that Nix could not quite make out.

Nix's body went cold, the vitality draining out of him. He stumbled, his body nearly numb. Beside him, Egil and Jyme groaned and staggered. Jyme went to all fours, retched onto the ground. Egil grabbed him by the back of his shirt and half-lifted, half-dragged him toward the tunnel of buildings.

Nix plodded on, each step a labor, until all three stood under the sheltering roofs of the dilapidated buildings, shivering and cold.

"Good?" Nix asked.

Jyme nodded, spitting away the taste of vomit.

"Good," Egil said, hefting his hammers and eyeing the automatons. "What the Hells was that?"

"Wizard shite," Nix said. "More comin', no doubt. Listen, I'm going to clear a hole in those constructs around Kerfallen. You get ready to throw and you to shoot, yeah?"

Nods from both Egil and Jyme.

"Do it quick, Nix," the priest said.

From each side of the alley, the automatons started advancing at last, their dead eyes fixed on the three of them.

Nix scrabbled in the dirt of the alley, collecting a handful of pebbles. When he had a fistful, he said, "Get ready. Follow me out and be ready to shoot. Don't fakkin' miss."

"Do it," Jyme said. He bounced on the balls of his feet, his crossbow at the ready.

Nix yelled out, "Leave or I'll destroy the plates, Kerfallen!"

The wizard's laugh answered Nix's idle threat. "They can't be destroyed, you imbecile! They're fundamental! They are forever, existing to tempt us!"

The wizard's voice gave Nix an idea of where he was in the air, so he darted out from the protection of the tunnel of buildings, Jyme and Egil on his heels. The moment he could see sky, he saw Kerfallen. The wizard hovered low over the alley, surrounded by the cloud of his constructs, at a height slightly below the roofline of Cobert's place. The moment he saw them Kerfallen's face twisted into a leering smile. He leveled his staff; the automatons coming down the alley broke into a stiff run.

Nix threw the stones as hard as he could at the wizard. As he'd hoped, the constructs protecting Kerfallen from missile fire were unthinking, and therefore unable to distinguish between a projectile that presented danger and one that didn't, and they reacted quickly. They flitted and darted here and there to block the pebbles, and their occupation with the stones opened Kerfallen up to Jyme and Egil.

Egil roared and hurled his hammer. Jyme's crossbow sang.

Nix grinned at the sight of Kerfallen's surprised gawp, but his smile disappeared when the crossbow bolt struck the wizard in the chest and deflected away, the shaft splintering under the impact. Egil's hammer, meanwhile, struck Kerfallen in the head and rang off so hard it sounded like a gong. The wizard's head should have been pulped, his heart skewered by Jyme's bolt, but he appeared unharmed.

Still, the impact of Egil's blow knocked him backward and the abrupt movement caused a few of the constructs holding him aloft to lose their grip on his straps. He dangled there for a moment, a marionette with broken strings, before spiraling toward the ground, the attempts of the remaining constructs to keep him airborne made futile.

"He's either warded against steel or a construct himself," Nix said and ran for the downed wizard. "I have him! Destroy those automatons!"

"Aye, that," Egil said, and charged in one direction at the advancing constructs. Jyme joined him, their shouts echoing off the walls of the alley.

Before Nix could reach the wizard, Kerfallen, on his rump on the ground, spoke a word and the small flying constructs swarmed toward Nix. He slashed and stabbed as he ran, slapped at them with his free hand, and did not slow his advance. His blade knocked one of the insectoid creatures from the air, another, but there were so many that he couldn't avoid them all. One slammed into his head, opening a gash that leaked blood down the side of his face. Others locked into his flesh, one biting him in the arm, another in the back, another in the shoulder. He cursed, fearing they would transform him to stone or worse, and smacked them frantically away.

Kerfallen stood and pointed his staff at Nix.

Nix lunged the final few paces between them and slashed with his falchion, not at Kerfallen, since he knew his blade wouldn't hurt the wizard, but at the staff. His blow knocked the staff out of the wizard's hand. Kerfallen cursed, bent down to get it, but Nix grabbed him by his robes and flung him hard against the side of the building. The impact sounded like metal hitting stone, but the wizard bounced off the wall like a sling bullet, unharmed, and reached for something in his robes as he said, "The bag at his side! Take it!"

One of the constructs bit Nix on the arm. He cursed, slapped it to the ground, and stomped it into the earth with his boot. And that gave him an idea.

The remaining constructs, heeding Kerfallen's order, went for Nix's satchel, their claws and teeth clutching at the flap.

Nix slashed with his falchion, knocking another from the air, but half a score latched on to the bag and tried to lift it away.

Cursing, Nix tucked it under his armpit and held on as tight as he could. Meanwhile, Kerfallen withdrew from his robes a thin stick of ivory or bone and started uttering a phrase in the Language of Creation.

Desperate, Nix, still holding his satchel with one hand and arm against the pull of the metal constructs, lowered his shoulder and charged, slamming into the dwarf wizard and again driving him hard against the wall. The blow did no harm but at least knocked Kerfallen backward and fouled whatever incantation the wizard had intended. He dropped the wand and Nix ground it underfoot while using his greater weight to keep the wizard pressed against the wall.

"Egil!" Nix called over his shoulder.

Jyme and Egil waded into the dozen or so of Kerfallen's automatons. The creatures came at them from both directions. The constructs, slow-moving, ponderous creatures, grabbed for them, tried to overwhelm them by sheer force of weight and numbers. Their fists rose and fell, one of them striking Jyme in the shoulder and causing his arm to go numb. He stabbed the creature through the midsection, his blade grating against metal and wood and whatever else the wizard had built them from.

As the automaton started to fall, he jerked the blade free and crosscut the head from another. A hand closed on his biceps and squeezed, sending a shock of pain along the length of Jyme's arm. He cursed, kicked at the automaton, but the thing was so heavy the kick barely registered. He twisted in the creature's grasp and stabbed it through the face. It fell but another one struck him in the back, knocking the wind from him and driving him into the reach of another, which tried to punch in his skull. Jyme ducked under the blow, spun, and slashed weakly at the creature as he backed off.

Not far from him Egil's remaining hammer rose and fell in a destructive two-handed rhythm that crushed chests and heads and put a shattered automaton on the ground with each blow. The priest roared or grunted with each strike, ignoring the blows of the creatures that struck him while his hammer reaped them one after another.

Nix's shout from behind them brought Egil up short. He kicked an automaton away from him—his kick actually moved the thing backward—and looked over at Jyme. A vicious bruise had already risen above Egil's left eye.

"Finish them," the priest said, then turned and ran back toward Nix and Kerfallen.

Jyme stabbed another automaton through the chest and twisted the blade to scramble whatever composed the thing's innards. A hand closed on his free shoulder, squeezed and pulled him toward it. A fist struck him above the right ear and sparks exploded behind his eyes. He managed to keep a grip on his blade as he staggered. He pulled the weapon free of the construct he'd stabbed and as he did he lashed out blindly with a hilt. The pommel struck the face of the automaton that had punched him. It seemed to stall for a moment, and Jyme took the opportunity to run his sword through its chest.

He backed off, gasping, trying to reorient himself, as the remaining few continued their relentless advance, arms outstretched.

Nix, still struggling to hold on to his satchel, heard Egil's heavy strides and slid to the side when he deemed the priest within striking range, clearing the way to Kerfallen. Egil swung his hammer and it rang off the wizard's head so hard it sounded like Ool's clock striking the first hour. Egil's arm vibrated under the impact and the blow knocked the wizard head over heels, but did not seem to otherwise harm him. Down on all fours, Kerfallen scrabbled in the dirt for the wand he'd lost.

"He's warded against weapons, Egil," Nix said, hugging the satchel to his chest and trying to twist and turn away from the buzzing constructs. "Don't let him get his wand back!"

Egil dropped his hammer, grabbed Kerfallen by the shoulders, and heaved him up. The wizard started to say something in the Language of Creation but Egil hurled him against the side of the building. Bricks cracked and the wizard's warded frame bounced off the wall to land again at Egil's feet.

"Kill them, my creatures!" Kerfallen said.

The constructs left off pulling at Nix's satchel and attacked him outright, biting his hands, and trying to sting his eyes. He careened backward, waving his falchion and free hand before his face. Egil bellowed, no doubt similarly afflicted.

"I'll have the plates one way or another!" Kerfallen shouted, then began to intone in the Language of Creation.

"Weapons can't hurt him but he has to breathe!" Nix shouted. He knocked one of the constructs to the ground, screamed as one tore a finger out of joint and opened a gash to the bone. But Egil heard and understood. The priest ignored the tiny creatures attacking him, enduring their bites and stings, and charged Kerfallen. The wizard's incantation died on his lips as Egil drove him to the ground, forced him over, and shoved his face into the soil. The wizard scrambled, temporarily slipped his head free of Egil's grip, turned his dirt-caked face sideways, and screamed, "Kill this one!"

Every flying construct still remaining buzzed toward Egil. The priest ignored them and forced Kerfallen's face back into the dirt. The little wizard kicked and squirmed in Egil's grasp. In moments half a dozen or more of the creatures were latched on to Egil's arms and hands, with another dozen or so seeking purchase.

The priest had the wizard down, straddling him from the back, driving his face into the earth with both hands, trying to suffocate him in the dirt. Kerfallen's small body spasmed, the hands forming fists, pounding the earth, the legs kicking.

Nix slashed at the creatures attacking Egil, slapped one off the priest's back, stomped it with his boot. "Jyme! Over here!"

Jyme had gutted the last automaton and ran to help. Fatigue caused him to stumble but he kept his feet and slashed as soon as he was within reach, though he hit none of the creatures.

"Help me keep them at bay, Jyme!" Nix said, knocking another off Egil's shoulder with the hilt of his sword and stomping it.

"Easy to fakkin' say!" Jyme said, cursing. He swung his sword left, right, crosscut, finally struck one of the creatures, and sent it spinning to the ground, fluttering.

Nix did similarly, swinging his falchion in one hand, drawing his dagger in the other, and spinning, slashing, trying to keep the creatures off Egil. The creatures were all around him, their wings a metallic buzz, a swarm of biting iron insects.

Another one of the creatures latched on to Egil, bit through his shirt, and tore into his flesh. The priest cursed but did not try to shake it off, enduring the pain to keep the wizard down. Nix slammed the hilt of his dagger into the buzzing construct, knocking it loose, revealing a bloody gash in Egil's skin. Another latched on to Egil's calf, his shoulder, his back. He was bleeding from multiple wounds, his clothing getting soaked with blood, but still he held on to Kerfallen. Somehow the wizard was still alive.

Cursing, Nix dropped to the ground and covered Egil's hands with his own, lending his strength to drive Kerfallen's face into the earth.

"Keep them off, Jyme!" Nix said.

Egil grunted, leaning all his weight onto the wizard, pressing his face several fingers' width deep into the ground. Nix did the same, teeth gritted. Had the wizard not had wards to protect him from physical harm, Nix had no doubt his neck would already have snapped from the force they were applying.

"Will. You. Just. Fakking. Die," Nix said.

Jyme, slashing and cursing, gasping with fatigue, stood over them, swinging and chopping and kicking and cursing, downing several of the creatures. He knocked one off Egil's back but before he could stomp it, it fluttered its wings, took back to the air, and slammed itself into Egil's temple. The priest's grip did not lessen. He shook the bucket of his skull and did not relent.

Kerfallen's legs kicked and his entire body spasmed.

"Die, damn it!" Nix said.

And then, finally, Kerfallen went still. The moment he did all of the automatons went inert and fell to the earth like leaves from a tree, those falling off Egil leaving bloody gouges and gashes in their wake. Jyme stomped them as fast as he could, bending or snapping wings and bodies.

Egil did not let up his grip, but drove Kerfallen's face into the ground awhile longer, just to make sure.

"He's done," Nix said. He released the wizard and stood on weak legs.

"Aye," Egil said, breathing hard. He let the wizard's head go and started to stand, but fell to his knees, bloody and gashed. Jyme sagged to the ground beside him, his face blotchy, out of breath.

Nix knew they had little time to recover. He quickly rummaged in his satchel, his gaze lingering for a moment on the plates, before he grabbed the only three healing elixirs he still had, each contained in a stoppered metal vial, and tossed one each to Egil and Jyme.

"Put it straight on the wounds. A little goes a long way, so don't bathe in it." He nodded at Kerfallen's corpse. "And seeing that Kerfallen was my source for these, these last three may be it for a while."

"Obliged, wizard," Jyme said, nodding at Kerfallen's corpse. He bit the stopper off the top of the vial.

Egil and Nix did the same and the three of them carefully poured drops of the oily red liquid onto their wounds. Nix winced; Jyme gasped. The elixir burned like a brand where it touched blood and bruised flesh and cracked or displaced bones, but the magic accelerated healing and the holes and slashes and bruises knit closed and healed, even Nix's displaced finger.

"Around your eye, too," he said to Egil, and the priest smeared some onto his face.

When the elixir was gone and they seemed as well as they were going to get, Nix said, "Two wizards in one night. That's a first."

"Gonna get a reputation," Egil said. He stood and tilted his head from side to side to crack his neck. He removed his blood-soaked shirt, revealing the scarred, hairy, muscular terrain of his torso. "Thieves' Guild now, I suppose."

"Aye," Nix said, thinking about the creature that was still on their trail. "And quick, I'd say."

Jyme looked around the alley at the pile of tall humanoid automatons, the flying insectoid constructs, the wizard's corpse. "Watch'll have a time figuring this."

"Not the first time we've left them a mess to clean," Egil said. He gathered his hammers, placed them in the loops at his belt. "Let's go."

They hurried out of the alley, scanned the street to either side, saw nothing, and hurried on.

CHAPTER NINE

Egil, Nix, and Jyme stayed at street level, dodging the dung-sweepers, drunks, and fishermen as best they could as they traversed the final stretch toward Mandin's Way. Nix felt something building in him as they moved, a dread that put a hole in his stomach. He almost hoped Rusk refused them. He feared opening the book again. He had to learn more, but what he'd learned already was almost too much to carry. While they'd been fleeing across the city and fighting Kerfallen and his creatures, he hadn't had time to think much about what awaited him. Now nearing Mandin's Way, he found himself reluctant to face it. Kazmarek's words rose to the front of his mind.

The weight, once placed, is never lifted.

And that's what Nix felt—heavy, weighted down.

How could anyone know what he knew and not surrender to despair, or nihilism, or hedonism, or some kind of excess to give existence meaning? It seemed . . . pointless.

"You're too quiet," Egil said. "Tell me when you're ready. You need to. I can see that."

Nix looked at his friend, the friend with whom he'd shared and endured so much. He started to shake his head but it came out a nod. He did need to share it, to have someone help him bear the weight. "When we reach the Vault."

"Aye," Egil said.

Jyme looked at them, bemused. "You going to tell me, too? Because I have no idea what the two of you are talking about."

"Sure, Jyme," Nix said. "I'll tell you, too. I'll tell you both. It doesn't matter. But once you know, you're fakked."

Egil grunted.

Jyme shook his head. "The two of you jest while we fight wizards but get grim when we walk the street. You make no damned sense."

Nix grinned at that, a genuine grin. Egil, too.

Nix clapped him on the shoulder. "I'm glad you're with us, Jyme. I just hope you're glad of it when all's said and done."

Soon they reached their destination and Mandin's Way stretched to their right and left, the streetlights long since burned out, the wide, twisting avenue dark and quiet in the predawn gray. Voices carried from the docks, sailors and teamsters loading or unloading ships ahead of a dawn launch, the fish market gearing up for the day. A few fishmongers' wagons already rolled down the street, making their way to the fish market, a tent and stall city at the terminus of the road near the Archbridge. The moment the sun lit the sky, street vendors would pop up on Mandin's Way like watered flowers, hawking smoked fish and river eel. But for the moment, for the next hour perhaps, the street appeared deserted. Nix knew better, of course. Rusk's guild men would be stationed along the road, on roofs and in shadowed doorways, their numbers getting thicker nearer the Squid.

"We go," Nix said, and led them out of the alley on Mandin's.

They walked down the center of the street to make themselves obvious. After a couple of blocks, the rooftop spotters saw them coming. Nix didn't bother with signs or any other damned thing. The guild men would recognize him and Egil.

Nix suddenly picked up his pace and their accelerated approach caused a scramble: signs from the rooftops, cocked crossbows. Nix wanted someone to alert Rusk.

"Probably have ten bolts ready to fire," Jyme said. "Can we not be rash possibly? Hate to end the night shot in the street after everything else we've survived tonight."

"I guess we'll see," Egil rumbled.

The guild men manning the door of the Squid stepped hurriedly off the porch and onto the street, hands on their blades. Others fell in behind the trio, but at a distance.

"Don't you dare shoot, you bunghole slubbers!" Nix shouted up at the rooftop snipers. "We're on Rusk's business!"

"No you ain't," said one of the men from the door. He raised a hand to stop them. "Hold right there."

Nix did nothing of the kind, didn't even slow.

"Rusk's business," he bluffed, and he, Egil, and Jyme plowed through the men.

To Nix's surprise, he didn't hear the twang of loosed bolts or the sound of drawn blades, but another four guild men rushed out of darkened doorways on either side of the street to intercept them. That put five around them, four before, and not less than four behind, with half a dozen snipers on roofs.

One of the men who'd stepped down from the porch had a thick mustache and sideburns and he put himself in front of the three and held his ground. A man stood to either side of him. The rest fell in around.

"You'll be stopping there."

"I don't have time for explanations to anyone but Rusk," Nix said, but he did stop. "Get him."

"Please," Jyme said.

"Get him," Egil said. The priest slid two steps away from Nix and Jyme, presumably so he'd have room to work the hammers should the need arise.

"We can't kill our way through everyone," Jyme said to them.

"I think maybe we could," Egil said, eyeing the guild men.

The guild men tightened up around them, more than a dozen in all.

Nix controlled his frustration and tried to speak calmly, even as he mentally started picking the places he would stab first. "You tell Rusk we need inside right now."

"I thought you said you were on his business," said the mustache. "That don't sound like you are."

Nix went on as if he hadn't spoken. "You tell him we need the same shelter as before. He'll know what we mean."

Mustache made no move to obey, and the sneer was answer enough.

"Gentlemen," Nix said, "and I use that appellation in full knowledge that it has applicability to none of you."

"Appellation," Egil said softly. "Nice."

"It's been a very long night and we're a bit too tired for another fight, but not so tired we wouldn't gut each of you, if it came to it. So unless you enjoy bleeding, you go tell Rusk the Hells are on our heels and it'll come to the Squid and all of you if we don't get the same consideration we got earlier. You tell him it'll take down the guild house. All of it. There's no doubt, and you're hearing that from the two of us who marched through it and all of you not a year ago. You'll tell him we'll pay, whatever he asks. Yeah?"

Mustache crossed his arms over his chest, his expression defiant.

Nix's impatience got the better of him so he took the man by the arm. "We'll walk with you so you can tell him. Let's go."

"Let go of my fakkin' arm," the man said. "Or we'll see who ends up bleeding."

The other men grumbled, moved in, and Nix thought he might have to stab a few to make clear his sense of urgency. Egil tensed, too, violence promised in his coiled limbs. Jyme whispered a curse under his breath.

Nix leaned in toward the mustache. "I'm asking one more time: Can we walk? Otherwise . . ."

The man shook himself free of Nix and stared into his face. "Otherwise what?"

"That'll do," said a voice from within the darkness of the Squid's entryway. Rusk's voice. Nix relaxed.

Mustache called back over his shoulder. "Eighth Blade, this little pissdrip is—"

"I heard it all, Ullger," said Rusk, and stepped out onto the street. He was dressed exactly as he had been when they'd seen him earlier in the day.

The guild men around them eased off half a step.

"You keeping long hours now, I see," Nix called to Rusk.

Rusk chuckled. "Eighth Blade, Nix Fall. Comes with the office. Who's that other slubber with you two?"

"This is Jyme," Egil said. "He's in the shite with us now."

"Still deep and dark, I'm guessing," Rusk said.

"You have no idea," Nix said. "Listen, we need to move, Rusk. Everything I said is true."

"Best hurry in, then," Rusk said, then a bit louder, "Payment will be steep, gentlemen, and I use that appellation as loosely as you did. Very steep indeed."

The guild men around them smiled and chuckled. Rusk had made his point. Nix let it stand.

"Fair enough, Eighth Blade," Nix said.

He, Egil, and Jyme moved past the men toward Rusk.

"Extra sharp, men," Rusk said to his guild men. "And that's well done, Ullger." To Egil and Nix he said, "What do they need to watch for?"

"You get us to the Vault quickly and they won't have to watch for anything," Nix said, then, for the benefit of the guild men in the street, "Won't be any missing it. It's big. Listen . . ."

He considered whether to tell them that weapons couldn't hurt it. They probably wouldn't believe him. But if they did, if Rusk did, he might not take them to the Vault.

"It's hard to hurt," Nix said.

"We'll see," said Ullger, and the other men muttered agreement.

With that, Rusk led them into the guild house. He moved quickly, evidently taking Nix's words to heart.

"You bring something down on the house and the cost goes up," he said, as they half-ran through the halls.

"Of course," Nix said. "Sorry for this. But we've nowhere else to go. This thing can track us and I need some time to figure things out. Vault's the only option. Once we're in, it'll lose us and you and yours won't be bothered."

"Seems I'm helping you two a lot," Rusk said. "First in the swamp, then earlier tonight, and then now."

Egil grunted. Nix bit his tongue. In truth, Rusk hadn't helped them in the swamp at all. Egil and Nix had helped him, in a way. He'd had false memories of events placed in his head by a mindmage. But Nix and Egil could never tell him. The fewer people who knew the truth, the better.

"We appreciate the help you've given," Nix said, trying not to choke on the words. "Here's hoping third time's lucky."

"You called it a thing," Rusk said, hustling them along. They passed a guild man now and again, who nodded respectfully at the Upright Man, but looked with curiosity at Egil and Nix and Jyme.

"How's that?" Egil asked.

"What's chasing you. You called it a thing. What is it?"

"We don't know," Nix said. "And that's truth. It's not human and it's big and it's hard to hurt. That's what we know."

Rusk grunted, plainly not believing them entirely. "How long in the Vault?"

"Hours. Full sun in the sky and that thing won't show itself," Nix answered.

"Well enough," Rusk said. "We'll talk payment with the dawn."

They moved through two concealed doors and entered the

tunnels under the Meander, taking the winding turns, their feet walking the circular, spiral path of the corridors, tracing the shape of the ward that protected against detection. At the end of it they reached the door of the Vault. Rusk unlocked it and allowed them in.

Nix and Jyme filed in, but Egil hesitated. He stood before Rusk, looked him in the face, and extended a hand. Rusk hesitated a moment, but took it. Egil pulled him in for an embrace. Rusk's shocked expression mirrored Jyme's.

"We appreciate the help," Egil said. "We won't soon forget it."

"You two want your own room or something?" Nix said.

Rusk shoved him away. "The fak, man? This is business. We're not friends."

"Even so," Egil said, and entered the Vault. "Even so."

"I'll return in a few hours," Rusk said, and closed the door.

Jyme stared at Egil, dumbfounded. "In a night that makes no sense, that . . . embrace made the least sense of all."

"Sure it does," Nix said. "What'd you lift, Egil?"

Egil held up the magical talking key Nix had paid to Rusk to use the Vault the first time. "This. In case we need to get out. We'll give it back to him when the time's right." He tossed the key to Nix.

Nix snatched it out of the air. "Nicely done, priest. Picking the pocket of the head of the Thieves' Guild. Impressive." He put the key in his satchel with the book and plates and other needful things.

Egil sat in the chair he'd sat in the first time. "So here we are. You going to tell us?"

Nix nodded. "I am. But not until I've read more, yeah?"

"Sounds like more delay," Egil said.

"No," Nix said. "I'll tell you. As you said, I need to. But first, the book."

"Suit yourself," Egil said. He interlaced his fingers behind his head and closed his eyes.

Jyme looked from one to the other. "Read what? The plates? And are you going to sleep, Egil?"

"Not the plates, no. This book," Nix said, and took the ancient tome from his satchel.

"Just resting my eyes," Egil said. "Catch as catch can. I'm tired. Aren't you?"

"To the bone, but that don't mean I can sleep," Jyme said. He sagged to the floor, his back against the wall, his arms on his knees. "You two," he said, shaking his head. "You two."

Nix stared at the book a moment, knowing that when he opened it the magic of the script would allow him to read and understand it quickly. He wanted to ensure he was ready. He wished he had a drink.

"What is that? A spellbook or some such?" Jyme asked.

"Some such," Nix said, then, "Here we go."

He opened the book. He picked up where he'd left off before, and, as before, he felt apart from himself as he read, an observer, not a participant. The knowledge he gained tempted despair, but despair wasn't in Nix and he fought it back.

Instead, he read, he understood, and he began to plan.

The soaring bridge of white stone, the monumental bones of an earlier world, rose above the rooftops of the city and colored lanterns dotted its sides, bouncing in the predawn breeze, and the breeze carried the sound of distant gongs and chanting, prayers to gods unknown to the Afterbirth. He continued forward through the alleys and streets, never slowing, his feet sticky with the gore of the dungsweeper he crushed, and he passed the corpse of a small man and mechanical creatures that lay in ruins and smelled of magic and soon he was on a wide, winding street that tracked the wobbly course of the river. The scent of the Great Spell was thick in the air, tracing the line of the street.

Large, multistory buildings lined up on the river side of the street, places for men and their clubs and societies and guilds, and the Afterbirth ran along in their shadow, under the soulless eyes of their windows, hunched and mumbling. The smell of the spell led into a low, two-story wooden building ahead, a building that had been expanded many times, a building that splayed out on its lot like a sleeping drunk, limbs askew.

He could smell the men lurking around the building, the stink of their leather and steel and sweat, the smell getting more acute as their tension grew. They'd seen him. They were preparing for him but the Great Spell was not among them because the aroma of it was still too attenuated and the men he'd been chasing must have carried it into the sprawling building and left these men to ambush him.

There were men on the roofs and on the street and in the doorway of the building and he didn't care or slow. The city would soon be awake and alerted to his presence, perhaps it already was, and the authorities would come if they weren't already there. He'd left a trail of broken buildings and broken bodies in his wake, and they would have to come after him and because they could not kill him they would try to hold him and he would not be held. Day would reveal him and he thought that it would not matter if he obtained the Great Spell, which entered the sprawling building but did not exit it. He had the two men penned in the building and the river was to their back.

The twang of crossbows announced the men's attack and three bolts sank deep into the flesh of his middle, the ends shuddering with the impact. He pulled them free and did not slow, growled, and ran pell-mell toward the building. Men stormed off the porch, blades drawn, and men ran from alleys, brandishing steel, and shouts came down from atop the buildings. More men in hidden alleys and doorways darted out, a march of steel and resolve and none of it would matter because the Afterbirth would not slow or stop and he would kill them all.

"It's hard to hurt, men!" said one of the men. "Mind your-selves, now!"

"Look at it!" said another.

"It's a horror!"

He crashed into them like the tide and his weight knocked two of them down and he stomped them, crushing them under-foot as blades rose and fell and stabbed and thrust. The sharp edges of steel opened his flesh, spilled his blood, but he felt nothing except purpose and hope and anger and nothing would stop him. His fists rose and fell, smashing jaws and skulls, and anyone who fell to the ground he stomped underfoot. The men around him shouted, first in rage, then in disbelief, and finally in fear. He smelled the stink of their growing terror as he left bloody smears in the street, broken, groaning men, a gory trail that was leading, inevitably, to the door of the sprawling build-ing. Gashes and cracked bones knit closed as he continued his roaring, bloody march toward the doors. He muttered and drooled and crushed and stomped and broke and killed and soon found himself on the porch, the men on the street having either retreated or died, and he put his hand, slick with blood, some his own, much of it not, to the handle, and found it locked.

He began to beat on the iron-reinforced door, the sound of his blows booming through the night's quiet. Shouts sounded from behind the door, men issuing orders to other men. Cross-bow fire continued to rain down on him from the rooftops, some thudding into his flesh and scraping against bone, others slamming into the doorjambs and skittering along the paving stones.

He stepped back and charged the door, throwing the en-tirety of his weight against it, and the door cracked and metal re-inforcing bands creaked. Shouts of surprise and alarm sounded from behind it. He repeated the process, slamming into it a second time, a third, and then it gave way, tearing free of the hinge mounts and falling inward. He lumbered in, flattening the door the rest of the way as he entered and finding himself face-to-face with a crowd of men who stabbed and slashed and shouted.

"Kill it! In Aster's name, kill it!"

He answered their shouts with the roars of his many mouths and began again to crush and stomp and throw and bludgeon until the room was awash in blood and bodies.

The words in the book, written in Ool's steady hand, pierced Nix, burrowed through his eyes and into his brain and lifted him up and left him floating. Reading them, understanding them, separated him from the world, because he knew a truth of the world that no one should know, that seemed impossible and left him feeling disembodied.

The will of the caster determines the scale of the remaking. Thus, the most powerful of magics requires nothing more than an act of will. A first cause.

As he read, as each new revelation planted itself in his head, it struck Nix that the book, *The Account of Ool the Mad,* could have been from the world that immediately preceded Nix's, or it could have been from a world ten iterations in the past. The book could have survived each casting. Things did, or at least could, or so said the book. Ool's clock was a leftover. And so too was Ool's name, but all of it could have been a remainder from a world many worlds in the past.

The only things certain in each casting are that it must be done at the Fulcrum, the place that is no place, and that it results in the afterbirth, the palimpsest of the rewritten world. The greater the remaking, the more pronounced the afterbirth.

Nix realized that the imperfect remaking would work as a constraint on the amount of change wrought by the caster. Small changes would probably be the rule. A kingdom here. Beauty there. Wealth the next time. And that might explain why, if Ool were from a much earlier iteration, his imprint had survived.

Or could there be a different reason?

Nix remembered what Kerfallen had said, what Kazmarek had implied: The plates were eternal. They existed to tempt us. To tempt us. Because they'd been made that way.

Because Ool had made them that way?

Maybe that was why his name had survived, his clock, his book. They were as eternal as the plates. They couldn't be destroyed or erased, either.

Was Ool the Mad the *first* of the first causes? Was the Great Spell of his making? Or had Ool figured out a way to game the spell?

Nix focused on that last.

He would game the spell, too, find a way to keep the plates out of anyone's hands, but keep the world the same. Nix had gamed the world since as far back as he could remember. He could do this, too.

A thought struck him and it made him dizzy and he had to look up and he had to stop reading and he had to not think too hard about what it could mean.

He could have done all this before.

He could have been him, or some version of him, in a previous iteration. And he could have had these very same thoughts, followed this very same course, and he could have . . .

"No, no, no." He shook his head, consciously choosing not to descend too far into that spiral. He turned his mind back to the problem of preserving his world, this world. He realized that he would need to use the plates. He had to, despite his vow to Kazmarek.

He had to use them. He had to use them to isolate them.

Likely everyone who'd used them before had used them to gain something. Nix didn't want to use them for that. He wanted to preserve something. Maybe that would be a difference? If an act of will effected the spell, maybe the motivation for that act would allow it to work as he wished.

But he couldn't have been the only one to think of that over the course of . . . how many previous worlds? Others must have, mustn't they?

He realized that he was going to drive himself mad, that the possibilities for doubt and second-guessing were endless, and that entertaining them over and over would render him paralyzed or insane.

He had to act. He could do nothing else.

He turned the page to realize he'd finished the book. He didn't remember reading particular words. Instead it was as though the knowledge had just bonded with him. He looked up to find that Jyme and Egil were staring at him, their brows furrowed, questions in their eyes.

"Fak, man," Jyme said.

"You were shaking your head and muttering," Egil said.

Nix nodded. He looked down at the book, back up at his friends. He didn't even know where to begin.

"Just tell us," Egil said. "What's going on?"

"And what in the name of the Hells is that thing chasing us?" Jyme added.

Nix could feel a vein pulsing in his forehead. A headache formed behind his eyes, dug its roots farther back into his brain. "I'm not sure I can tell you."

"Things could go bad, Nix," Egil said. "Then what? If this is that important, you can't risk letting it die with you."

"I can't die," Nix said, waving a hand derisively. "Everyone knows that."

Jyme was nodding. "Egil makes a point. You probably should tell us."

"I know he does and I know I do," Nix said. "But when I say I'm not sure I can, I don't even know how to tell you. It's . . . unbelievable."

"Maybe that book is shite?" Jyme said, sounding unconvinced.

"No," Nix said. "It's not. I'm sure it's not." He looked each of them in the face. "If I tell you, it will change everything. I mean it. Everything. You still want to hear?"

Egil leaned forward in his chair, rubbing his hand along the stubble of his beard. Jyme cursed softly.

"Let's hear it," Egil said. "Jyme?"

Jyme squinted, sniffed, and nodded.

Nix gathered his thoughts and began. "Fine. The plates are inscribed with the words of a great spell. No, not a great spell. *The* Great Spell."

"That's what the creature was saying," Jyme said. "Back at the Tunnel."

Nix nodded. "Right. The spell is . . ." He sought for words, felt too ridiculous to say the ones that came to mind first. "It's powerful."

Egil stared at him. "Nix, what is this thing?"

Nix swallowed and dove in. "Imagine you could wish for something, anything, and you could have it."

Egil's eyes narrowed.

Jyme exhaled, said, "I can think of a few things. That what this does?"

"Yes," Nix said, then shook his head. "No. It does more than that. It does more than that." He exhaled and said it. "It remakes the world. That's what this book says. It remakes the world."

Jyme looked at him as if he were speaking a language he didn't understand. "What?"

Egil looked at Nix, off to the side, back at Nix. "The book could be wrong. Or it could be lies, as Jyme said. A wizard wrote it."

Nix heard the lack of conviction in Egil's voice. "Maybe. But Kerfallen wanted it. Kazmarek was terrified to have us learn about it. And that . . . thing wants it, too. And Jyme said the creature spoke of the Great Spell."

Jyme stood and started to pace. "Fak. Fak. What does that

even mean, 'remake the world'? As in the whole world? From the beginning of time? That doesn't even make sense."

Nix shrugged. "Those are the words. And I think they mean what we think they mean but I agree that it doesn't make sense. Can't be from the beginning of time. Has to be from the point of the first change, doesn't it?"

Jyme stopped pacing and stared at him.

"Doesn't it?" Nix asked.

"How the Hells should I know?" Jyme exclaimed. "I can't believe we're having this conversation."

"How is this possible?" Egil asked.

Nix sighed. "I don't know. It's wizard shite, Egil."

"No," Egil said. "It's more than that. Much more. Those plates are just sitting at the bottom of the Deadmire waiting for us to find them? How has no one ever used these before? That makes no sense either and . . ."

Nix stared at him, letting the silence serve as answer.

Egil tilted his head to the side. "Are you saying they've been used before?"

"I am," Nix said. "The book says they've been used before. Maybe many times."

Jyme waved his hands in the air, the gesture almost comical. "Wait, wait, wait. What the fak are you saying? You're saying . . . ?"

"Yes," Nix said. "Maybe."

Jyme stared at him a long moment, holding his breath. He blew it out. "You're saying this world, *our* world, was remade? Is remade?"

"That's what I'm saying. Worlds gone by, Jyme. Our world just another one."

Jyme's mouth opened, closed. He blinked, stared wide-eyed. "Worlds gone by? Worlds gone by! That doesn't . . . I can't . . . This doesn't make sense. Egil?"

Egil was staring off at the wall, his mind away on some thought of his own.

"No, it does make sense," Nix said. "There are leftovers from previous worlds each time the Great Spell is cast. The Archbridge. Ool's clock." He looked at Egil. "Some of the things we saw in the swamp. You remember?"

Egil's eyes refocused on the present and he nodded slowly. "The thing that's after us?"

"What do you mean?" Jyme said.

Nix saw the logic of it and pointed a finger at Egil. "Yes! That makes sense. That's why we can't hurt it. It's eternal, like the bridge and clock."

"Not eternal," Egil said softly.

Nix took his point. "No. In existence until the next iteration of the world."

"Wait, wait!" Jyme said. "Why can't we just use the plates and wish that creature dead? Then our problem is solved."

"It's not," Nix said, shaking his head and thinking it through. "The book says the remaking always leaves something leftover. A palimpsest."

"I don't know what that even means," Jyme said. He stopped pacing and put a hand to the wall, as if he might fall over. Nix understood the feeling.

"It's the ghost of old writing when you rewrite something," Egil said. "The impressions on the page."

"That creature is the ghost of old writing?" Jyme asked.

"Of an old world," Egil said, and nodded.

A long silence fell. Jyme broke it.

"This is insane!" He looked like he wanted to run. Instead he started pacing anew. "You two are discussing this like it's a love potion we bought at the Low Bazaar. This is a fakkin' cataclysm. Do you even hear yourselves? This can't be right, Nix. You read it wrong, or those wizards are full of shite or somethin'."

"I don't think so," Nix said.

"Nor I," said Egil.

"Damn it all," Jyme said. He sat, deflated. "What then? What do we do?"

"That's what I've been thinking about," Nix said.

"And?" Jyme asked.

Nix was still working through details, and what he had for a plan was uncertain at best. But it was what he had. "Understand that I'm working this through, yeah? We're going to make the plates, the Great Spell, go away."

"What do you mean 'go away'?" Jyme asked.

Nix spoke quickly to plow through his doubts. "We're going to remake the world. But we're going to remake it precisely the same way, except that these fakkin' plates will be locked away forever, or at least as close to forever as we can make it. Our world is the final world as far as we're concerned. No more Great Spell."

"I don't see how it can be precisely the same," Jyme said. "It's still a remaking, yeah?"

Nix saw where the question would lead. "Yeah."

Jyme looked up. "Then we won't be us. Or we'll be us, but different."

Nix was shaking his head before Jyme finished the sentence. "No, no. We'll be the same."

Egil cleared his throat. He'd taken out his dice and was shaking them absently in his hand. "We're not pots. We can't be broken and remade and still be the same thing."

Nix could not muster the conviction to gainsay him, not entirely. "Maybe we can if there aren't any cracks. We don't know."

"Fak," Jyme muttered. "Fak. It seems like we're saying everything is false, that nothing matters. There's another world coming after this one, and there was one before, or ten, or a hundred, and why the fak do anything at all? Gods. Gods."

"Calm down, Jyme," Nix said.

Egil put his dice back in the pouch at his belt. "That's not what he's saying."

"You sure?" Jyme asked. "Then what?"

"Yeah," Nix said. "Then what? Because it sure feels like

that's what I just said, though maybe not quite so bleak. Thanks, Jyme. You fakker."

Egil inhaled deeply, exhaled the same way. "All he said is that things are temporary. It doesn't mean nothing matters, and it doesn't mean nothing is real. It means it's . . . temporary. But then it's always been, hasn't it? We die and our world ends. It's no different if it's the whole world or just us. Temporary, yeah?"

Nix and Jyme stared at him.

"I like that," Jyme said. "Yes. I like that."

Nix nodded. "And I. I don't know if it makes sense or not but I'm hanging on to it."

"You should have a pipe or something, priest," Jyme said. "Waxing profound and all."

"He does that sometimes," Nix said. "I blame the fact that he's been hit on the head often."

"Ebenor's eye does make a nice target," Jyme added.

Egil grunted. "And now let me add some additional profundity and it goes as follows. Fak you. And also you."

Nix laughed aloud. "Didn't know you were signing on for this, now, did you Jyme? Ha!"

"I did not," Jyme said, and the words caused the mirth to wilt. "Wait, what about that thing? The leftover?"

Nix shrugged. "There will be a different one, I guess. There's always a leftover."

Neither Jyme nor Egil would make eye contact with Nix. Each was lost in his own thoughts, his own doubts.

"I'll hear other suggestions because I don't have anything else," Nix said. "Well?"

Neither Jyme nor Egil said anything.

"If we don't do this, or if we can't do this, eventually that thing is going to get these plates. Or if not it, then someone else. Kazmarek or someone like him. Too many people know about them now. And they . . . want to be found. That's what the book says. The need to create and destroy and create anew, it's . . . inexorable. Eventually they'll be found and someone will use them. And then who knows what the world will look like. It's us or them."

"Gods," Jyme said.

"Fak," Egil said softly.

"I wish I'd left them in the swamp," Nix said. "I'm sorry I didn't. They must have been protected there or something. But now they're out and it's too late to put them back in a box. Unless, unless . . ."

"Unless we make a new box," Egil finished.

"Yes. Yes."

Jyme's face was red and blotchy. "It's not a fakkin' box. It's the world. You're talking about the world."

"Yeah," Nix said. "Yeah."

Egil stood, exhaled. "So how do they work? The plates, I mean."

Jyme gave a start and his expression looked panicky. "You're not going to do it here?"

Nix almost laughed, Jyme sounded so panicked. "No. I can't do it here. It only works in one place—though *place* seems the wrong word—called the Fulcrum."

"And where's that?" Egil said.

"You warming up to this?" Nix said.

The priest shook his head. "No. But things are what they are. I'm with you. I don't see another way."

"Things aren't what they are," Jyme said. "I don't feel fakkin' real. I feel like a player in a play all of a sudden. Gods."

"Of course you're real," Nix said, but Jyme's words planted a seed of doubt. Were they just the outcome of a spell, the spawn of someone's wish long ago? Players in someone else's play?

"How can you say we are when—"

Nix stabbed the air with a finger to silence him. "That's enough, Jyme! Enough! We're real. I've lived, you've lived, everything that's happened has happened. As Egil said, we've always been temporary. What does it matter how we started or who started us? We are what we are."

"Anyway," Egil said in an even tone. "The location of the Fulcrum?"

Nix was glad for the change in conversational direction. "The Fulcrum is not a where, exactly. The Fulcrum is the fixed point of the world, a place that doesn't change with each iteration. The spell can only be cast there."

Jyme was shaking his head, just shaking it over and over, as if he could knock loose everything he'd heard. Nix didn't think he even realized he was doing it.

"So the Fulcrum could be anywhere," Jyme said. "We're just going to keep running from this thing until we happen to find it."

Egil stared at Nix.

"Say it," Nix said.

"Jyme makes a point," Egil said.

"You're jesting now?" Jyme said. "Still? After this? Gods, men. Gods."

"Breathe, Jyme," Nix said. "I find it helps. Just breathe."

Jyme stared at him, nodded, and took a deep breath. "I cannot believe we are talking about this. I can't."

Nix couldn't, either. He'd awakened yesterday morning and the day had been just another day.

Egil spoke softly. "How does the spell work?"

Nix consulted the knowledge imprinted on his brain from the book. "You activate the plates with the Language of Creation, read the words, and the rest is as much an act of will as a casting. You think about what you want and that is what you get."

The furrow in Egil's brow announced his skepticism. "That's all there is to it?"

Nix shrugged. "It seems so."

"This is a weighty damned matter for a 'seems,'" Jyme said.

"Agreed," Nix said. "But 'seems' is all I've got. The only thing we change is that the plates are hidden somewhere very hard to find. Everything else stays the same. A little change."

"Little," Jyme scoffed.

"And in the process we make a new leftover?" Egil asked. "A new creature?"

"Yes, I think. The remaking is never perfect, that's what the book says. There's always a leftover. Maybe it's something like that creature every time. Maybe it's something else. But we take that risk, yeah? We already know what we have this time around. Can't be worse next time."

"Aye," Egil agreed.

A lengthy silence followed. Jyme broke it. "Will we remember?"

"Would you want to?" Nix asked.

"Maybe not," Jyme said. "But could we?"

Nix shrugged. "Certainly. Ool did. Remember or forget. It's the will of the caster."

"Would you remember or forget?" Jyme asked.

Nix ran a hand through his hair. "I don't know. It's heavy to carry. But knowing now, I think I'd rather stay knowing. You?"

Jyme scoffed. "I want to forget this and never have to think about it again."

Nix laughed. Egil did not.

"We could have done this before, more than once," the priest said.

"What?" Jyme asked.

Nix took Egil's point. "Why would we do it again?" It came to him almost as soon as he asked the question and he nodded. "Because we failed. Shite."

Jyme held up his hands. "You're telling me we did this before and don't remember?"

"It's possible," Egil said.

"No, no," Nix said. "Wait, wait. If we remade it, then we didn't fail."

Egil shook his head. "No, we still could've. A contingency built in."

"What?" Jyme asked.

Nix saw it and nodded. "Shite. That could be. The spell is limited only by the will of the caster. We could have done it before contingently." For Jyme's benefit, he explained: "Maybe we got to the Fulcrum before and cast the spell. And when we cast it we tried hiding the plates forever but also built in a contingency: If they aren't or can't be hidden forever, or if this or that is the case—something we don't want, yeah?—then remake the world precisely as it was, except make this or that easier next time around so we do it correctly that time."

Jyme just stared.

Egil said, "That spiral never ends. It could go on a long time. Nested contingencies."

Nix nodded. "Little changes. Slight differences maybe to help us along and get it right finally? I don't know."

"But . . ." Jyme began. "We couldn't help us along unless we remembered."

"No, we could. We could not remember—maybe there's a reason why we shouldn't—and yet we changed the world to make a wall easier to climb or ourselves a better shot with a sling or whatever. Keep in mind that we'd be standing in the Fulcrum, looking back on how we got there, trying to remake the world without the plates, but knowing how we got there and knowing what we could change to make it easier next time. So if the remaking of the world without the plates didn't work, the contingency takes effect."

"You're saying we remade the world so we can better climb a wall?" Jyme asked, skeptical.

"I don't know," Nix blurted. "Maybe. Little changes. If I was doing it right now, I'd want to make as few changes as I could. Because I want me to stay me, this world to stay this world. So, yeah. Maybe we changed everything but a wall. Or who knows what else? But maybe we didn't change things enough and we failed. So here we are again, not remembering, the world changed in some small way we'll never know, but going at it again. Hells, maybe having this conversation is the change!"

"Shite," Jyme said. "I'm getting tired thinking about it."

"I see it now," Egil said.

"See what?" Jyme asked.

"We didn't remake the world to help us along. We remade it because one of us died."

Jyme and Nix sat for a long moment in silence.

"Shite," Nix said softly. "Of course. Of course."

"You're saying one of us died?" Jyme said.

Egil shrugged.

"That would make sense," Nix said, and tried not to think about the way he might have gone out. "Probably it was you, Jyme, being a clumsy oaf and such. But listen, whether we did or didn't die is irrelevant at this point. We just have to proceed as planned. If we did it before and failed, or one of us died, let's do it better this time, yeah? We think too hard about previous iterations and what we may have done or not done and we'll paralyze ourselves. We'll get it right eventually."

"Or fail altogether," Egil said.

"Always uplifting you are, priest," Nix said.

"We could all die," Jyme said. "Then there's no one to remake anything and we're fakked."

"Likewise uplifting," Nix said. "You two should stop talking now."

"Hells," Egil said to Nix. "Maybe in a previous world you're charming."

"And maybe you're handsome and less fakking dour," Nix answered, then shook his head. "No, that'd be asking too much of even the Great Spell. Little changes, I said. Not turning the world upside down."

"Ha," Egil said, and grinned.

"See, now we have the right attitude," Nix said.

Jyme massaged his temples. "This is insanity. How can this not be insane? We're talking about changing the world, about already having died, and you two sit here trading jests."

"That's how we manage," Egil said seriously. "And here's

how you're going to manage. You're going to carry this, Jyme. Because you can. We're all three going to carry it together, yeah? And eventually we're going to get it right."

"Yeah, all right," Jyme said, visibly propping himself up. "Yeah."

"Now," Egil said, brandishing the morphic key, "let's go fix this. Again if that's the way of it. Wake up, key."

The end of the key's barrel elongated and opened, as though in a yawn, then the key said, in its high-pitched voice, "Give us an apple."

CHAPTER TEN

A distant impact caused the walls to vibrate. Another followed, then a third.

"Shite," Jyme said. They could all could guess the origin of the sound.

"That thing has tracked us," Nix said.

"How? We're in the Vault!" Jyme said. "That was the whole point."

Nix shook his head. "It must be able to follow our scent in the air or the like. Maybe it can't sense *us* right now, but it can sense whatever we left on the air behind us and that's enough for it to know we're in the guild house."

"Shite," Jyme said. "It's like a fakkin' hound."

"Seconding shite," Nix said, and tossed Egil an apple that he took from his satchel. "For that key."

Egil held the apple, brown and wrinkled, in front of the key.

"Give us a carrot instead," the key said in its high-pitched voice.

Egil frowned and looked back at Nix, who rifled through his satchel. He didn't have a carrot. He shook his head.

"A carrot," the key repeated.

"We're having an argument with a fakking key and that thing is here!" Jyme said. "Give it a fakkin' onion or something. We get caught in here there's nowhere to go."

"Give us a carrot," repeated the key.

"It's temperamental," Nix said. "I left it unfed too long."

Egil's eyes narrowed in anger. He held the key up to his face and stared down the barrel. "There is no carrot. So you will open this lock or I will bend you into a fishhook."

A long pause, in which Nix imagined the key thinking, then, "Give us the apple."

Egil held the apple before the key and it took several bites.

Another impact shook the walls, the boom something Nix felt as vibrations in his teeth. He imagined the creature throwing its monstrous form against the doors and walls of the guild house, its senses linked in some arcane way to the plates, drawing it toward the Vault, toward them. They needed to get clear.

With the key having eaten, Egil jammed it into the locking mechanism and waited. One moment stretched into another.

"Come on," Jyme said, shifting on his feet, while the key did its work. "Come on."

"Open the fakkin' lock," Egil growled at the key.

Nix looked around at the walls, the metal door, the high ceiling reinforced with beams to hold the weight of the river at bay. An idea struck him.

Egil fiddled with the key, grumbling at it, and finally it turned and the lock clicked open.

"You're fortunate," the priest said to the key, and shoved it into his belt pouch.

Without another word, all three of them drew their weapons, for whatever good they would do. They shared a collective nod and Egil pushed the door open. A breeze wafted in but nothing else. The hallway was empty.

"Let's go," Egil said, but Nix had already laid his satchel on the ground. He crouched beside it and opened the flap.

"You two go," he said, and took out the plates, the plates on which were inscribed words that would end the world. He lingered over them a heartbeat, the fact of what they were giving him pause, but he forced himself not to linger on it. He snatched the thin reel of cordage he always kept in the satchel and pulled that out. "I'm going to trap that thing in here."

"Say again?" Jyme said, incredulous.

Another boom sounded from somewhere in the guild house, a dull crash that echoed for a moment like a dying heartbeat. Jyme looked like a horse ready to bolt. "Are you mad?"

"Nix . . ." Egil said, but even as he was saying it the priest studied the room, the ceiling, and the beams.

Nix unreeled the cordage, started tying a cross knot around the plates. He worked fast and made damned sure the line was secure. "Listen, I know where the Fulcrum is. Or think I do. We'll need a head start because we're going to look for a way in."

"A way into where?" Jyme said.

Egil waited, eyebrows raised.

"Ool wrote the book," Nix said, testing the knot on the plates, finding it well secured. He stood and the plates dangled like a lure from the cord in his hand. "And that's his clock that's chimed every hour since anyone anywhere can remember. And if anything isn't of this world, it's that clock."

Another boom, closer this time. Dust fell from the ceiling beams.

"I have this," Nix said. "Go. Hurry."

Neither Egil nor Jyme moved.

"You're telling me this Fulcrum just happens to be in Dur Follin?" Egil said. "That bit about the clock is a weak table to set your theory on."

"Agreed," Jyme said, looking over his shoulder down the hall. "Seems awfully convenient."

A sound carried from somewhere in the guild house, not a

boom but a roar, the creature's roar, closer and diffused by walls, but coming.

Nix slid the plates along the floor to the far side of the Vault, and eyed the ceiling for a likely perch over the door. "Unlikely unless there's something special about Dur Follin, yeah? Some way of accessing the Fulcrum here that you can't do in other places?"

Nix ensured the cord made a straight line along the floor, from the plates at the far end of the Vault to the doorjambs, taking care that nothing obstructed them. He'd have to yank them in and get the door shut quickly. "Think of everywhere we've been, Egil. Anything like Ool's clock anywhere else?"

Egil rubbed the top of his head. "No. Nor the Archbridge, though, for that matter."

Egil's observation brought Nix up short. He hadn't considered the bridge. "Shite."

The bridge, too, seemed just as likely to be a remnant from a previous world. Now that Nix thought about it, so too did the tunnels under Dur Follin that predated the city by who knew how long.

"Shite, shite, shite," Nix said, his conviction starting to fade. He thought he'd had it but Dur Follin could have been made and remade a dozen times. Even if the Fulcrum were accessible from the city, it needn't be in or about Ool's clock.

"We could've made it that way," Jyme said thoughtfully. His eyes were wide, like he'd struck on something profound. "Last time? We could've made Ool's clock the Fulcrum."

Nix shook his head. "The Fulcrum doesn't move. It can't move. That's the point of it. It's a fixed spot in all worlds. Maybe it's the clock, maybe it's the bridge, or maybe it's on the other side of the world. Shite, Egil."

"No, no," Jyme said, warming to his words. "I don't mean we made the Fulcrum in a particular place. I mean we made you realize it's in the clock."

"That's a damned thin thread of a theory, too," Egil said,

but Nix liked it and grabbed hold. He had nothing else. The book was written in Ool's hand; that had to mean something.

"Thin thread or not, I'm going with it," Nix said, moving to the wall and feeling for purchase. "If it's wrong, we blame Jyme, in this world and the next. Then we fix it next time through. Agreed?"

"There won't be a next time if we're wrong," Egil said. "But agreed. We'll wait for you down the hall at the first turn."

"Aye," Nix said, and started to climb. "Mind that thing's nose, though. Don't let it sense you."

"Bah," Egil said. "It'll be the plates it follows, not us. Speaking of, this is an awful risk, Nix. You don't get clear in time . . ."

"It'll have the plates, yeah. And you and Jyme won't be able to get them back from it. But we can't get to the clock without a lead. That thing will catch us easily. Comes to it, I'll lock myself in here with it, then you try and bring the house down on us. Or the river. Yeah?"

Egil looked at Nix, the ceiling, the cordage on the floor tied to the plates. "You're going to have to be fast," he said. "Very fast."

"I'm Nix the Quick," Nix said. "Now go. And don't disturb that cord as you do."

"We'll be close if you need us," Egil said, and he and Jyme hurried out of the Vault.

The proximity of the Great Spell drove the Afterbirth mad. The smell-taste of it saturated his senses, propelled him onward. He threw himself against doors, knocking them from their hinges. Now and again he smelled an occupant of the building, but only faintly. The scent of the spell—soclosesoclosesoclose—overpowered everything else. He ranstumbled through hallways and rooms, inhaling, muttering, drooling. He reached a stairway and started up, the treads groaning under his weight, but the scent of the spell faded and he stopped, his hearts beating hard, his breath coming fast. The smell was not up the stairs. He scrambled down and stood in the hall at the bottom of the stairs, inhaling deeply, mouths groaning. The smell lingered in the room but went no farther. He roared his frustration, stomped the floor so hard the floorboards cracked. He fell to all fours, the mouths in his abdomen groaning, and put his head to the floor, inhaled deeply, and followed the scent along the wooden planks until he bumped up against the wall. He felt the faint movement of cooler air leaking from under a crease between the wall and floor and realized there was a door and stood and slammed his fists into the wood until the panel gave way to reveal the opening.

Chuffing and muttering, he ran into the dark hallway beyond. The aroma of the spell hung thick in the air, so thick he felt he could almost touch it. He murmured hopefully as he ran on, the narrow hallway turning and twisting in ways for reasons he could not understand and did not care to understand for the spell was at hand and so too was his freedom from pain.

He lumbered so quickly through the narrow labyrinthine hallways that he bounced off the walls. The air was damp, the smell of it bearing the hint of the river, but he focused on the scent of the spell. Ahead he saw an open door, a room, and the scent and feel of the spell was so strong that it caused his body to shudder. Moans racked him and he rushed forward, through the door and into the room.

Nix levered himself between ceiling beams, looking down on the Vault, his boots pressed against one beam, his hands against the other, the tension keeping him up, his muscles straining with the effort. He heard the creature coming long before it entered the room: the heavy tread, the wet breathing. Despite himself, his heartbeat jumped. He held his breath as the creature burst into the room, and hoped that the plates distracted the creature enough that it didn't notice him perched above it.

It moved with surprising speed, its body lurching in an abrupt, awkward flail of limbs. Wet, sloppy groans leaked from its mouths, though it somehow sounded like several voices instead of one. Blood and filth covered the oversize, ragged cloak it wore. The cloak and hood also shielded the creature's bulbous, lumpy form and face from view, and for that Nix was grateful. He had no desire to see what lay beneath the fabric, some residual horror stitched together from some wizard's remaking of the world.

The plates lay at the far end of the Vault, tied with the line he'd left stretched across the floor, waiting for Nix to grab it up and reel it in.

Sweat formed on his brow, ran down his face, wicked to his nose. The creature was standing right under him and he could do nothing. He watched, cross-eyed, as the drop of sweat gathered on his nose tip, stretched, and started to fall.

The creature saw or smelled or sensed the plates and its muttering took on a whine. It lurched forward—the drop of sweat fell and formed a tiny wet stain on the floor—and in its eagerness to reach the plates plowed through the chair on which Egil had sat and knocked one of the guild's chests to the side.

Nix wasted no time. He dropped from the wall, hit the ground in a crouch, grabbed the end of the rope, and yanked, thinking to pull the plates through the creature's legs, slam the door, and get clear.

But the rope jerked taut and then moved not at all because the fakking creature was standing partially on it.

Nix cursed as the creature, having heard him land, started to whirl, growling. Nix caught a glimpse of the deformed, lump-covered face underneath the hood but only a glimpse, because as it turned, it lifted its foot off the rope.

Nix reeled in the plates as fast as he could while backing rapidly out of the Vault.

The creature saw the plates skitter across the floor and

quickly realized what was happening. It muttered and squealed, issuing forth a desperate, slobbery group of syllables that Nix could not parse, and charged after the plates. It stumbled over the chair it had tipped, crushing it and nearly tripping as Nix backed through the doorjambs.

Nix snapped the rope to pull the plates through the doorway and started to swing the metal slab closed. The creature, screaming, flung the chair at the door as it lurched forward. The chair caught between door and jamb, preventing it from closing.

"Shite, shite," Nix said, kicking it clear and trying to slam the door closed, but before it latched the creature slammed into it, hitting with the force of a battering ram. The impact drove the door back, knocked Nix on his rump, and pushed the door halfway open.

"Fak!"

The creature answered his curse with a roar of its own and Nix knew he'd not get the door closed. He scrabbled for his blade, planning to die fighting, when a growl and shout sounded from behind him and he turned to see Egil and Jyme charging down the hall at a full run, their faces red with effort. Nix rolled out of their way. Egil hit the door first, followed immediately by Jyme, the two of them striking with such power that the door snapped shut. Nix jumped up and turned the large handle that secured the lock.

On the other side, the creature slammed its body against the door so hard the metal groaned, again, again, again. Its shrieks and screams sounded almost pitiable, as though it were terrified to be in such a small space. It was screaming something, the words unintelligible.

"Little earlier next time, yeah?" Nix said to the priest, thumping Egil on the shoulder. He grabbed the plates and shoved them and the rope back into his satchel. "Let's go. This door won't hold."

"Aye," Egil said.

"Where?" Jyme asked. "The clock?"

"Aye," Nix said. "Like you suggested."

"*You* suggested it," Jyme protested.

"What do you say, Egil? Seems to me old Jyme's trying to slip the blame should things go wrong."

"I'd agree," Egil said.

"Fak you both," Jyme said.

"And that's well told," Nix said. "Now let's go."

They sprinted back through the tunnels, the boom of the creature against the Vault door chasing them the while. Halfway through the tunnels that formed the warding symbol they ran into Rusk—literally.

Egil, in the lead, plowed over the Upright Man and knocked him down. Rusk had a blade in hand, and his shirt and cape were covered in blood.

"Shite," Egil said. "Sorry, Rusk."

Egil and Jyme helped Rusk, whose face was flush, to his feet.

"Where is that thing?" Rusk said. "It can't be hurt. It can be cut, but it doesn't hurt it."

"I told you that—" Nix began.

"You told me it was *hard* to hurt!" Rusk said, almost taking Nix by the shirt but thinking better of it. "Not impossible to hurt! I've got twenty dead in the street and the Watch on its way."

Another boom sounded from behind, the creature assailing the door. Rusk's eyes widened at the sound.

"Do you have a way to flood these tunnels?" Nix asked. "Collapse them?"

Rusk looked at him as if he were stupid. "What? No."

Nix had figured. "The creature is locked in the Vault—"

"The Vault!" Rusk exclaimed. "We have valuable swag in there!"

"Go get it if you want," Jyme said.

Rusk stared blades at him.

Nix continued. "That door won't hold, Rusk. You oughta

clear the guild house. Just get everybody out. When that thing gets loose, it'll come after us. It'll only bother you and yours if you get in its way."

"So don't get in its way," Egil said, then, "Wait, were you running here to help us? Or to have a go at that thing yourself?"

Rusk clamped his mouth shut and didn't answer.

"Maybe he just figured whatever we have that the creature wants must be worth having," Nix said.

"Maybe," Egil said, eyeing Rusk. "But ballsy either way."

"I got no shortage of balls, priest. Now, where're you three planning to go? If what you say is right, there's nowhere to run from this thing. It'll tear down the city. No one will be able to stop it."

"Best you don't know where we're going," Nix said.

"Sorry about this, Rusk," Egil added, sincerely.

"Fak you," Rusk said, making a cutting gesture with his gloved hand. "And give me back that morphic key you stole, priest. Yeah, I know you lifted it. But I'll have it back, just in case the city isn't in ruins by midday."

Egil handed over the key as another boom shook the walls.

"And speaking of what it wants?" Rusk asked.

Nix shook his head. "You wouldn't believe me if I told you."

"You wouldn't," Jyme said.

Rusk studied their faces. "Well then, fak you again, and that's for all three of you, and meant sincere. You remember that you owe me when this is done. Owe me big."

"We owe you," Nix agreed.

"When it's done," Egil said.

They stared at each other for a moment, then all of them turned and ran, the booms of the creature assaulting the door still echoing behind them. On the first floor, they found doors hanging crookedly in jambs, broken bodies of guild men strewn here and there, pools of blood, toppled furniture.

"Gods," Jyme said. "Watch'll have a day with this."

"I have enough of them I pay that I can keep them out of

here. It's the street I'm worried about. Anyways, I'm clearing the house," Rusk said, and diverted down a hallway. "Luck to you three."

"And you," Nix called after him, as Rusk started shouting for everyone to get out. To Egil and Jyme, Nix said, "We remake the world, maybe we have him forget we owe him?"

"I don't know," Egil said. "I'm thinking he earned it."

"Fair point," Nix said.

The front door of the guild house, thick and reinforced with iron bands, had been knocked from its hinges and lay flat in the foyer. Bodies of guild men, heads and faces crushed and bloody, lay on the ground around it. The creature's bloody footprints led a path back into the guild house. From outside in the street, Nix could hear the commotion of a gathering crowd, the whistles of the Watch.

"Straight to the clock if we can," he said.

They strode out of the guild house and stopped. A dozen or more bodies littered the streets, all of them leaking blood or innards or brains, bones poking through flesh. People had gathered in small groups, checking on the corpses, hands before their mouths or pointing or turning away, disbelief and shock in their eyes. Members of the Watch, noticeable among the gathering crowd in their orange tabards, moved among the gawkers, issuing orders, but looking upon the carnage with their own expressions of disbelief. One or two of the Orangies blew their whistle, as if summoning more members of the Watch would somehow spread thinner the horror of the slaughter. Nix spotted a couple of surviving guild men among the throng. When they saw Nix, they pointed and shouted.

"That's them that brought it!"

"Shite," Nix whispered under his breath.

"Just go," Jyme said, pushing at him to move.

But Nix knew he couldn't. They had to get the street cleared. The door to the Vault would not hold that creature and he'd seen what it had done to the guild house. It would kill everyone within reach in its madness.

"Everyone needs to get out of here now!" Nix shouted.

"What are you doing?" Jyme said.

More faces turned in their direction and Nix imagined how the three of them must look in the predawn light—he and Jyme covered in filth and blood, Egil shirtless and likewise stained. Murmurs ran through the crowd, mumbled accusations, knowing nods. An Orangie turned from looking at one of the corpses in the street, and Nix recognized the short gray hair of the Watch sergeant they'd seen earlier at the Slum Gate.

"You!" Nix called, and raised a hand in a hail. "Sergeant!"

He needn't have called. The sergeant seemed to register Nix at the same time that Nix registered him. He said something to the other Orangie standing near him and the man moved off, issuing orders to the other watchmen nearby. Meanwhile, the sergeant strode briskly toward Nix. As he approached, he took in their appearance.

"Another scrum, I'm guessing," the sergeant said.

"Like you wouldn't believe," Egil said.

"You need to clear the street, Sergeant, and—"

The sergeant was shaking his head. "Just slow down. Let's take it slow for a moment."

"Listen to me," Nix said. "The thing that slaughtered those people in the street? That thing is still in the guild house and it's only a matter of time before it gets out again—"

"What thing?" the sergeant said, looking past them at the guild house.

Nix went on: "And if it gets out again, it will kill everything in its way. It's after us and if you just clear a path—"

"Why is it after you? I've got ten men out here. We can stop—"

"You can't," Egil said. "It can't be hurt with weapons. I know how that sounds, but that's truth. All those men dead in the street thought they could hurt it, too. But nothing you can do will stop it. You just need to get everyone out of the way."

Other Orangies must have caught sight of the body language and sharp gestures punctuating the exchange. One of them called over.

"All well, Sarge?"

The sergeant waved at him to move on, never taking his eyes from Egil.

"We can stop it," Egil said.

"How? You said it can't be hurt."

"We have a way," Nix said, losing patience. "I'm asking you to trust us, or at least believe us. But we need to go right now. The thing will come after us and only us. If no one is here, no one else will be hurt."

The sergeant sniffed, considered, and looked at Jyme. "You got nothing to say here?"

"Just clear the street," Jyme said. "Everything Nix said is true."

The sergeant looked past them, back at them. "Fine." He pointed a finger at Nix's face. "But don't fak me over, gentlemen. Or I will find you."

Egil thumped him on the shoulder. "Good man."

Nix, Jyme, and Egil sprinted off toward Ool's clock, the towering spire like a dark line splitting the predawn sky. Behind them, the sergeant and the other Orangies started shouting for everyone to get clear.

"Next time through maybe we ought to make him have rank or wealth or something, yeah?" Nix said, jesting.

"Yeah," Egil said, apparently not jesting.

They ran through the streets, the tall spire of Ool's clock their guide. The farther away they moved from the slaughter on Mandin's Way, the more ordinary became the activity in the predawn streets—wagons and carts, donkeys and merchants, buskers and hawkers arguing over street corners, and pedestrians getting about their daily business. Nix took it all in and could not shake the feeling that it was all a fiction, something made, rather than something grown. He forced the thought from his mind.

"Keep moving!" Egil said, pulling him along.

He'd drifted to a slow jog without realizing it. He picked up his pace, focusing his mind on the task.

"Both of you listen now," he said, as they turned onto Non's Boulevard. "I'll activate the plates when we reach the clock. If something happens to me, you two carry on, yeah?"

"Yeah," Egil said.

"Shite, man, I figured you'd at least protest the thought of me dying," Nix said. "Anyway, once they're activated, they should stay that way. But nothing can be done with them until they're within the Fulcrum. That's what the book said. If it's you and not me doing the casting, just read what's on the plates. It'll be like Ool's book. The script will appear strange and un-readable at first but then it will start to . . . sink into you. You'll know what to say."

A loud, piercing scream sounded from a block or so behind them. Another joined it, another. Nix imagined the creature bursting out of the guild house and onto the street, tracking them in its way.

"It's coming," Jyme said, glancing behind them.

"Aye," said Egil.

Nix kept talking as they ran, cutting through an alley toward Cobbler's Row. "Remember, in the Fulcrum, as you cast, you just think of what you want, you wish it, but small fakking changes. Small. Our plan is to remake the world ex-actly as it is except that we found something else in that tower in the swamp, something interesting but harmless, and these plates are hidden away somewhere else. I'd planned for me to remember, but you don't have to. How do you want it?"

"Yes," Egil said without hesitating. He must have already thought it through for himself.

"No," Jyme said. "I don't think . . . no."

"Good enough," Nix said. "Final thing. I think the remaking has to go back to the point in time of the first change wrought by the spell. The world doesn't start again from the beginning. It starts from the change as though it'd always been that way." He paused, then said, "And that's a maybe."

"A maybe?" Egil asked.

"Fak," Jyme swore.

"Yes," Nix said. "A maybe. Hells, I don't know. This is the most powerful spell ever made, Egil. It's like being a god. Not even a god, *the* god, the only one that matters, at least in that moment. Maybe lots of things are possible. Maybe the world does restart from the get. I'm making an assumption. And anyway, how would we know? We'll be here when we were meant to be here."

"Gods," Jyme said softly as they ran. "Gods. This is fakking maddening to think about."

"If one of us dies, we go again," Egil said. "That's our rule."

"That's our rule," Nix said, nodding. "One of us dies, we go again. We are not coming through this worse than we started. Jyme?"

"Agreed, yes, of course," Jyme said. "All of us or we go again. But . . ."

"But what?" Nix asked.

"Why not just cast the remaking and make us all alive and hide the plates? Solves all the problems in one go."

"No," Nix said, trying not to feel overwhelmed by the scope of the conversation. "No. Because that remaking could fail or get fouled somehow."

"So?" Jyme said.

"So," Egil said, picking up Nix's thinking, "maybe one or two of us are dead and the remaking doesn't bring us back but does secrete the plates in some unknown corner of Ellerth. Then what?"

"Then someone is dead and there won't be another remaking," Nix said, finishing for the priest. "At least not by us."

"I don't get it," Jyme said. "Why would it do that?"

"How the fak would I know, Jyme?" Nix said. "Half of this is guesswork. I only know we have just established a rule, and that rule is that if someone dies, the change we make in the next casting is remaking the world to bring him back. Until and unless we all three make it through alive and stand in that Fulcrum together, we do it again, plates and all. And then again, if need be. Maybe just make a small change to help us along the next time."

"Hells, this entire conversation could be the change from last time," Egil said. "Helping us along."

Nix knew and thinking about it made his head light. He decided that they had their plan, such as it was, and he'd stick to it because he had nothing else. He was risking their lives on a hunch, on an awful lot of unknowns. He hoped the hunch was right, or maybe had a basis in a previous world. Otherwise, they could all three die, never reaching the Fulcrum, never remaking the world, and that would be the end for them.

"I'm just going to say," he said, "that this is not an ideal damned discussion to be had at a full run while pursued by a monster."

"Aye, that," Egil said.

The clock rose before them, the breaking dawn stretching a faded shadow of the spire across the city. They ran as directly for it as Dur Follin's haphazard street layout allowed. Heads turned to watch them pass, surprise or questions or indifference etched on their faces.

The clock stood on a foundation of huge gray blocks of stone. The stones were of a kind that couldn't have been quarried near Dur Follin, and were said to have been brought to Dur Follin by giants. Nix knew better now.

Age and weather had left the foundation stones pitted, and lichen stained them green in irregular patches that made them look like maps of worlds that never were. Scrawled vulgarities marred the stones where the lichen offered a blank space, all of it written in chalk or paint.

Atop the base stood the tower of Ool's clock, and nothing marred its rough surface. The spire stretched skyward, twisting and narrowing as it ascended, the architectural flourish giving it a warped, unfinished look, like a mistake, like a leftover. Four thin spires rose from the corners of the tower's concave top. Somehow it had always reminded Nix of a bird's nest. In the predawn quiet he could hear the sound of flowing water from somewhere within the spire, the sound faint and diffuse behind the stone. No one knew how the water clock worked, or why or how the water within kept flowing. It was a mystery, or at least it had been.

"Where would it be?" Jyme asked. "Right here? Inside?"

Nix didn't know. He was working on faith. He eyed the area, looking for a clue or association to trigger something he'd learned from Ool's book and let him discern the location of the Fulcrum. There was nothing but the same ground he'd walked on and past for decades.

"Has to be inside, doesn't it?" he said.

Egil's voice was calm. "There's no way inside. We've checked before, Nix. There may not even be an inside for anything other than the water and the clockworks."

"Not helping," Nix said, though he knew the priest spoke truth. He and Egil had scoured the base of the spire years earlier, on a drunken lark, hoping to find a way in, convincing themselves in their stupor that the fabled clock tower had to hold some ancient treasures. They'd found nothing then and they'd find nothing now.

All at once the clock started to toll, the sound of its gongs ringing down in resounding waves from the peak of the spire, the volume like a weight on them.

Nix lifted his eyes, blinking into the sound, the twisting lines of the tower momentarily making him feel dizzy. He looked up near the tower's top, where the round metal slabs of the huge gongs hung suspended in a row that circumnavigated the spire, twelve in all, one for each hour of day and night. A jointed mechanism jutted from the spire above or below the gongs, each ending in the hammer that tolled the metal. Nix watched as the hammers tensed and struck, one after another, announcing the sixth hour, presaging the dawn. A new day, and the world would either be remade or not.

He let his eyes drift higher, to the pronged peak of the spire.

"I've never heard of anyone climbing the clock," he said.

"Of course not," Jyme said. "It's fakkin' tall."

"But rough," Nix said. "And it thins as it rises. Not that hard a climb but for the height. And yet . . ."

"No one has ever climbed it," Egil said. "You're thinking that's built into the making somehow."

"I am."

"Then the Fulcrum would be?" Egil said.

"There," Nix answered, pointing at the bird's nest with his chin.

"There?" Jyme asked. "There! Shite."

Nix dropped his satchel to the ground and started emptying it of everything save the plates. He also shed the dagger at his back, the one in his boot, the one on his thigh. He considered dropping his falchion but thought better of it, though it would make climbing more difficult. He would feel naked were he without his blade.

"You sure?" Jyme said.

"No," Nix said. "But we go up anyway."

"Shite," Jyme said.

"You said you could climb," Egil said to Jyme.

"I didn't say it," Jyme said. "I showed it. But this thing is . . ." He looked up. "A hundred fifty paces tall, maybe more. The surface is rough but . . ."

"Nix," Egil said. "We start up this thing . . . we can't be wrong. We'll be cornered."

"I know," Nix said. "And I might be wrong. But I think I'm not. I can always do this alone."

"You're not going alone," Egil said, as though it were the plainest fact in the world. He started dropping equipment to the ground.

"We don't have any climbing gear," Jyme said. "Wouldn't we have suggested gear?"

"Maybe," Nix said, standing. "Or maybe we never made it this far yet. Go light." He patted the hilt of his falchion. "But keep your weapons."

"Shite," Jyme said again, looking up at the spire as he stripped himself of gear.

Nix took the plates in his hand, spoke a word in the Language of Creation to activate them. They vibrated in his hands, almost humming. They felt slippery, and the script on them swirled.

"One of you do it if I die," he said, and put them back in his satchel.

"What're you boys doing?" said a middle-aged woman who sat on the driving board of a horse-drawn wagon. She drew on her pipe, blew it out.

"I really don't know what we're doing," Nix said to her, and grinned.

Screams from down the street announced the approach of the creature.

"Best clear out of here, goodwoman," Nix said to her. "The Hells are on our heels and closing fast."

The woman started to smile, saw Nix was serious, and flicked the reins of the horse.

"You take care then," she said as the wagon rolled off.

"Get a drink at the Slick Tunnel," Nix called after her. "Tell them Egil and Nix sent you."

She raised a hand so he knew she'd heard.

More shouts from somewhere around the corner, a deep roar—the creature.

"Here we go," Nix said, and moved to the base of the spire. Egil and Jyme fell in with him. They each found purchase on the wall and started up. Nix would lead, finding the path. Jyme came next, followed by Egil. The stone of the clock felt cool under his grip. The pyramidal bricks out of which it was built provided ample ridges and edges so he made good progress.

"You ever climb anything this tall, Jyme?" Egil called.

"No," Jyme said.

"Eyes on the wall mostly, not up or down, belly close but not flat to the tower; the wind will get tough once we get above the city's rooflines."

"Once I feel the direction of the wind, I'll circle around so we're lee of it," Nix called down.

"I'll be all right," Jyme said, though Nix thought he caught some nervousness in the tone. "Though I feel compelled to ask whether there's anything the two of you *haven't* done."

"He's still funny," Nix said. "I like it."

At twenty-five paces up, a growl sounded from below. Nix looked down. The city stretched out below him, piers jutting into the Meander, a forest of sails, a thicket of scows and ships at anchor. The sprawl of Dur Follin's roads zigged and zagged in all directions like the scrawl of some cosmic madman. Wagons and pedestrians, smaller from this height but still readily visible, roamed them, and to the north, back toward the guild house, Nix saw the creature as it came. It lumbered down the street at an alarming speed, clots of pedestrians and wagons fleeing before it like goats before a wolf. The creature roared as it came, the sound carrying up to them, getting entangled with the screams of people and the distant whine of an Orangie's whistle.

None of the three said anything. They simply put their faces back to the wall of the spire and climbed. The wind picked up, gusting off the river, snapping Nix's shirt. Jyme cursed.

"Going left to stay out of the wind," Nix called down.

Below, the creature reached the foundation stones of the

tower. It looked up at them, its mien hidden by the hood, which seemed to stick to its head as though fabric and flesh had congealed into one. It screamed something at them, the gibberish of its words made even more incomprehensible by the sound of the wind.

"Sounds angry," Nix said.

"Aye," Egil shouted.

Nix figured the creature's bulk would prevent it from climbing, so they would be safe as long as none of them fell.

The creature bounded up to the foundation stones, felt at the wall, and started to heave its bulk up the surface. It climbed awkwardly, but with a speed and agility that Nix would not have thought possible.

"Fak," Nix whispered, and refocused on the climb.

"It's coming up!" Jyme shouted.

"Just keep going," Egil said. "Deliberate, though. No panic, Jyme. You fall, you're going to take me with you."

"I'm not fakkin' falling anywhere," Jyme said.

The wind whistled in Nix's ear. He focused on the face of the spire, the gritty texture, the lay of its pyramidal bricks with their protuberant edges, each a foothold, a handhold, the sum of them a ladder, as if placed there for that very purpose. He concentrated on the task, his motion settling into the repetition of hand, foot, lift, hand, foot, lift, the words and motion the rhythm of his ascent. He was climbing to the edge of the world, to the tip of a stone finger that was pointing at the beginning and end of everything.

"Nix," Egil called from below.

Nix pretended to not hear. He shook his head and kept climbing.

"Nix!" Egil said.

Nix stopped, placed his cheek to the cold stone, then looked down.

Jyme was a pace or two behind him, the wind causing his

shirt to flutter. Egil was below Jyme, looking up, the eye of the priest's tattoo staring up at the unending sky. The creature was below Egil and coming up fast.

"We can't outpace it," Egil said. "We delayed too long at the bottom."

"Not standing fakkin' still we can't," Jyme said. "Go, Nix!"

Nix's arms screamed with fatigue. He stared at the stone, white as bleached bone. Egil was right. They'd never reach the top before the creature.

"I'm going to stop it," Egil said. "You two will go on. Fix it next time, is all. Yeah?"

"No," Nix said.

"Nix," Egil started.

Nix was shaking his head. "Think of your wife, Egil. Your daughter."

Egil smiled. "I am. You preserve them for me. We go again, Nix."

They shared a look, one that bespoke a friendship that transcended time and worlds.

Nix couldn't speak so he just nodded.

Jyme looked up at Nix, wide-eyed, then down at Egil. "You're not . . . ?"

"I am," Egil said. "Just make it to the top and do what we came to do. Go."

"But we don't even know if we're in the right place!" Jyme said. "We're just fakkin' climbing!"

"If we're wrong, we're all dead anyway," Egil said. "I'm just going first. But if we're right, then you fix it, Jyme."

Jyme looked back up at Nix. Nix looked him in the face, turned, and started up again, leaving Egil where he was. Hand, foot, hand, foot, mind the wind, profile low, find purchase, keep moving. The wind sounded loud in his ears.

After a time, unable to help himself, Nix looked down and saw the creature rapidly scaling the wall, nearing Egil. The wind caused the creature's cloak to whip and flap but it hung on the wall as if its hands and feet were affixed to the stone.

Even Egil looked small compared to it. The priest, looking down, maneuvered himself sideways to intercept the creature's ascent. Nix could hear it babbling over the wind, its voices frantic and slobbery.

Jyme and Nix both stopped, looking down, unable to not watch. They had to bear witness, if nothing else.

Egil hung on with one hand, flattening himself against the stone while he carefully pulled one hammer from its thong. He held it by the haft and waited, waited, and dropped it when the creature was below him. The hammer fell true, struck the creature in the head, but whatever hope had flashed in Nix for a moment died quickly. The blow barely budged it and the hammer tumbled earthward. The creature looked up at Egil, growling and coming on fast.

The priest inhaled and nodded, as though he'd come to terms with something. He did not look up. He tensed, waiting for the creature to get closer, just below him. Nix knew what was coming; his heart thrummed, pounded his ribs.

"Egil!" Nix called, wanting to say something but not sure what, but the priest did not acknowledge him.

All at once Egil roared and launched himself at the creature, twisting in midair as he came so he hit head-on. He crashed into it, the impact dislodging it from the wall, and both of them plummeted in a tangle of limbs.

Nix could not breathe.

Halfway down Egil extended his arm and raised a defiant fist, the gesture purposeful, intended for Nix and Jyme.

Nix blinked and turned away before they hit the ground. He stared at the stone, noting every detail of its texture, gathering himself. The wind felt cool on the wetness on his face.

"Gods, Nix," Jyme said. "How can it—? Don't look, Nix, don't look! But that fakking creature survived the fall. And now here it comes again."

Nix nodded. He didn't look. He couldn't. He cleared his throat and looked up at the top of the clock. He blinked away tears.

"Climb like you're on fire, Jyme. Like you're on fakking fire."

"Aye," Jyme said. "I'm right behind you."

"We go again," Nix muttered as he climbed. "We go again."

CHAPTER ELEVEN

As they ran for the clock, Nix played out the next steps in his mind. Likely they'd have to climb and the creature would be hard after them. Maybe it could climb, maybe it couldn't. Nix would assume it could. The tower thinned as it rose, giving it a favorable incline. And the unusual bricks that composed it made for a scalable surface. Odd that he'd never heard of any- one climbing it, not even on a drunken dare. He started shed- ding gear as he ran, small blades, pouches.

"Keep a weapon, but get rid of everything else you can. We'll need to climb."

"Climb?" Jyme said, huffing at their pace. "The clock? Are you mad?"

"You said you could climb," Egil said, a smile in his tone.

"I showed I could climb," Jyme said defiantly.

"Just lose what you don't need," Nix said, dropping another belt pouch. "No stopping at all when we reach the clock. We go up."

Jyme and the priest hopped and skipped as they went, to

allow them to drop or cut loose equipment. The pedestrians on the street watched them pass with bemused expressions.

"Why up and not in?" Jyme asked.

"We know there's no way in," Egil said. "Tried it before."

"Aye," Nix said, recalling the night when he and Egil, half-drunk, had tried to find a way in. "There probably is no in. There's just up."

"To what?" Jyme asked.

Nix didn't bother answering. He was operating as much on faith as reason. If he ended up being wrong, they'd all die.

"Up to where, Nix?" Jyme asked again.

Nix didn't look at him. "You ever see anyone climb that clock, Jyme? No? Me either. Just trust me, yeah?"

To that, Jyme didn't answer.

They reached the clock, the twisting white spire seated on a foundation of stacked gray slabs of stone, a monumental finger pointing at the sky. Nix looked up, past the gongs that belted it three-quarters of the way up, to the four-pronged pinnacle.

"The top," Nix said. "The very top."

Without further ado they started climbing, Nix in the lead, then Egil, then Jyme. The wind would pick up once they broke above the city's rooflines.

"Follow my path," Nix said. "I'll get us lee of the wind."

The tower's face provided ample hand and footholds and they made rapid progress. Twenty paces up Nix circled left as he ascended, to keep the worst of the wind from them. Another ten and the city lay out below them: its tangled, nonsensical streets, the huge stone span of the Archbridge, the wide brown ribbon of the Meander.

Screams from below drew their attention. The creature was coming. Nix could see it moving at speed down the avenue, pedestrians parting around it like water around a stone.

"Faster," Nix said.

The creature reached the clock and looked up, its face still shrouded in its hood. It screamed at them, the particulars of the sound lost to wind and distance. It felt along the foundation, found a grip, and heaved itself up, another, another, and soon had a rhythm, ascending rapidly.

Nix looked up, past the gongs, to the uttermost top of the clock. He convinced himself the point at the top had to be significant, had to be the Fulcrum.

"Climb," he said.

Hand, foot, lift, hand, foot, lift.

The creature came up fast, very fast. It was well that they'd had such a large head start or it would have caught them quickly.

"No panic," Egil said. "Steady and sure but quick."

"Aye," Jyme said from below him.

Hand, foot, lift. Hand, foot, lift.

The creature was gaining, its slobbery words carrying up to them over the wind.

Nix kept going, felt the grit of the stone under his fingers and just kept climbing, as fast as he dared but not so fast as to risk a slip. A crowd had gathered in the street below, faces looking up, arms pointing.

By the time they reached the gongs, the creature was closer still. The gongs, along with the geared hammers that struck the hours, hung from a metal apparatus that jutted out from the stone of the tower's façade. Nix looked at them to see if he could see an easy way to release a gong to fall on the creature, but he would've needed a blacksmith's tools and time to get through the chains and metal arms on which the round slabs of metal hung.

"Little farther," Nix said, sweating, his shoulders and fingers aching, going past the gongs.

"Best hurry," Egil said.

"Move!" Jyme said.

Nix glanced down, saw that the creature was maybe ten paces below them, less perhaps, and coming up fast. It growled and muttered as it came.

Nix put it out of his mind, got his hands on the lip of the pinnacle, and heaved himself up.

He didn't know what he expected to find, but finding nothing wasn't what he'd imagined. Framed by the four corner spires, the top of the tower was just a concave stone surface shielded from the wind. Bird shit dotted it here and there. A spiderweb fluttered in one corner. Leaves had collected in a small pile in another. He stood there, looking around, lost.

"Is it there? Is it?" Egil called, the priest's hands cresting the lip. He pulled himself up, staring around. Nix stood in the center, hands slack. He saw nothing that could be taken for the Fulcrum.

"There's nothing here," he said.

The creature's babbling carried up, the sound ominously close and getting louder.

Jyme's head came over the edge, his eyes wide, face flush and slick with sweat.

"Did we—?"

"I'm sorry," Nix said. "Shite, I'm sorry."

Jyme's expression fell. He looked up sharply. "The plates?"

At first Nix didn't take Jyme's point, but then he understood. He opened the flap of his satchel, saw that the characters on the plates were glowing brighter, that the plates themselves were vibrating more noticeably.

"That's it, Jyme!"

Nix looked a smile at him and Jyme's eyes went wide with terror as the creature below him forcefully tore him loose from the wall and Jyme vanished from sight. His prolonged scream carried up as he fell.

One of the creature's hands, covered in calluses and scales and filth, the nails yellow and long, appeared over the edge.

Nix hurriedly pulled out the plates while Egil drew his hammers.

"We go again," Nix said, pulling out the plates and watching the veil of the world fall away. "We go again."

Nix put his hands on the lip of the tower's pinnacle. The creature babbled and moaned below them, coming up fast.

"Go, Nix!" Jyme said.

Nix felt the plates vibrating in the satchel, like it contained a swarm of bees. He knew he'd been right. He heaved himself and rolled onto the top of Ool's clock, the dawn painting the sky in orange and red. Jyme, breathing hard, pulled himself up after and drew his sword.

"Help Egil," Nix said, and opened his satchel and took out the plates.

Jyme fell backward with the effort of heaving Egil over the edge of the tower's top. Egil had his hammers drawn in an instant. The mutterings of the creature grew in volume.

"Stopstopstopstop," it said, getting closer.

Egil looked over the edge, hands white around the hafts of his hammers. "We face it here as it climbs. We knock it down and earn ourselves some time."

Nix had the plates in hand. They felt slippery in his grasp. They vibrated and hummed and the characters on them glowed as if they were aflame. He became conscious of a sound, like the roar of distant surf, growing louder, louder. His vision blurred, the entire world around him becoming indistinct. A bout of dizziness caused him to wobble.

He was cursing, cursing.

The sound of surf was coming from the plates, the hum getting louder, the tide of magic building.

Instead of ambushing the creature as it came over the lip of the pinnacle, Jyme and Egil fell to their knees, holding their hands to their ears, shouting something. The roar of the creature cut through the tumult, too, as it heaved its huge body over the side of the tower.

And the world spun and twisted and blurred and transformed and Nix screamed and shouted and feared he would vomit and the world dissolved and he closed his eyes and tried to stay on his feet while the plates thrummed and sang.

Nix felt a flurry of motion, not so much like he was moving, but rather like the world was moving under and around him. He felt dizzy, felt as if he were light and floating, or maybe falling. The sensation left him unmoored for a breath. He gasped, opened his eyes, and found himself standing on weak legs in a vaulted chamber of smooth dark metal. The still air felt heavy, thick in his lungs. The smell of ages seemed to hang in that air, stale and brittle.

Engravings were etched into the walls, seemingly by different hands, in different styles, but all of it depicting what Nix assumed to be people and events and creatures from other worlds, other times.

A column of translucent light, two paces in diameter, descended from a source high in the ceiling, ringing a declivity in the metal floor, a socket into which a man could stand—the Fulcrum, Nix assumed—the motionless center of the world.

Jyme and Egil lay on the floor beside him, both of them groaning. The creature was ten paces away, already on all fours, already getting to its feet. It looked up and saw Nix from out of the depths of its hood and roared. The plates, still in Nix's hands, keened at a high pitch, vibrated like plucked strings.

"Givegivegiveusthespell!" it shouted, its voice many voices. Nix considered making a dash for the Fulcrum, trying to complete the casting before the creature could get to him, but it might reach him first. Or Nix might get the casting done but not before it killed Egil or Jyme, in which case the casting would be for nothing more than another run-through.

Nix pulled Jyme to his feet while he nudged Egil with his boot.

"Get up!" Nix said to them. "Jyme, you're doing the spell. Egil and I will buy you time."

"What?" Jyme asked. "What?"

"You heard me," Nix said, and shoved the plates into Jyme's hands. "Egil, get up!"

The priest mumbled and rose, hammers in hand. Nix drew his falchion.

The creature reared to its full height, clenched its fists.

"Go, Jyme," Nix said. To Egil he said, "Yeah?"

Egil banged the heads of his hammers. "Yeah."

The creature charged them. They spaced themselves and readied for blood, as they had countless times before.

Jyme took the plates—they felt slippery, as though coated in oil, and vibrated in his hands—and ran for the column or light or whatever the Hells it was. A voice sounded in his head, very much like his own.

"No more. Pay the price. No more. Pay the price."

Behind him the creature growled and he heard the impact of blades on flesh, heard Nix curse, heard Egil snarl, heard the sound of something heavy slamming into flesh.

"Stopstopstop!" the creature said.

"Egil!" Nix exclaimed.

Jyme glanced back and saw the creature stomp on a prone Nix, crushing bones and organs, Nix screaming as he exploded like an overripe fruit. The creature started toward Jyme but Egil bounded before it.

"Oh, no," the priest said, his voice hard and sharp. "You get *me* first, Thing."

The creature threw back its head and roared, its hood falling away to reveal the deformed bulb of its head. Misplaced mouths, crooked rotting teeth, three dotting eyes, two overlarge vertical slits that must have served as its nose.

"Freeusfreeusfreeus," it said.

Egil hefted his hammers. "I intend to do just so."

Jyme glanced at Nix's broken body, the crimson paste of his innards staining the floor around his body.

The creature roared and took a step toward Egil, another.

Egil gave no ground. He spoke over his shoulder to Jyme. "Everything the same," Egil said over his shoulder. "Small changes at most. We go again."

Jyme remembered the plan. It felt like it had been written on the pages of his brain, easy for him to recollect as needed. And realizing that made him realize something else.

They'd done this before many times. And always they'd failed. His voice sounded in his head again.

"No more. Pay the price."

The creature's eyes fixed on Jyme and it charged. Egil, standing in its way, braced himself, his hammers whistling as he struck the creature's head and chest. The blows hit with a dull thud, snapped and cracked bone, and would have felled an ox. But the creature merely endured the blows and lashed out with a ham fist that struck Egil in the side and sent him careening across the floor, out of the creature's way.

"Giveusthespellthespellthespell," it said to Jyme.

One of Egil's hammers spun haft over head and slammed into the creature's deformed mien, shattering teeth and exploding lips. The creature turned to the priest, the wounds already starting to heal, and roared, spitting blood and saliva.

"You and me aren't done," Egil said, wincing at some pain in his torso. The priest looked past the creature to Nix, back to Jyme. "Go, Jyme. I can't hurt the damned thing."

Jyme nodded, his legs weak, and feeling as though he might vomit.

They'd done this before. But who'd done it? Him? Nix? Egil? All of them, maybe.

Either way they'd failed because here they were again.

"Little changes," he said. "Little changes."

The plates were fundamental. They could not be destroyed.

And they always sought to return to the Fulcrum, to have their power expressed, to rewrite the world.

How did he know that? Had Nix told him that? Which time through?

Egil circled the creature, crouched, coiled, trying to keep it distracted, occupied. The creature tracked his movements, muttering, drooling, its eyes darting.

Jyme turned away. Writing on the metal wall caught his eye, an inelegant scrawl scratched into the surface with something sharp. He cocked his head, digesting the words. They read: *Jyme Ehren was here alone and he tried.*

He closed his eyes and stepped through into the light, down into the Fulcrum, the socket of the world. The touch of the light caused his flesh to tingle. The moment he stood there he felt a weightiness settle on him, a responsibility, a sense of possibility that exceeded anything he'd felt before. He was connected to everything, floating on waters of possibility. He looked down at his hands, holding the plates, the glowing characters on them spinning, turning from indecipherable to the common alphabet.

He turned and looked back on the words he'd left himself on the wall.

Broken pots. Broken pots.

He had used the plates at least once before and it hadn't worked. Or maybe it had, inasmuch as they could. Maybe there was no way to do what they wanted to do.

Worlds gone by.

The plates could not be destroyed. The plates always worked in the world to return to the Fulcrum and be used anew. There was always a palimpsest, a leftover, an afterbirth of the creation.

Jyme could not know if what he thought he knew had been with him throughout or if he'd learned it only in the latest iteration of the world. Maybe he'd learned it, or understood, only upon standing in the Fulcrum this time.

Broken pots. Broken pots.

Why hadn't they remade the world and simply caused themselves to remember everything?

Maybe they'd tried that and it hadn't worked? Maybe they'd tried that and it had driven them mad or made them nihilists?

The possibilities were endless, a spiral without end, the permutations too slippery to grasp or understand. Jyme only knew certain rules.

If he wanted a world like his world, he needed to make only small changes. The world was remade via an exercise of will, the wishes of the holder of the plates. But how to deal with the plates, with the palimpsest, with the obvious fact that they'd tried and failed at least once but probably many times?

And then he had it—understanding.

And understanding made him weak.

He looked up, watched through the barrier of light as the creature lifted Egil over its head and the priest, helpless in its grasp, looked at Jyme, a long look, a hopeful look.

"Do it, Jyme," Egil said.

The creature slammed Egil down to the floor, the priest's body visibly shattering under the impact. Blood poured from his cracked skull, joined with Nix's.

Do it, Jyme.

It was for Jyme to do. Not Nix. Not Egil. Jyme.

Be the hero.

He briefly entertained the idea that he'd done this before and one of the changes he'd wrought had been to make himself a braver man. If he had, did that actually mean he wasn't brave? If he'd remolded the clay of his soul to make himself brave, wasn't he really just a coward?

He shook his head and decided he couldn't let it matter. He was who he was, at least this time through, and he knew what he had to do.

The creature looked at him, all of its eyes fixed on him, its malformed shape diffused by the light into a blurry grotesquerie. Jyme stared at it for what seemed a long time.

"Is the palimpsest always like you?" he said.

"Giveusgiveusgiveususthespell. Freeususus."

"What is your name?" Jyme asked, bracing himself for the answer.

"Namenamename. We are the Afterbirth."

Jyme nodded.

"One more time, then, Afterbirth. And perhaps after that you'll have your freedom."

The creature cocked the mass of its head. Perhaps it understood him, or perhaps not. It scarcely mattered.

Jyme stood in the place that was no place, in the time that wasn't time. He thought for a moment of Sessket, of Ziza. Those had been good months. Had they been there through each iteration, he wondered, or were they new? Had he made those for himself, too? He decided it didn't matter. They'd happened and he'd loved her.

He formulated his thoughts, looked down at the plates, and started to read the words that would remake the world.

The Afterbirth roared, charged him, but it was too late to stop what Jyme had begun.

Little changes.

Little changes.

But not for Jyme. Not this time.

The world stopped and grew blurry, but within himself he saw with perfect clarity.

Nix dreamed of Jyme's voice. Disembodied, it carried across a dark void.

"A price, Nix," Jyme said. "That's what we missed, or wouldn't face. A price had to be paid. I think we knew it. I feel like I knew it, maybe on a previous time through. It turns out that someone always has to pay. The remaking is imperfect and something has to be done with the leftovers. The remaking works best when the price is paid willingly. That's when the wishes of the caster are most fully realized. I understood that this last time. And that's why I'm not with you this time around. I may have been a coward most of the times, but not this last one.

"I willed that the plates be secreted away, so that there won't be another time. You'll have scrolls instead, and they'll be of no interest. I'll keep the plates here, with me, in the Fulcrum. I can't get out. The only way in and out is via the plates and the remaking and soon I won't be able to use them. The price will change me.

"It's funny, Nix. The creature chasing us, he couldn't have used the plates he was after. The mind of the leftover gets too cluttered to use them, too filled with . . . everything. He was just desperate and hopeless and afraid and looking for a way out. I've given him rest, too.

"I'm leaving you this because it's important to me that you know what's happened, even if only for a moment. I'll take solace in you knowing. You'll wake and you'll remember and then you won't. I can't let you remember permanently because then you'll try to save me and the whole thing will start over again. I built this remembrance, and much else, into the remaking. Hells, I can't be saved anyway. I don't want to be. Egil had me right. I wanted to be the hero. I wanted a purpose. And now I've found it. Maybe you made me that way one of the times through, maybe I made myself that way, or maybe I was genuinely born that way. It doesn't matter. I'll stay here, apart from time, forever, and the world will go on."

"Jyme?" Nix said. He couldn't open his eyes. He existed in a void. "Can you hear me? Don't do this."

"Goodbye, Nix. We were friends through many worlds. I'm glad of that."

"Jyme, don't!"

———

Nix opened his eyes to see blue sky above, clouds, a lone gull winging along. He blinked. His eyes were crusty, stinging. Jyme's words echoed in his brain. His head felt thick, like it was filled with feathers, like a doll's head. For a moment he could not remember where he was, who he was, his mind seemed empty of everything. . . .

The tide of memories came in, the events at the Fulcrum, the creature, Egil, Jyme. He'd been crushed, a sharp blast of pain. He sat up with a gasp, blinking in the sun. His ribs, his body . . .

. . . did not pain him.

He prodded his abdomen and found the bones were healed. He looked at his arms, took the measure of his frame. No wounds. He smelled the Meander and the faint familiar rot of the Deadmarsh.

He shielded his eyes and looked north. Dur Follin's walls rose gray and dark in the distance, maybe a long crossbow shot away. He was sitting on the grass beside the southern road, the Meander to his right, its sluggish brown waters making their way south. Egil lay still near him. He saw no sign of Jyme. But then he wouldn't.

"Fakking heroic-minded idiot," Nix said, meaning Jyme, as he scrambled to Egil's side and shook him, fearing him dead. Egil groaned. Nix kept shaking him.

"Get up," Nix said. "Jyme has done something stupid."

"Enough," Egil finally said, pushing Nix's hands away, opening his eyes, and sitting up. "Stupid you said?"

Nix sat back and nodded.

Egil ran his hand over the tattoo on his pate, squinted in the sun. "That's Dur Follin. What happened?"

Nix was still working it through, though realization was dawning.

"Jyme happened." He looked hard at Egil. "Because you told him, too."

Egil's thick lips pursed. He nodded. "You're right. But I

wasn't telling him anything he didn't want to hear. He wanted to be the hero, and so he was."

"Damn it," Nix said. "We had an agreement. All of us or none."

Egil just stared at the Meander. "Couldn't be done that way. He must have realized it and . . . made a different decision."

"He brought us back," Nix said. "Saved everything."

"He did," Egil said.

"And we remember it all."

Egil nodded. "We said we wanted to."

"I'm not as sure now," Nix said, feeling unmoored.

"Nor I," Egil agreed.

"Is this even real?"

"Real . . ." Egil shook his head. "Real enough, I guess. How can we even ask the question now that we know what we know?"

"That supposed to be flippant or profound?"

"Fak if I know," Egil said. "I mean that, too. I don't know, Nix. I don't know that there is a 'real' at all."

Neither did Nix. *Know* and *real* seemed useless words. How could they know anything, ever? It was all relative, wasn't it?

Other than what he felt. That was real. Whatever it was built on, truth, lies, fiction, the feelings were real. He held on to that, dug his fingers in and held on tight.

"The world is made and unmade with words," Nix said softly. "Fakking wizards."

"Aye that. But then you were almost a wizard yourself till you quit."

"I was expelled," Nix said, the words a reflex. He sighed. "Drink?"

"Gods. Several."

"And so the world is righted," Nix said, thinking of Jyme. "Maybe. Let's go see what Jyme got up to."

They stood and the moment they did Nix remembered Jyme's words.

"You'll remember and then you won't."

He cursed, looked at Egil. He felt wobbly, dizzy, and a rushing sound filled his ears. He put his palms to the sides of his head, fell to his knees, groaning. He was vaguely conscious of Egil beside him, doing the same.

"No, no, no, no!" Nix shouted.

The world spun, grew dim, darker. He cursed, fell, and the world went dark.

Nix woke to Egil's snores. He opened his eyes and found himself staring up at the night sky. The murmur of the Meander's current carried from his left, the sound of crickets and insects.

He sat up and looked around, confused.

Egil lay beside him sleeping, snoring, stinking of alcohol. Nix prodded him awake. The priest grunted, stirred, and opened his eyes.

"I'm sleeping," he said.

"Get the fak up," Nix said, and stood.

Dur Follin's walls rose in the distance, lantern lights glowing at intervals along them. Lamps and torchlight glowed the length of the Archbridge, which spanned the dark, slow-moving Meander. The sound of instruments carried intermittently on the wind.

Egil, groaning and creaking, rose and stood beside him.

"What the fak are we doing out here?" Egil said. "The last two days are . . . ?"

"Gone?" Nix asked. "Likewise. I'll wager ale and women fit in somewhere. We got those scrolls we found in the Deadmire identified by Kerfallen's automaton, they proved to be nothing, and then . . . ?"

Egil shook the bucket of his head. "I don't know. I do know an ale is in order." He ran a hand over his head, sniffed, winced. "I stink."

"No argument," Nix said.

Egil took out the short wooden pipe he always carried in a

pouch at his belt. He struck a match and took a long draw. He exhaled a cloud of smoke and said, "Whatever happened, I'm sure we accounted well for ourselves."

"Little doubt," Nix said. He felt thoughtful, melancholy for no reason he could name. "Put out that fakkin' pipe, yeah? I've always hated that smell. Let's get back to the Tunnel. Tesha will be wondering after our health, having been gone a day or two."

"Agreed," Egil said, and the two friends started back down the road to Dur Follin. "I have an odd thought."

"That's different than usual how?"

Egil went on as though he hadn't spoken. "You remember that merc we met a long way back? The one who stayed behind in the desert after we fought that creature in service to Rose and Mere's brother?"

Nix rifled his memory. "I remember him. 'Jyme,' was his name, I think."

"Jyme," Egil said, rubbing at the whiskers on his cheeks. "Aye, that sounds right. Wonder what happened to him?"

"Why in the name of the Gods are you thinking of him?" Nix asked.

Egil shrugged. "No reason. Like I said, an odd thought."

They made their way to the road and back toward Dur Follin. As they journeyed, the sound of Ool's clock carried across the distance, tolling the hour of the world.

The rush of memories and fragments and images and knowledge poured into Jyme at an accelerating rate. He paced the metal room, the room from which he could never exit, groaning and moaning and mumbling as the leftovers entered his mind, changed him. He stared at the wall, saw his words.

Jyme Ehren was here alone and he tried.

He was losing himself in the mnemonic flood. Struck with an idea, he hurriedly drew his dagger and scratched new words into the metal. He gritted his teeth as he wrote, trying to keep himself against the tide of voices that had begun clamoring in his head. He felt his body changing, too, appendages forming, mouths opening, new eyes blinking into being, feathers, scales. He could not hold on to himself against the tide and started to slip, to drift, to lose and to fall into the cacophony of voices and events and parts of people and things that had been imperfectly rendered in the remaking and so had been made manifest in him and he'd had a name once and he'd had a name once and he'd had a name once and now he was the leftover, the after-birth, and he was the seal and he had secured the world and that is why he was, what he was, and he was alone and there was writing on the wall and a part of him recognized the words and he could read them but not understand them and he said them aloud and his voice was many voices.

"I . . . am . . . Jyme."